SPACE BATTLE
LUNCHTIME

VOLUME ONE:
LIGHTS, CAMERA, SNACKTION!

ONI
PRESS

AN ONI PRESS PUBLICATION

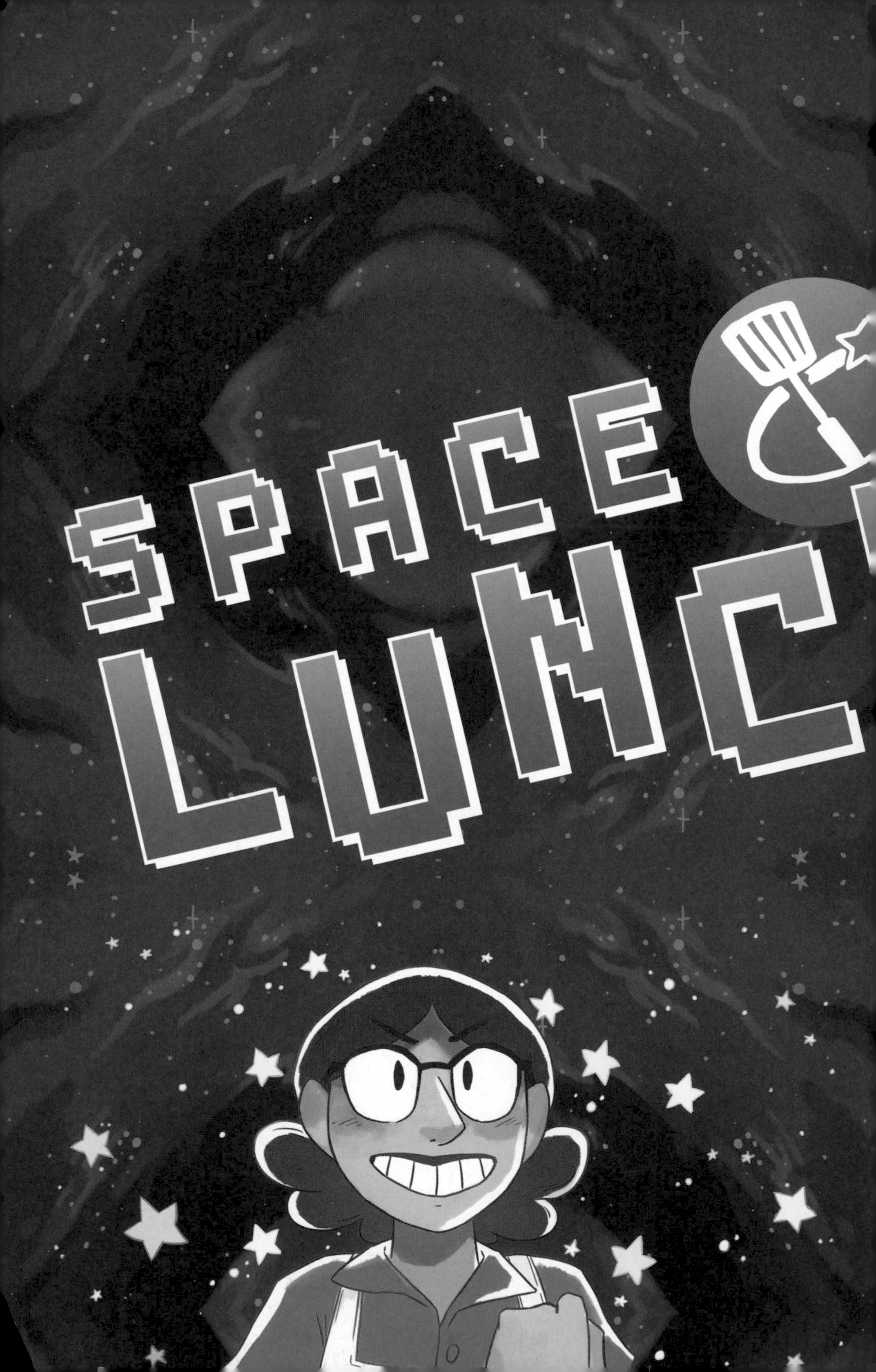
SPACE
LUNC

BATTLE TIME

VOLUME ONE: LIGHTS, CAMERA, SNACKTION!

BY NATALIE RIESS

EDITED BY ROBIN HERRERA
DESIGNED BY HILARY THOMPSON

PUBLISHED BY ONI PRESS, INC.

PUBLISHER JOE NOZEMACK
EDITOR IN CHIEF JAMES LUCAS JONES
V.P. OF MARETING & SALES ANDREW MCINTIRE
PUBLICITY COORDINATOR RACHEL REED
DIRECTOR OF DESIGN & PRODUCTION TROY LOOK
GRAPHIC DESIGNER HILARY THOMPSON
DIGITAL ART TECHNICIAN JARED JONES
MANAGING EDITOR ARI YARWOOD
SENIOR EDITOR CHARLIE CHU
EDITOR ROBIN HERRERA
EDITORIAL ASSISTANT BESS PALLARES
DIRECTOR OF LOGISTICS BRAD ROOKS
LOGISTICS ASSOCIATE JUNG LEE

ONIPRESS.COM
FACEBOOK.COM/ONIPRESS
TWITTER.COM/ONIPRESS
ONIPRESS.TUMBLR.COM
INSTAGRAM.COM/ONIPRESS

ORIGINALLY PUBLISHED AS ISSUES 1-4 OF THE ONI PRESS COMIC SERIES
SPACE BATTLE LUNCHTIME.

FIRST EDITION: OCTOBER 2016
ISBN 978-1-62010-313-5
EISBN 978-1-62010-314-2

1 3 5 7 9 10 8 6 4 2

LIBRARY OF CONGRESS CONTROL NUMBER: 2016937918
PRINTED IN CHINA.

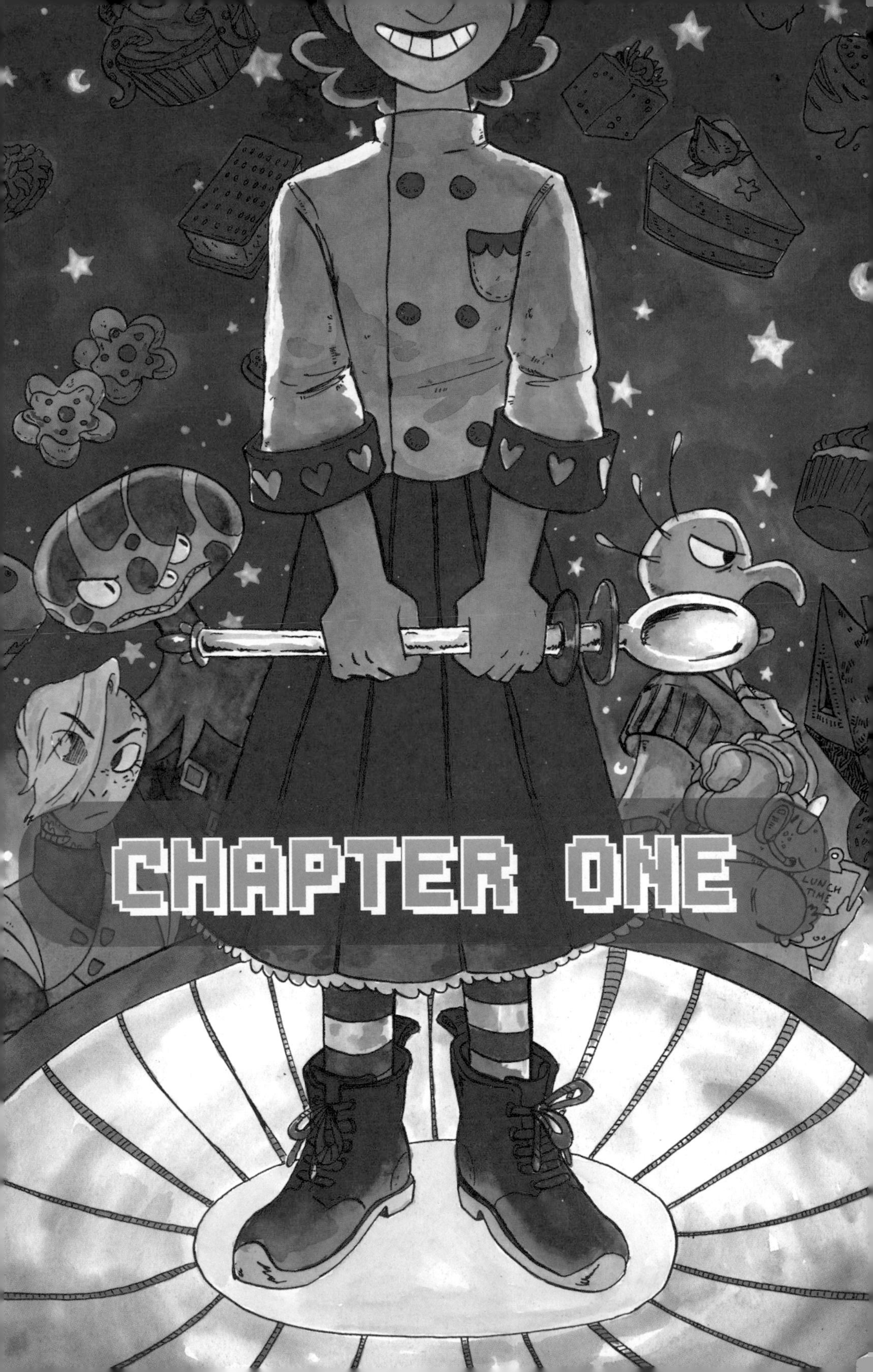
CHAPTER ONE
LUNCH TIME

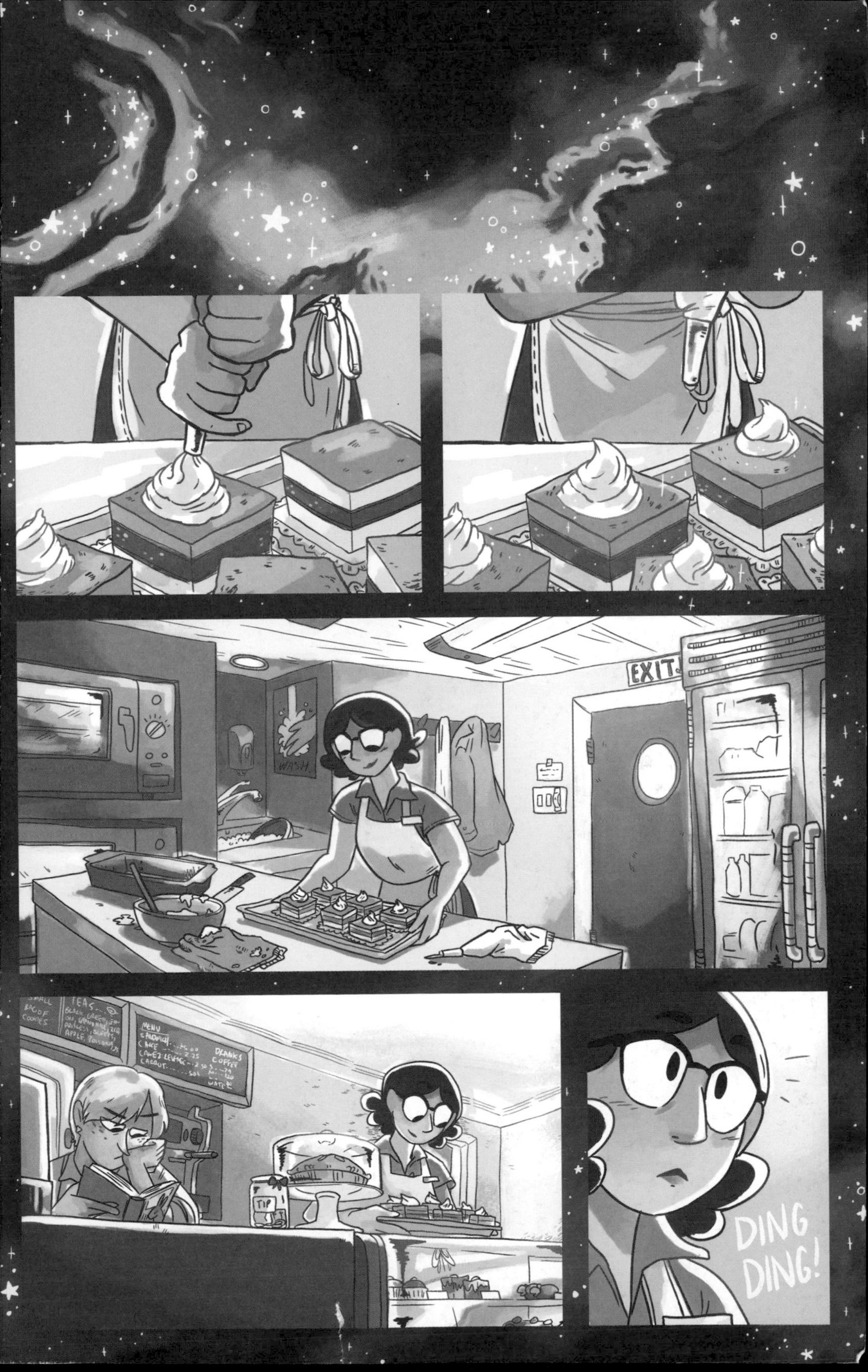
EXIT
WASH
BAG OF COOKIES
TEAS
MENU
DRANKS
COFFEE
TIP
DING DING!

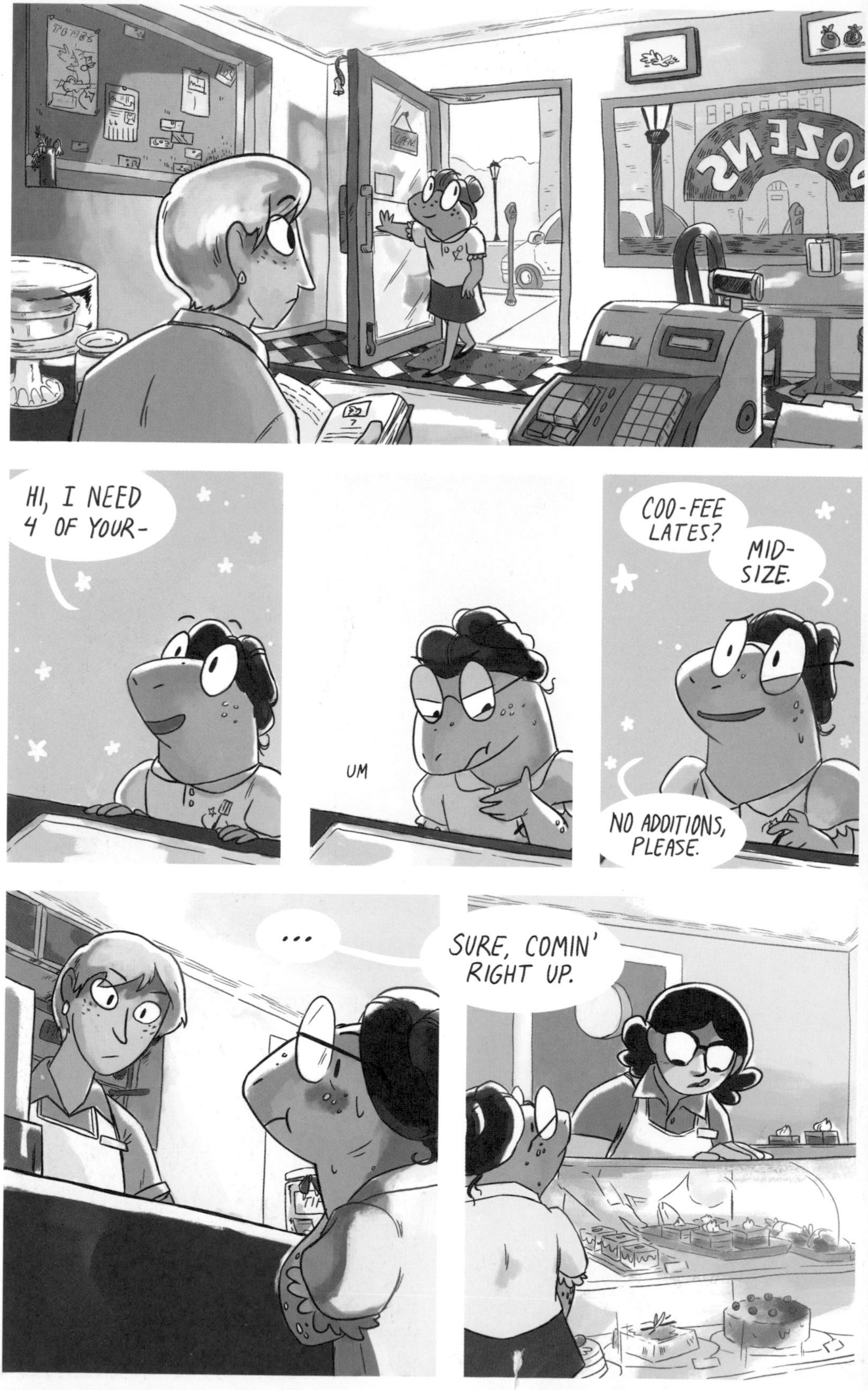
HI, I NEED 4 OF YOUR-
UM
COO-FEE LATES?
MID-SIZE.
NO ADDITIONS, PLEASE.
...
SURE, COMIN' RIGHT UP.

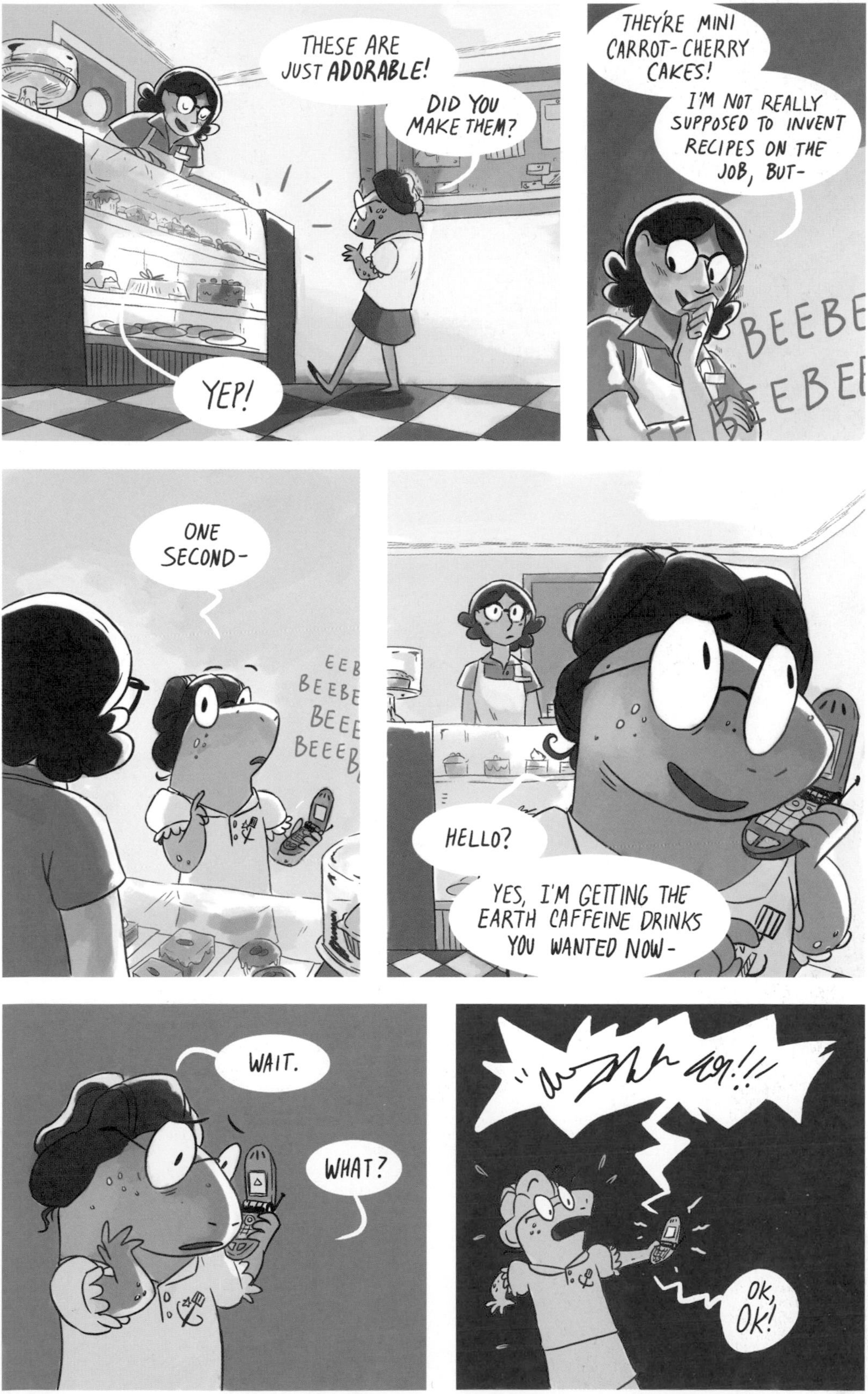
THESE ARE JUST ADORABLE!
DID YOU MAKE THEM?
YEP!
THEY'RE MINI CARROT-CHERRY CAKES!
I'M NOT REALLY SUPPOSED TO INVENT RECIPES ON THE JOB, BUT-
BEEBE
BEEBEE
ONE SECOND-
EEB
BEEBE
BEEE
BEEEB
HELLO?
YES, I'M GETTING THE EARTH CAFFEINE DRINKS YOU WANTED NOW-
WAIT.
WHAT?
OK, OK!

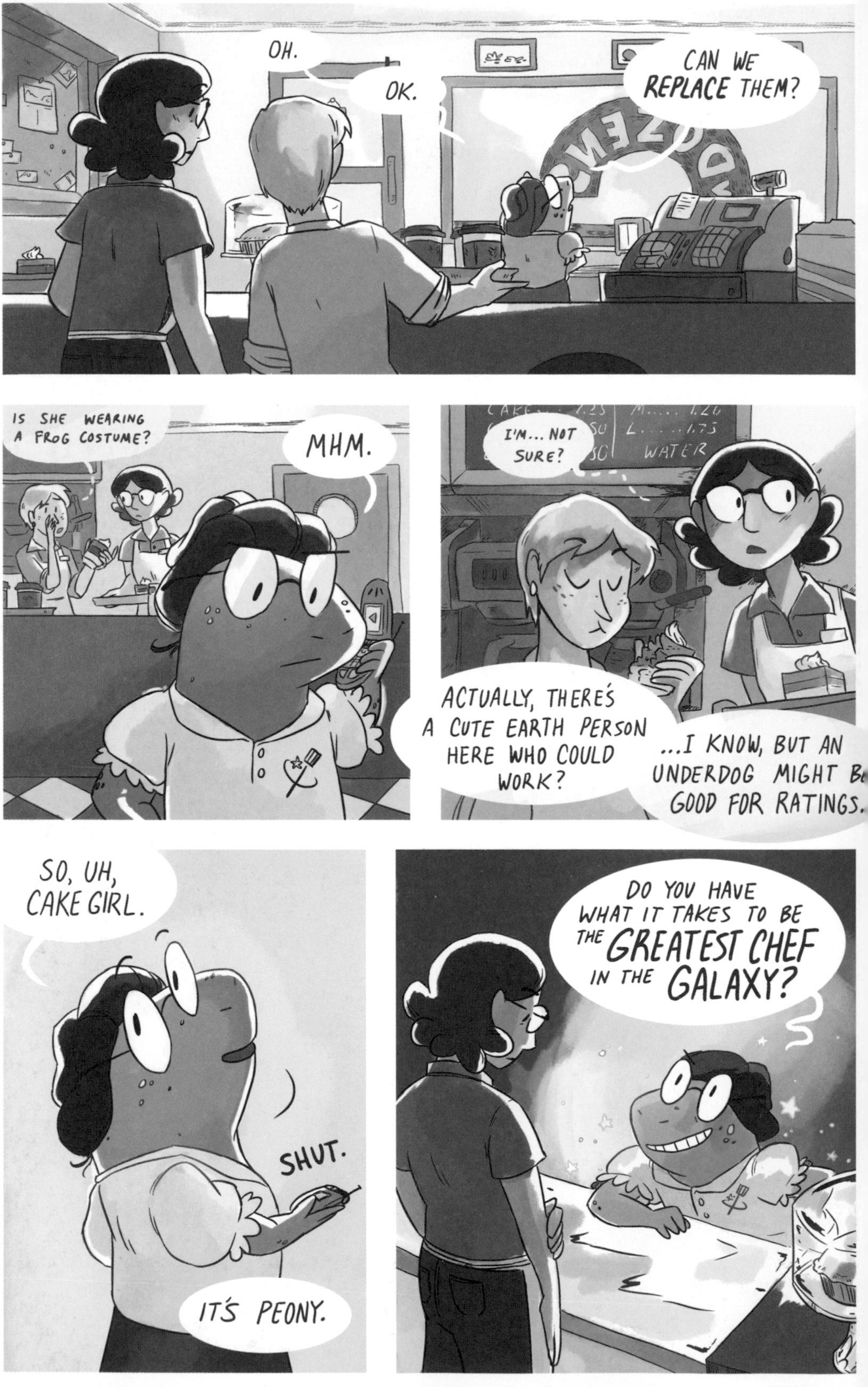
OH.
OK.
CAN WE REPLACE THEM?
IS SHE WEARING A FROG COSTUME?
MHM.
I'M... NOT SURE?
ACTUALLY, THERE'S A CUTE EARTH PERSON HERE WHO COULD WORK?
...I KNOW, BUT AN UNDERDOG MIGHT BE GOOD FOR RATINGS.
SO, UH, CAKE GIRL.
SHUT.
IT'S PEONY.
DO YOU HAVE WHAT IT TAKES TO BE THE GREATEST CHEF IN THE GALAXY?

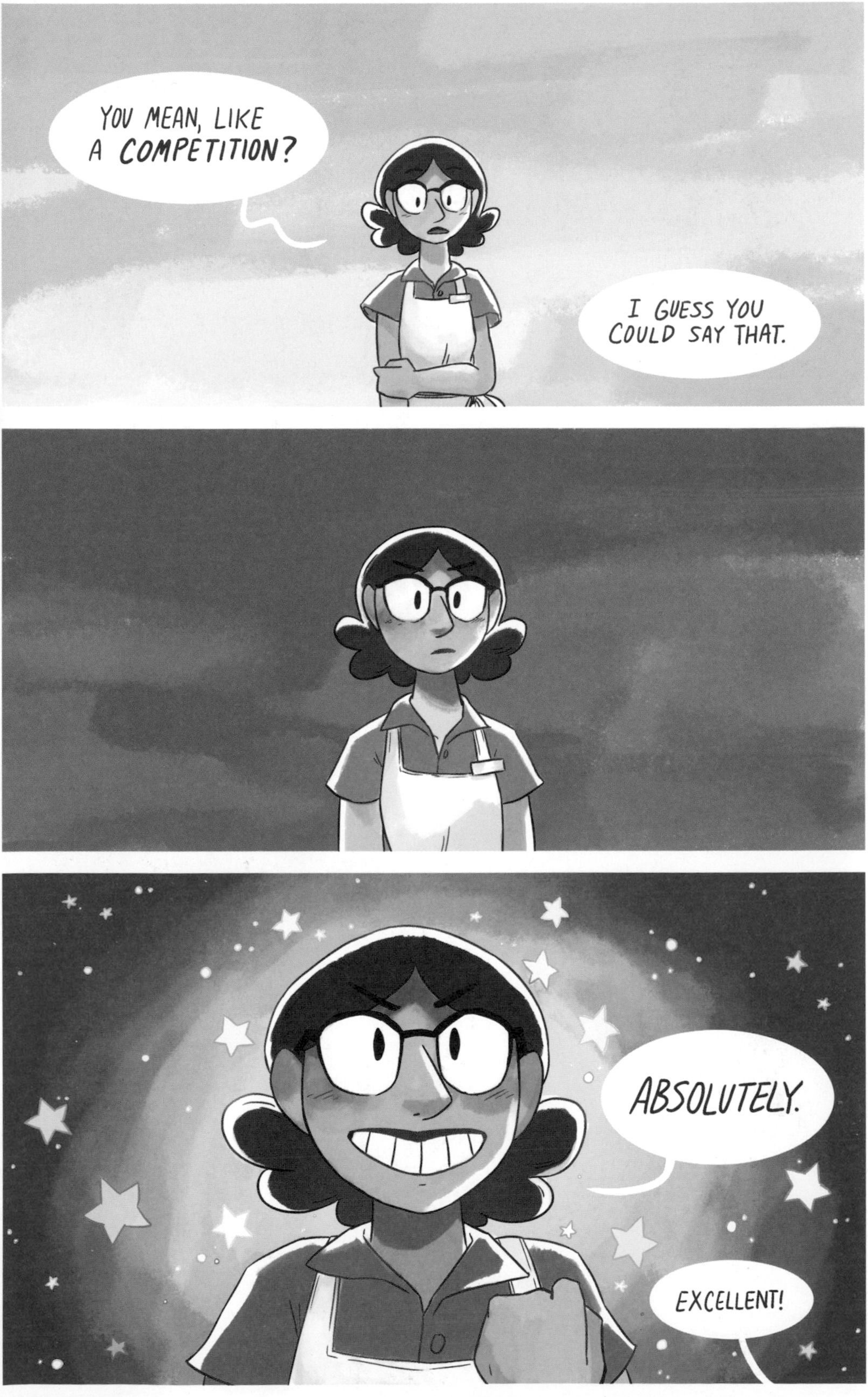
YOU MEAN, LIKE A COMPETITION?
I GUESS YOU COULD SAY THAT.
ABSOLUTELY.
EXCELLENT!

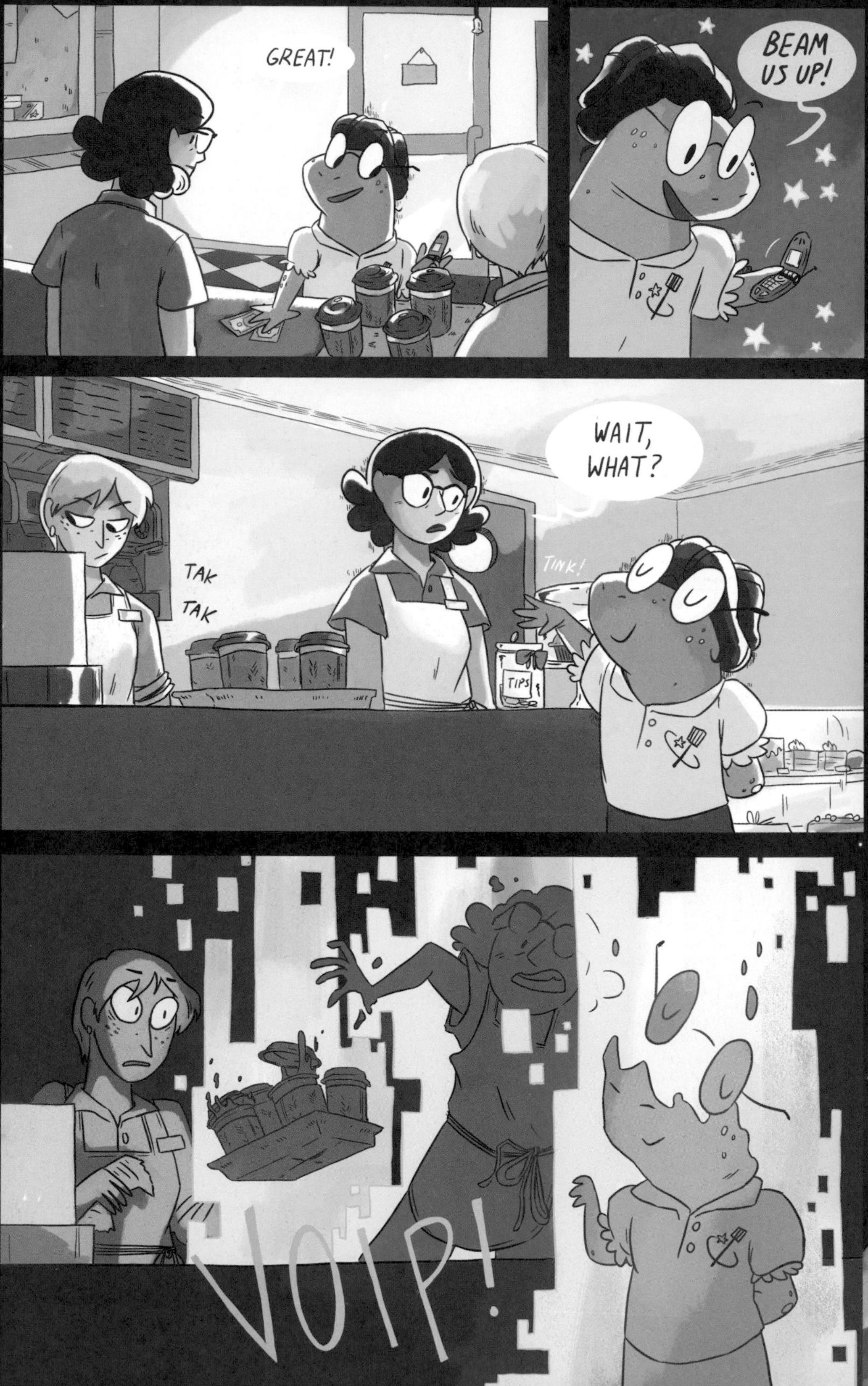
GREAT!
BEAM US UP!
WAIT, WHAT?
TAK
TAK
TINK!
TIPS
VOIP!

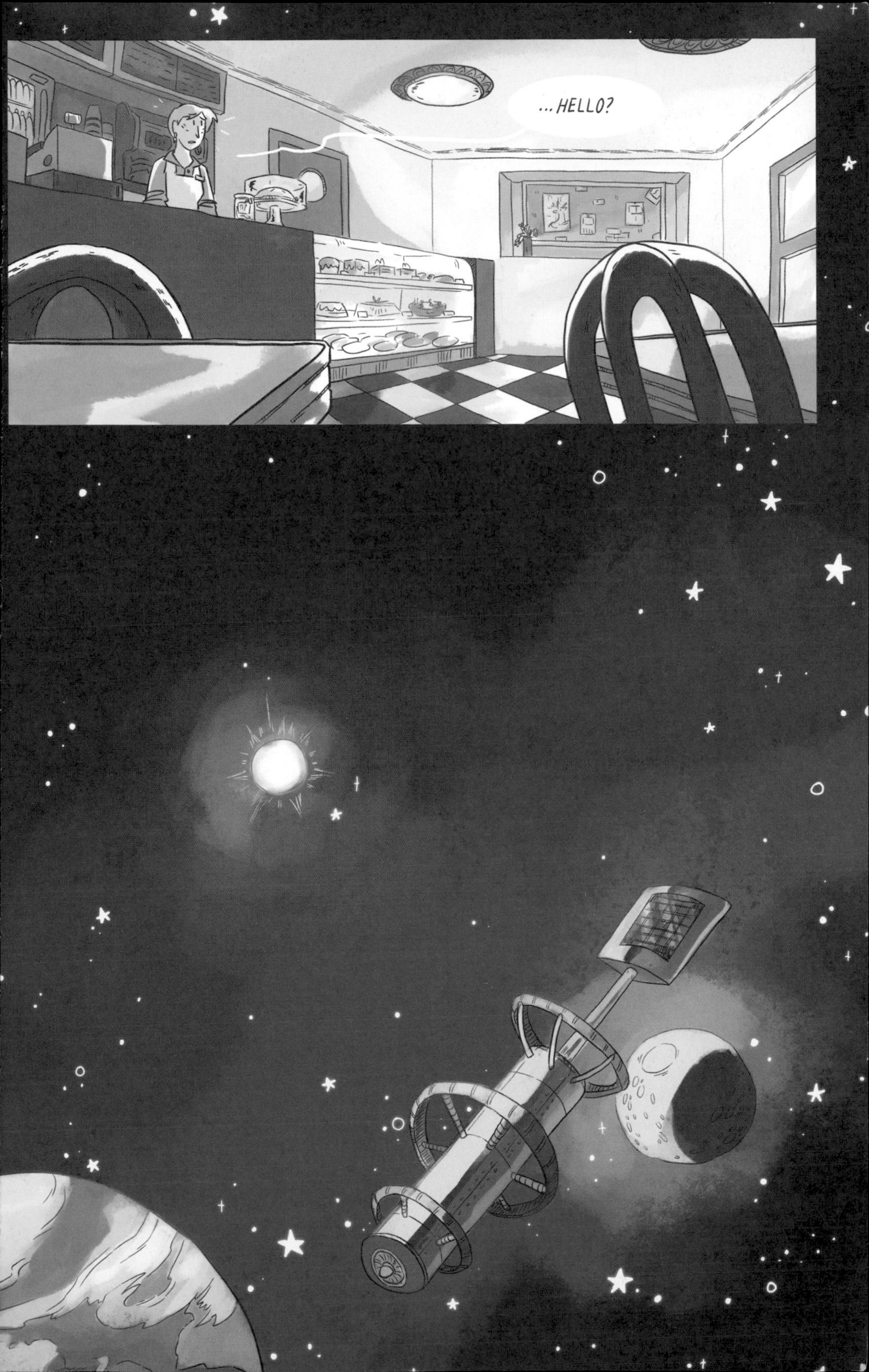
...HELLO?

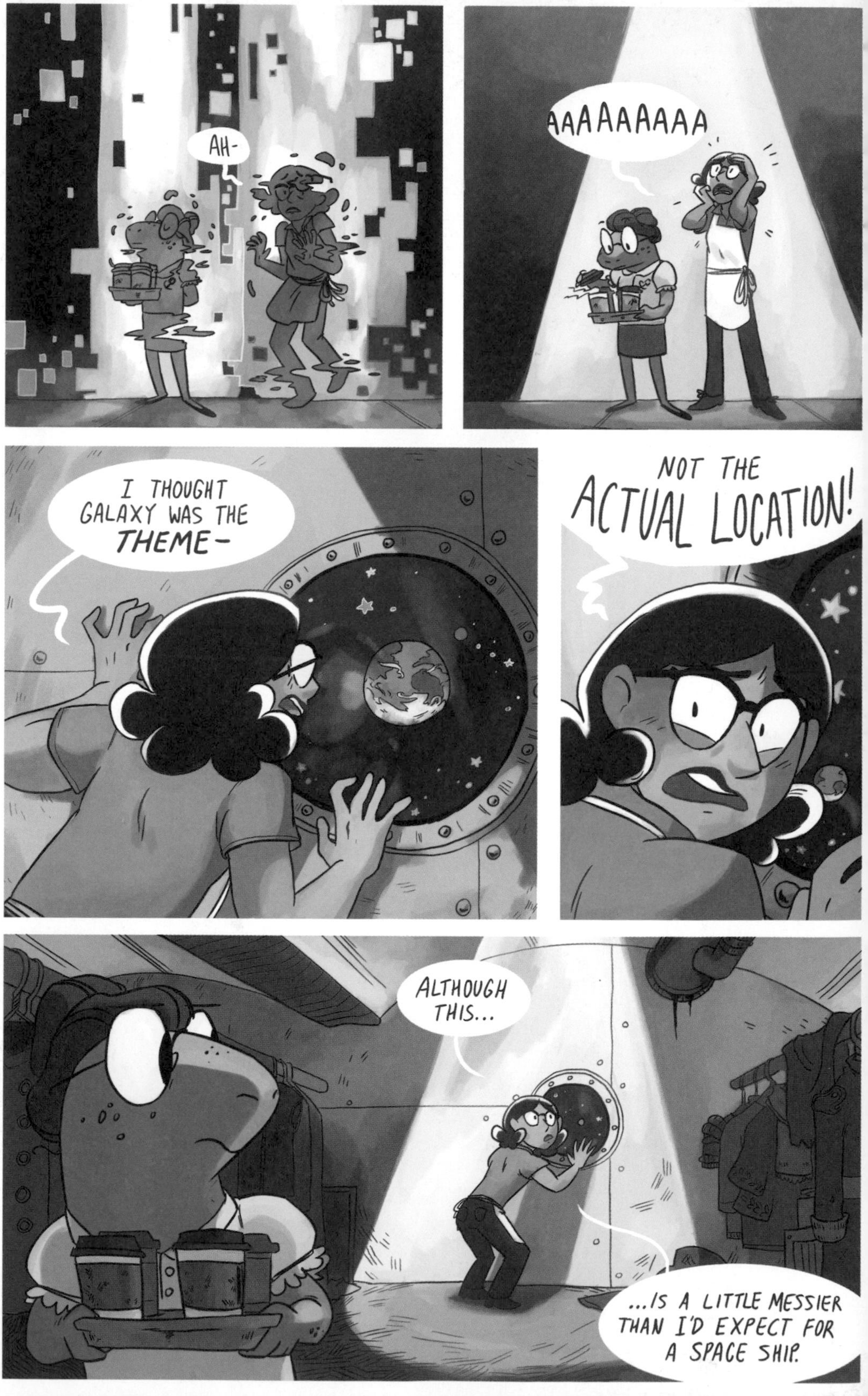
AH-
AAAAAAAAA
I THOUGHT GALAXY WAS THE THEME-
NOT THE ACTUAL LOCATION!
ALTHOUGH THIS...
...IS A LITTLE MESSIER THAN I'D EXPECT FOR A SPACE SHIP.

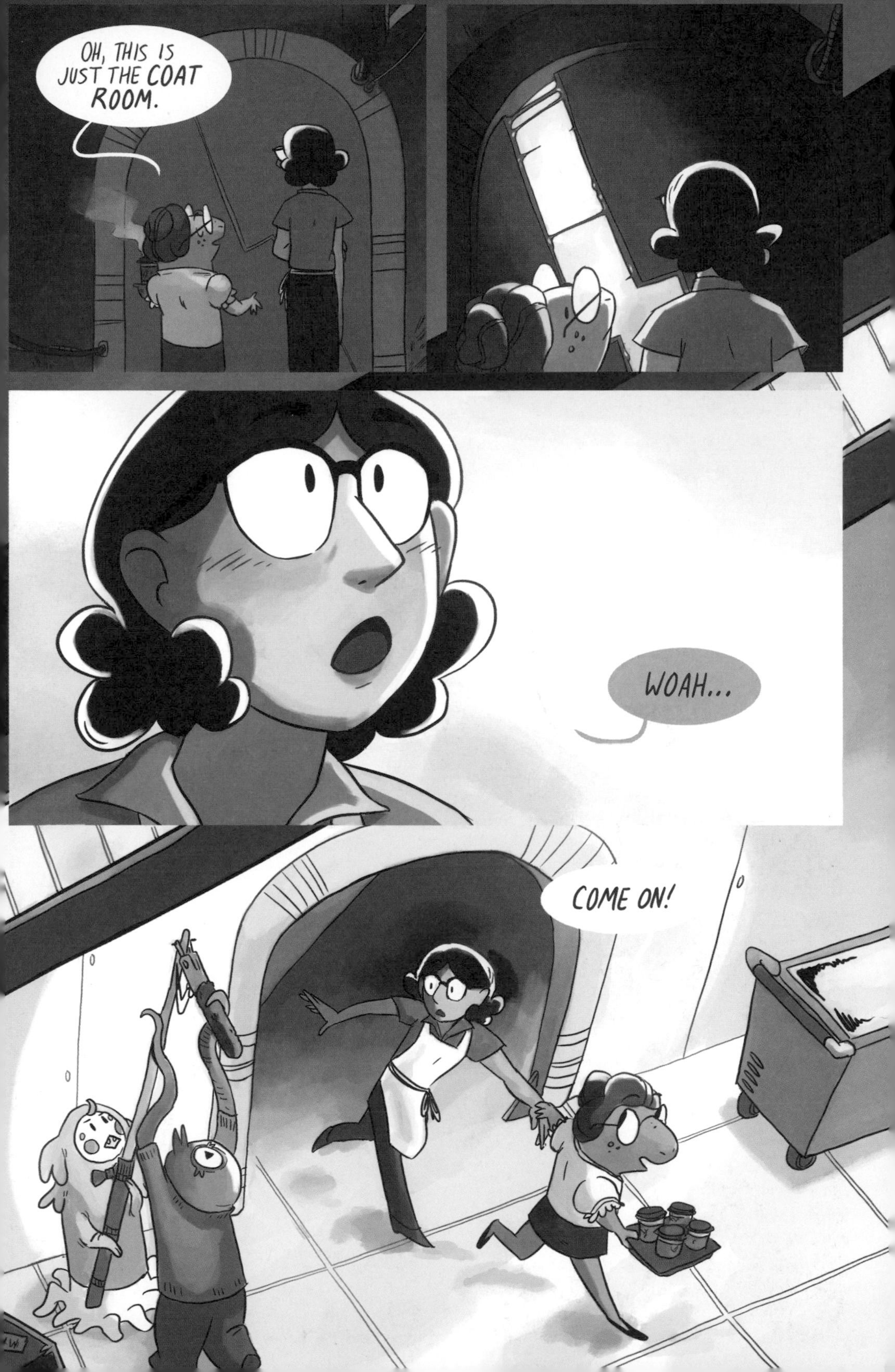
OH, THIS IS JUST THE COAT ROOM.
WOAH...
COME ON!

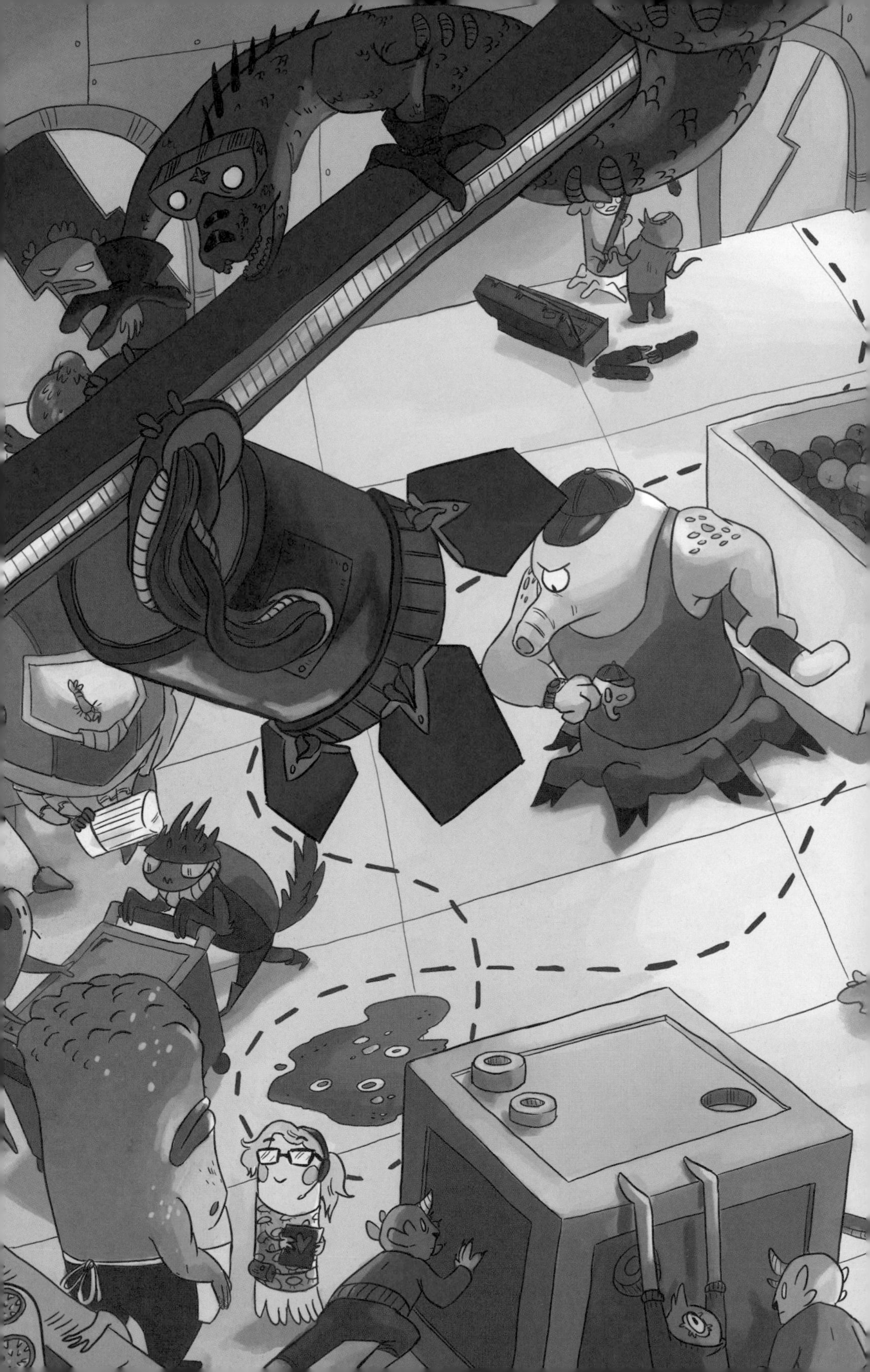

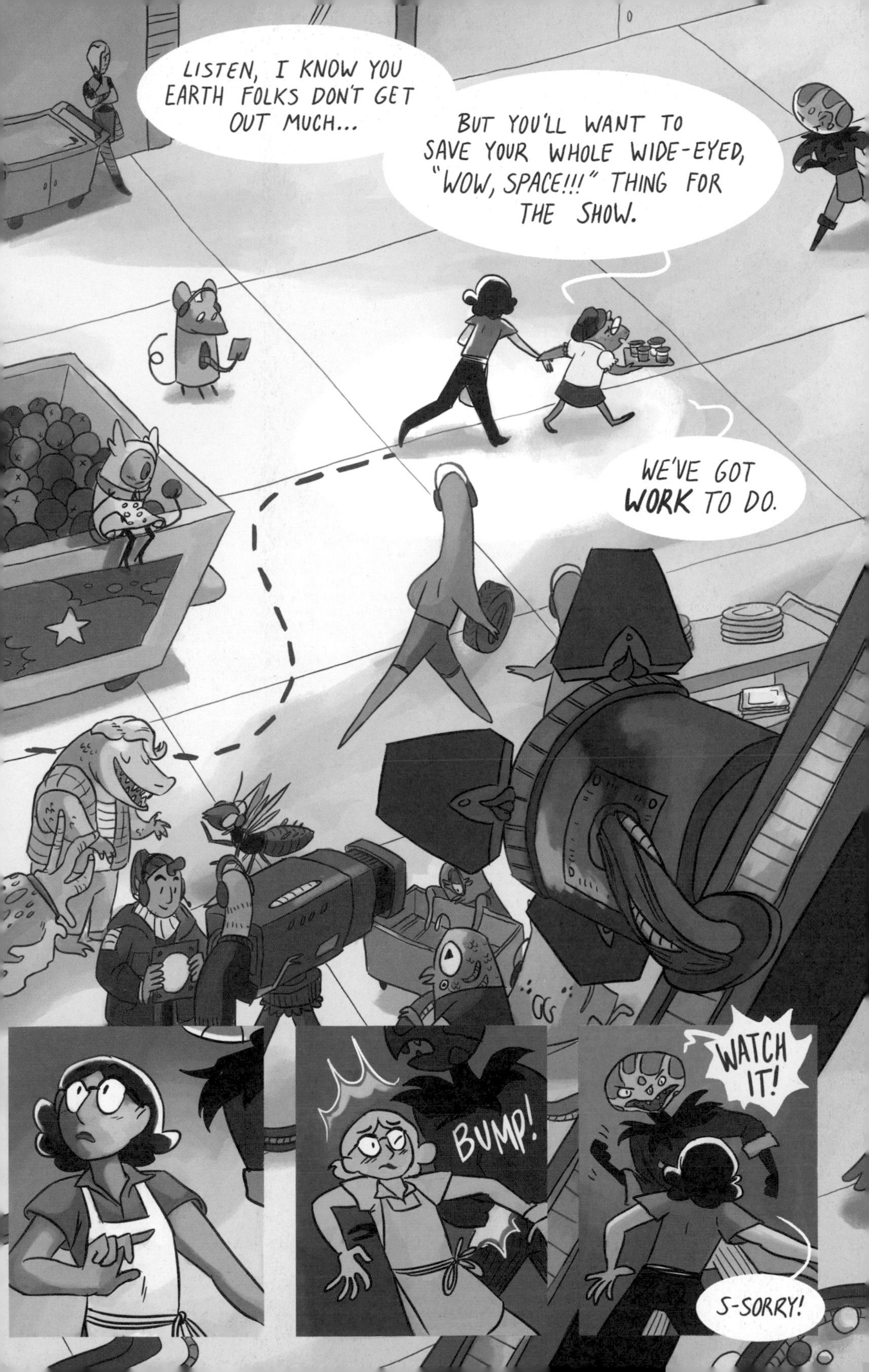
LISTEN, I KNOW YOU EARTH FOLKS DON'T GET OUT MUCH...
BUT YOU'LL WANT TO SAVE YOUR WHOLE WIDE-EYED, "WOW, SPACE!!!" THING FOR THE SHOW.
WE'VE GOT WORK TO DO.
BUMP!
WATCH IT!
S-SORRY!

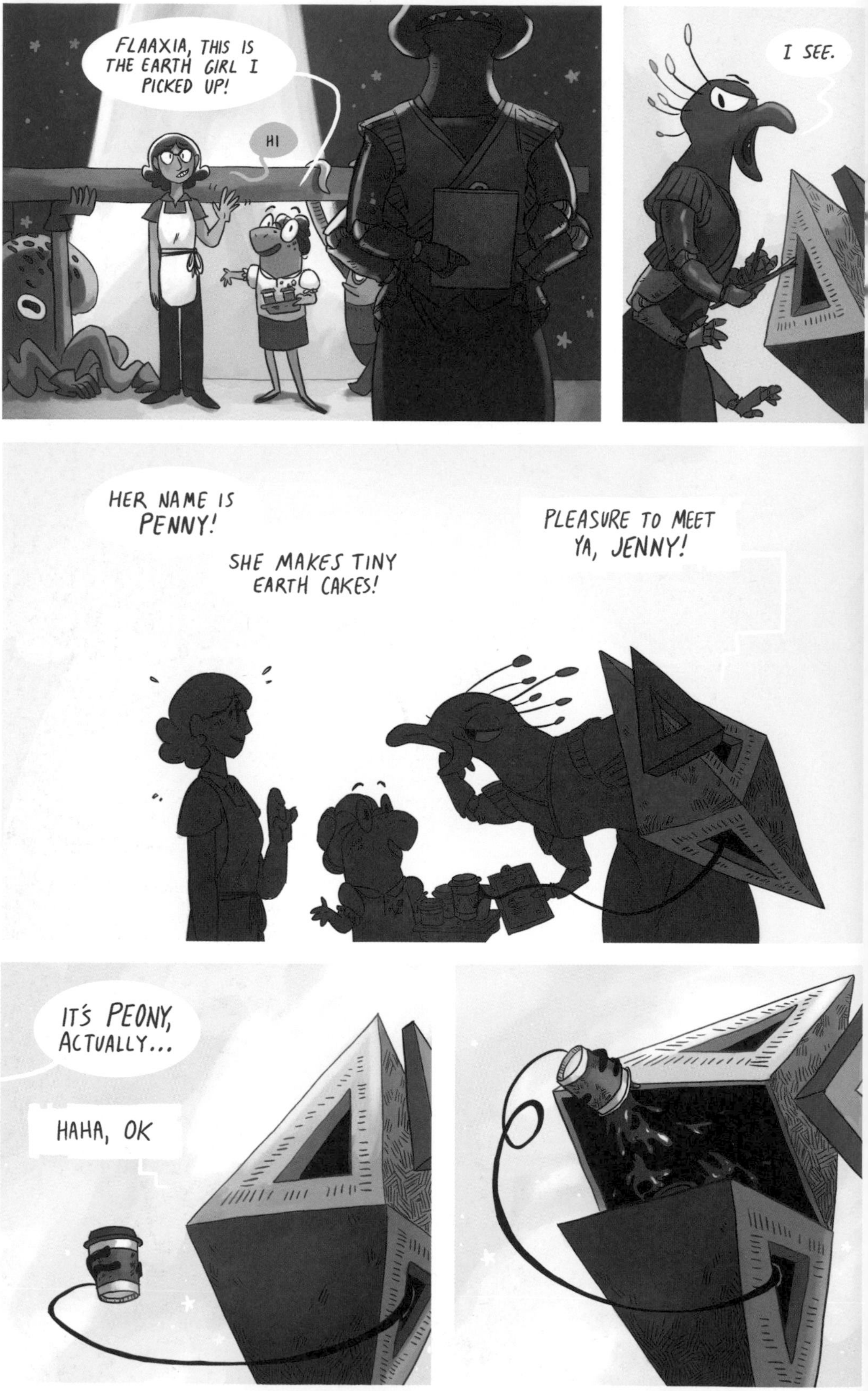
FLAAXIA, THIS IS THE EARTH GIRL I PICKED UP!
HI
I SEE.
HER NAME IS PENNY!
SHE MAKES TINY EARTH CAKES!
PLEASURE TO MEET YA, JENNY!
IT'S PEONY, ACTUALLY...
HAHA, OK

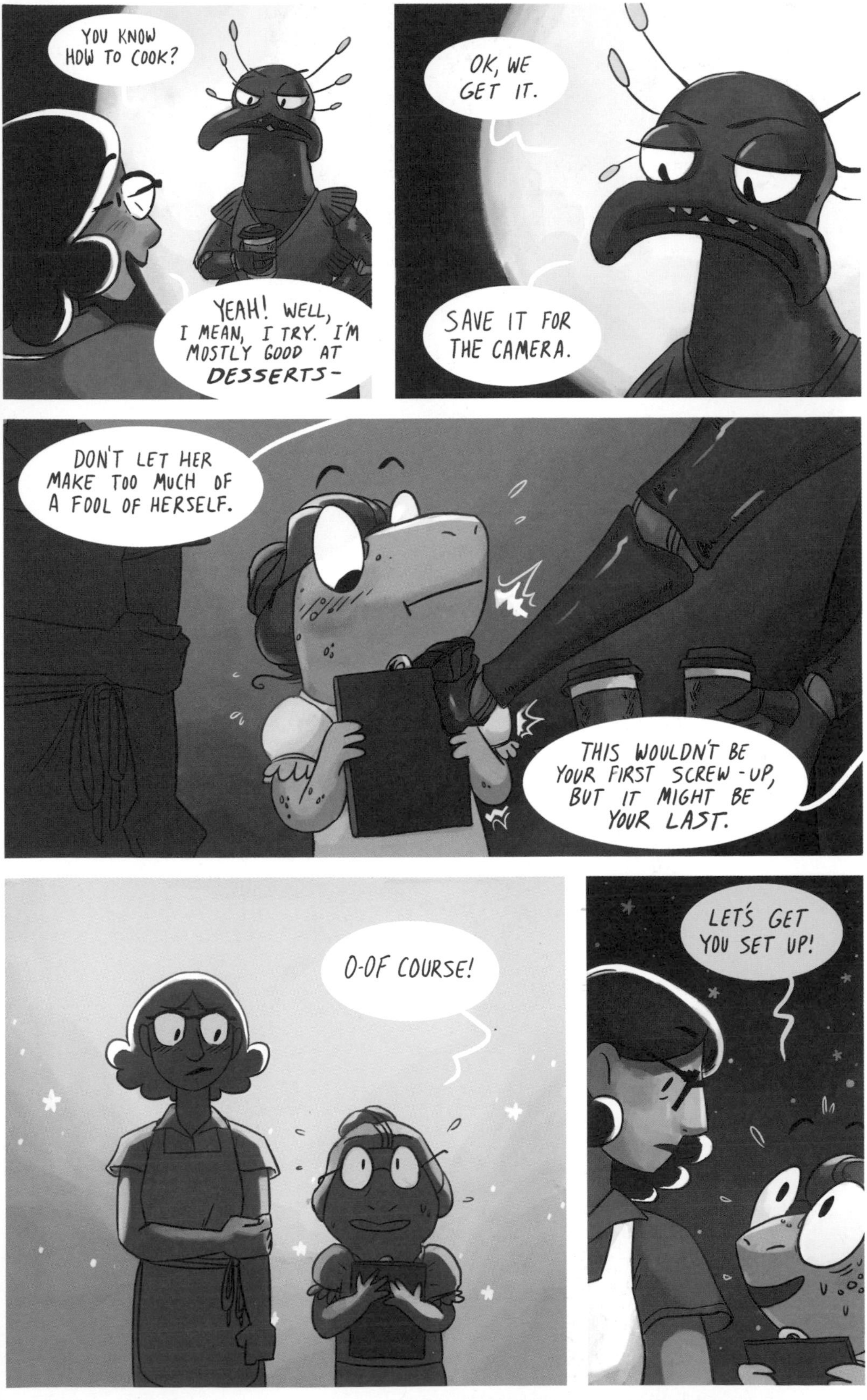
YOU KNOW HOW TO COOK?
YEAH! WELL, I MEAN, I TRY. I'M MOSTLY GOOD AT DESSERTS-
OK, WE GET IT.
SAVE IT FOR THE CAMERA.
DON'T LET HER MAKE TOO MUCH OF A FOOL OF HERSELF.
THIS WOULDN'T BE YOUR FIRST SCREW-UP, BUT IT MIGHT BE YOUR LAST.
O-OF COURSE!
LET'S GET YOU SET UP!

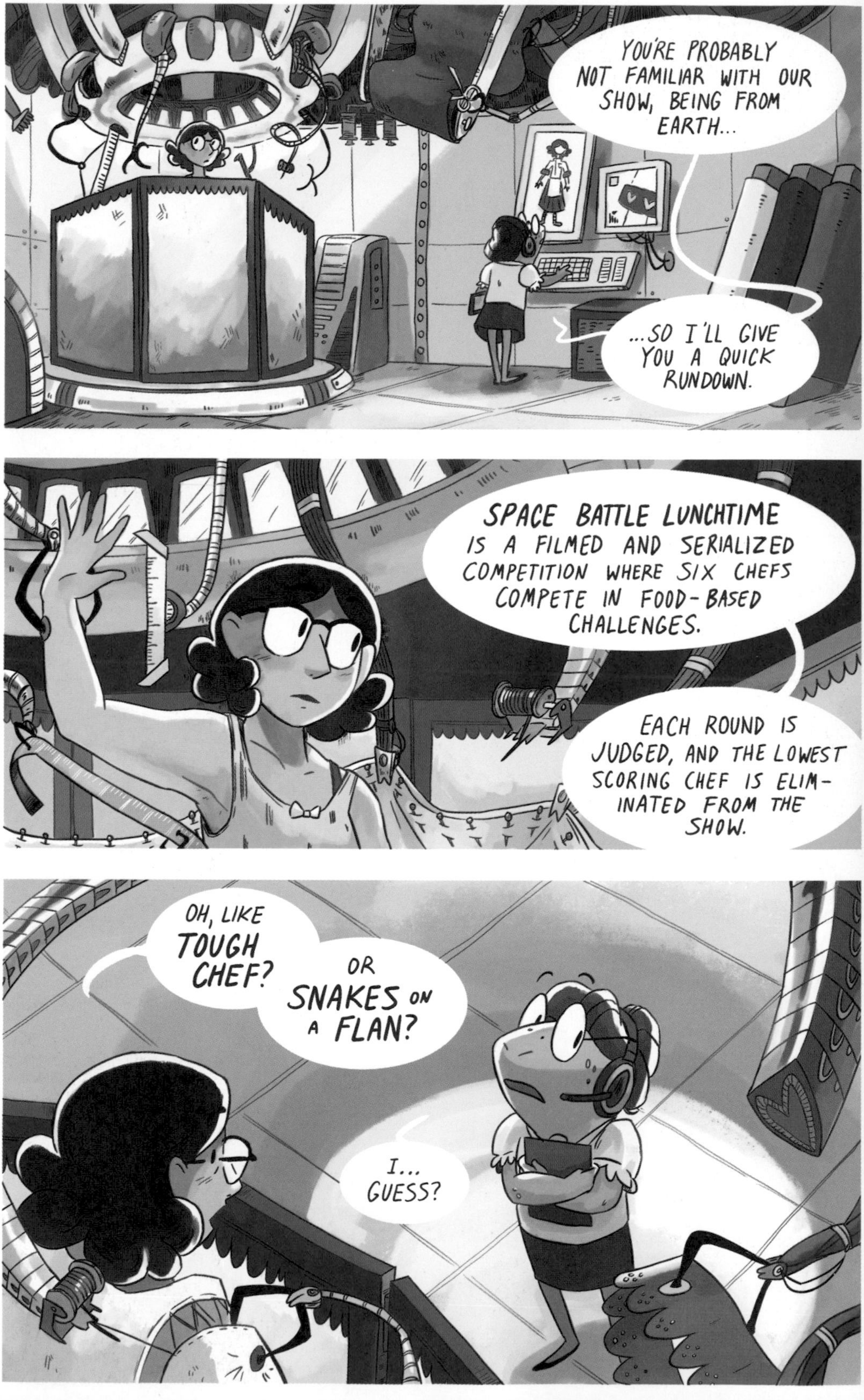
YOU'RE PROBABLY NOT FAMILIAR WITH OUR SHOW, BEING FROM EARTH...
...SO I'LL GIVE YOU A QUICK RUNDOWN.
SPACE BATTLE LUNCHTIME IS A FILMED AND SERIALIZED COMPETITION WHERE SIX CHEFS COMPETE IN FOOD-BASED CHALLENGES.
EACH ROUND IS JUDGED, AND THE LOWEST SCORING CHEF IS ELIM-INATED FROM THE SHOW.
OH, LIKE TOUGH CHEF?
OR SNAKES ON A FLAN?
I... GUESS?

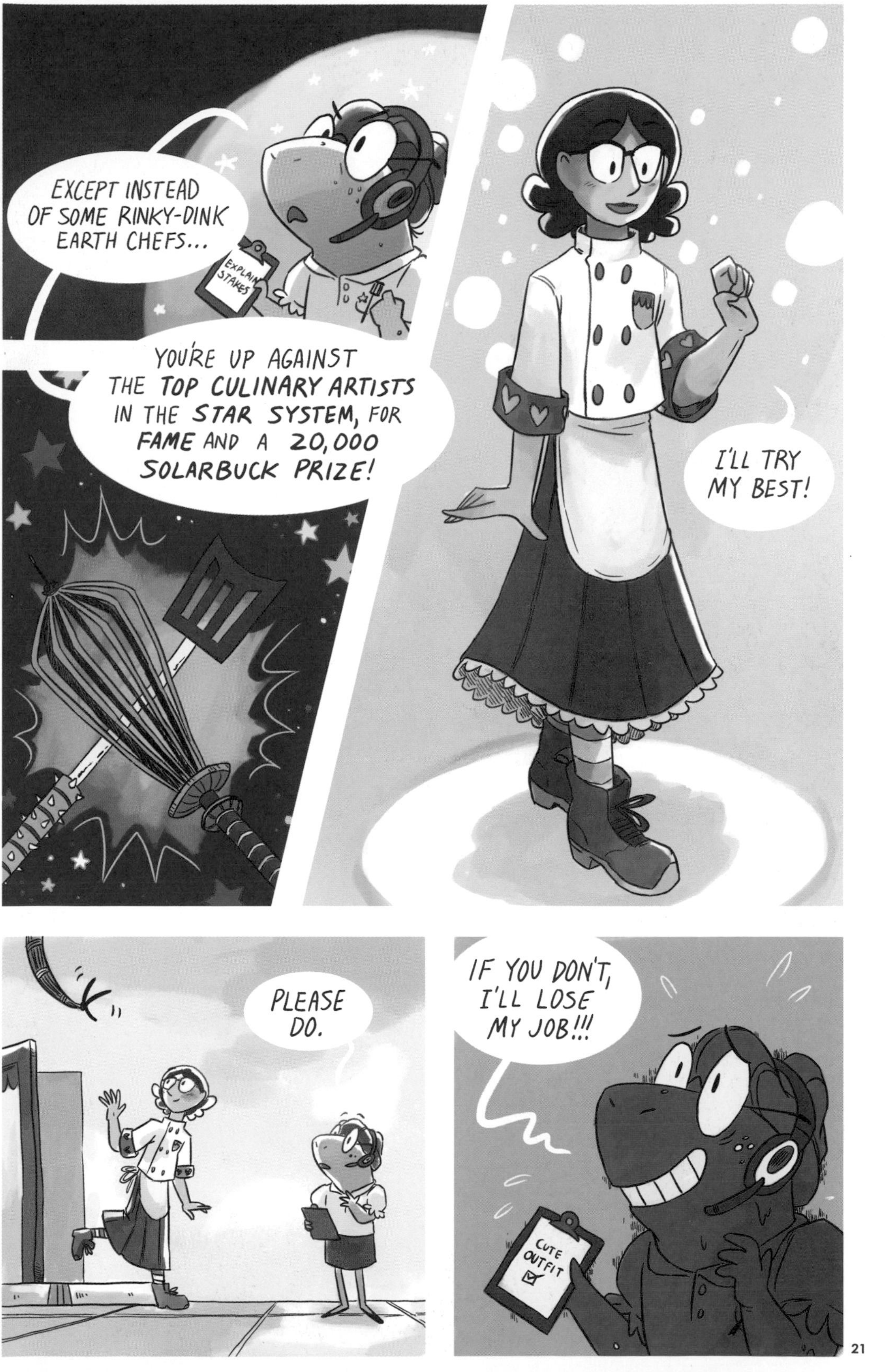
EXCEPT INSTEAD OF SOME RINKY-DINK EARTH CHEFS...
EXPLAIN STAKES
YOU'RE UP AGAINST THE TOP CULINARY ARTISTS IN THE STAR SYSTEM, FOR FAME AND A 20,000 SOLARBUCK PRIZE!
I'LL TRY MY BEST!
PLEASE DO.
IF YOU DON'T, I'LL LOSE MY JOB!!!
CUTE OUTFIT

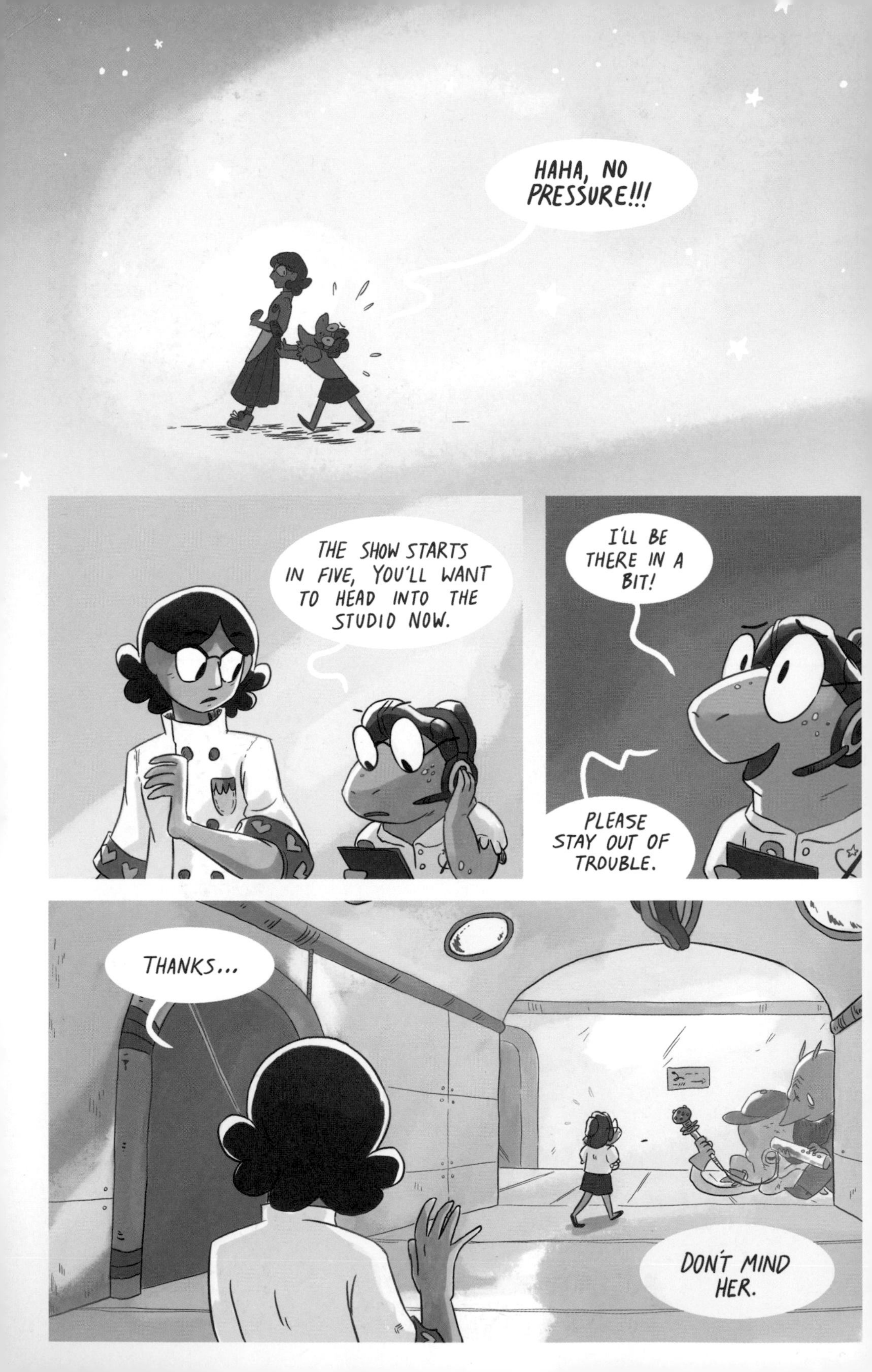
HAHA, NO PRESSURE!!!
THE SHOW STARTS IN FIVE, YOU'LL WANT TO HEAD INTO THE STUDIO NOW.
I'LL BE THERE IN A BIT!
PLEASE STAY OUT OF TROUBLE.
THANKS...
DON'T MIND HER.

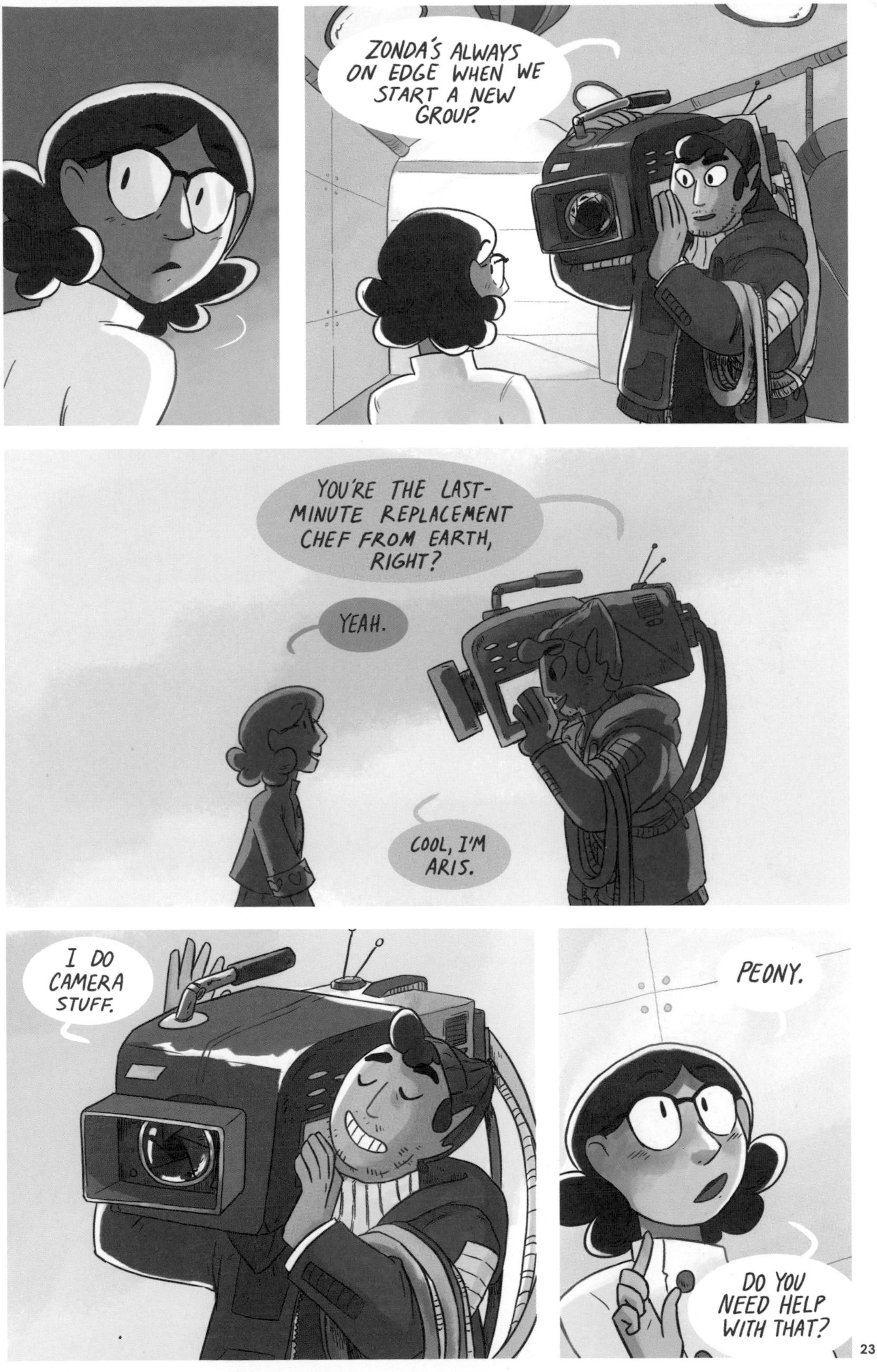
ZONDA'S ALWAYS ON EDGE WHEN WE START A NEW GROUP.
YOU'RE THE LAST-MINUTE REPLACEMENT CHEF FROM EARTH, RIGHT?
YEAH.
COOL, I'M ARIS.
I DO CAMERA STUFF.
PEONY.
DO YOU NEED HELP WITH THAT?

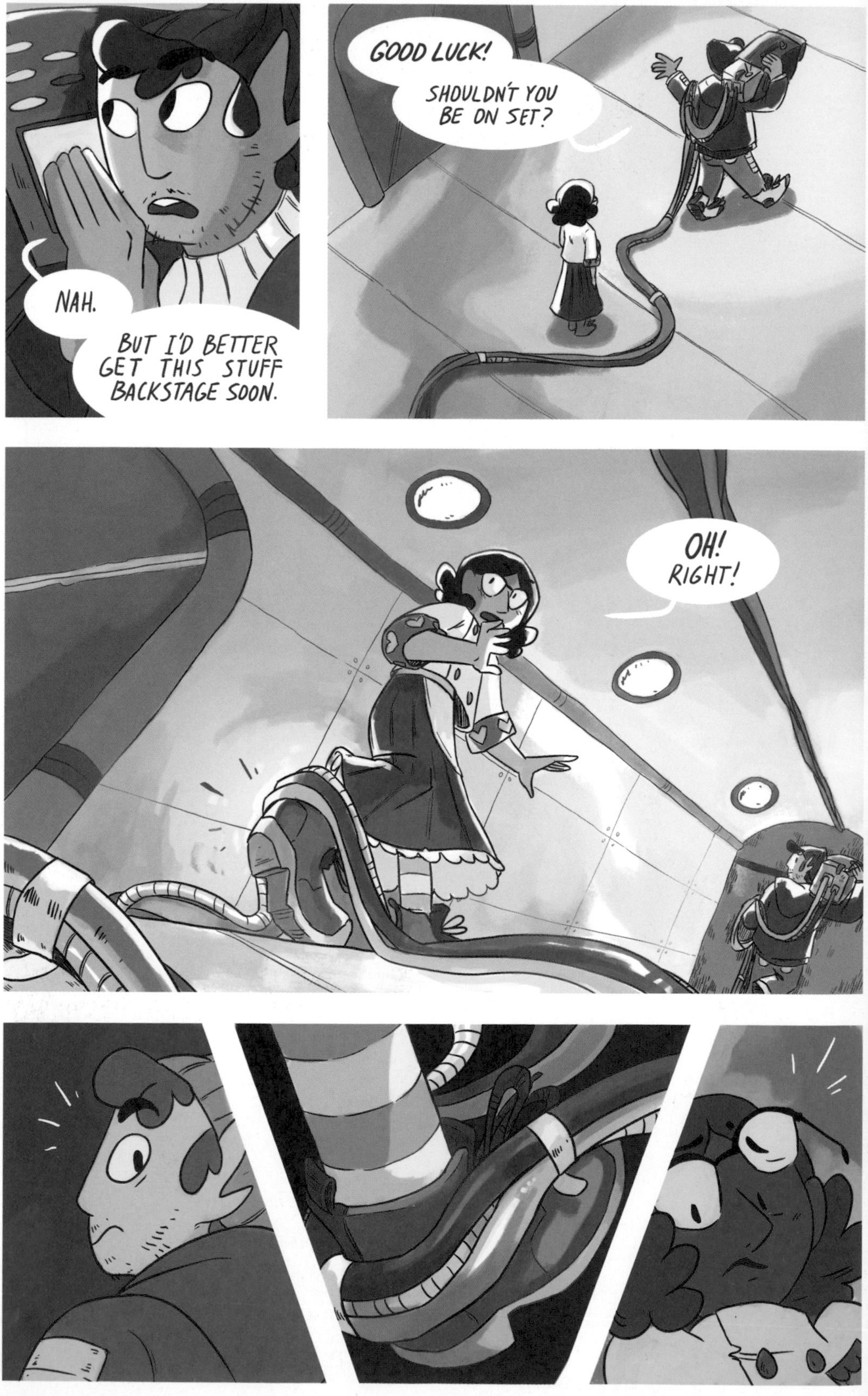

GOOD LUCK!
SHOULDN'T YOU BE ON SET?
NAH.
BUT I'D BETTER GET THIS STUFF BACKSTAGE SOON.
OH! RIGHT!

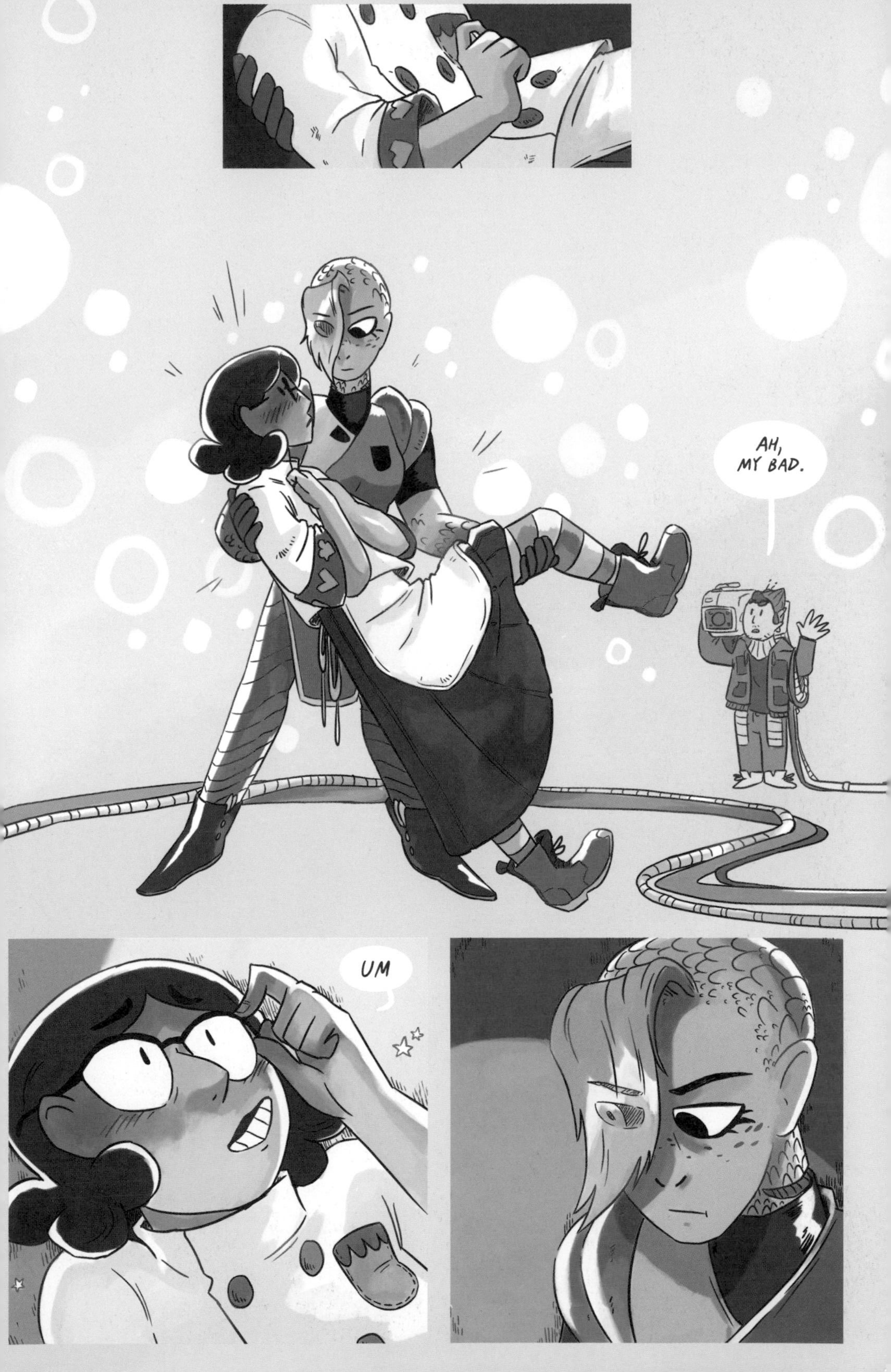
AH, MY BAD.
UM

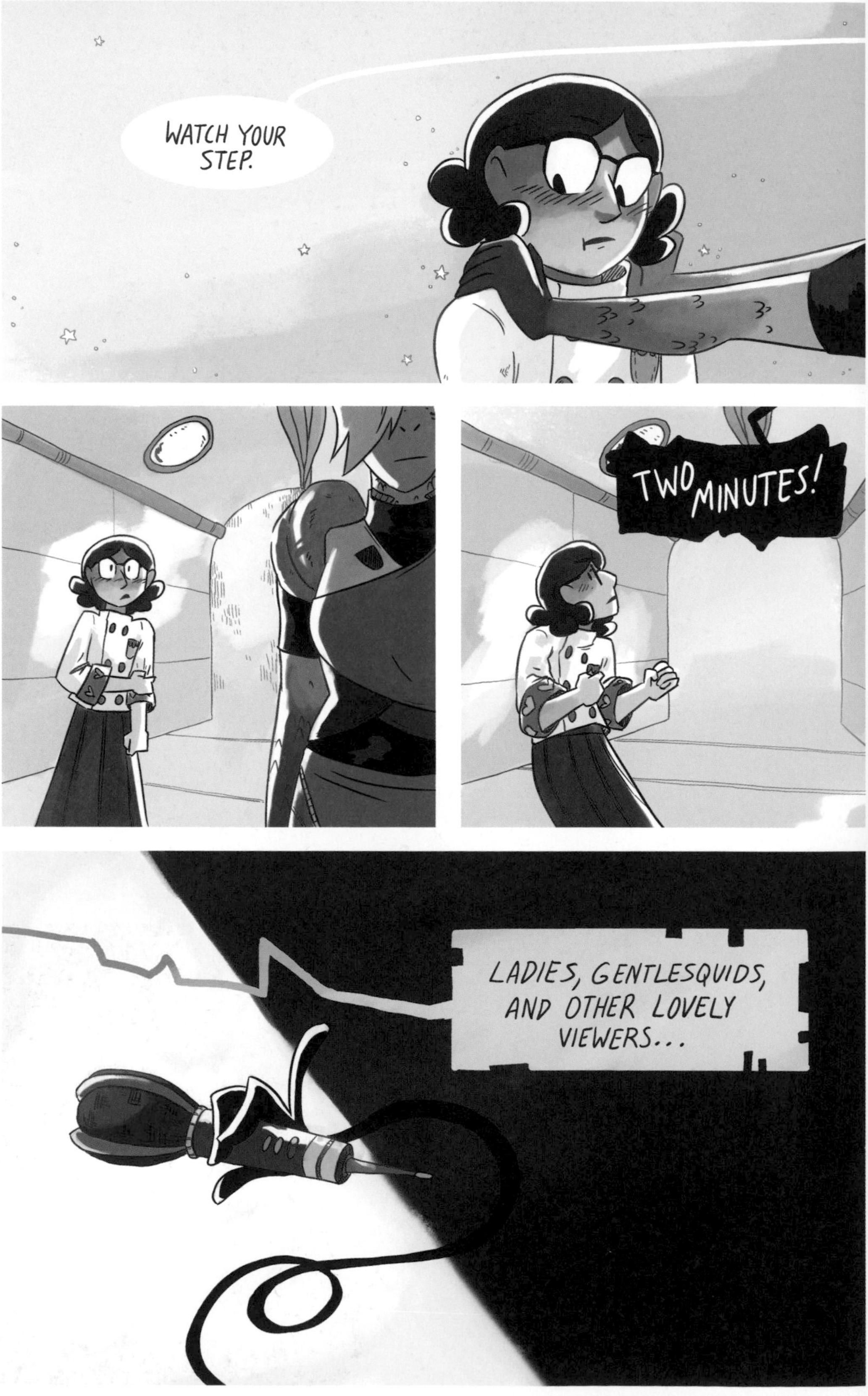
WATCH YOUR STEP.
TWO MINUTES!
LADIES, GENTLESQUIDS, AND OTHER LOVELY VIEWERS...

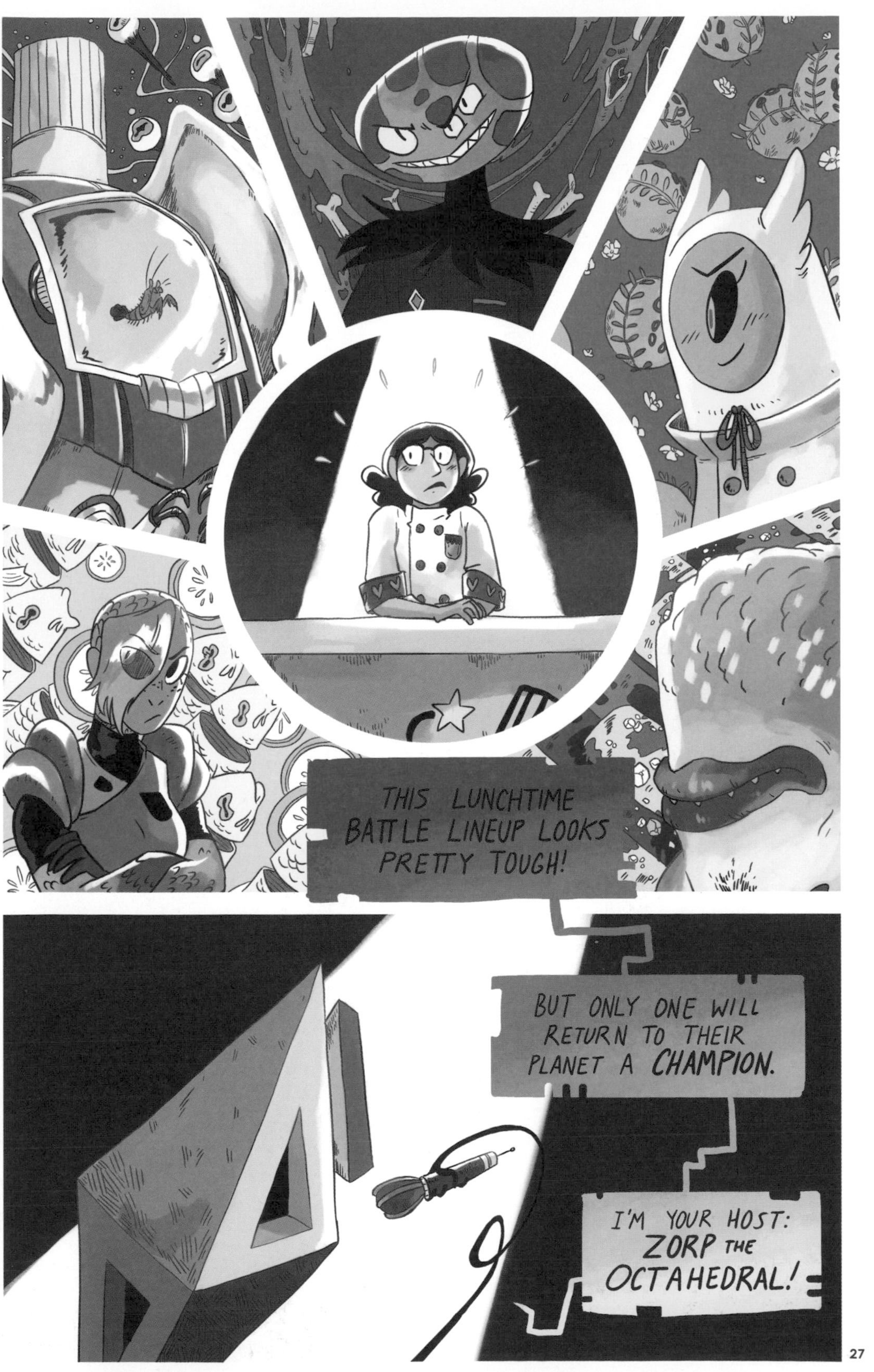
THIS LUNCHTIME BATTLE LINEUP LOOKS PRETTY TOUGH!
BUT ONLY ONE WILL RETURN TO THEIR PLANET A CHAMPION.
I'M YOUR HOST: ZORP THE OCTAHEDRAL!

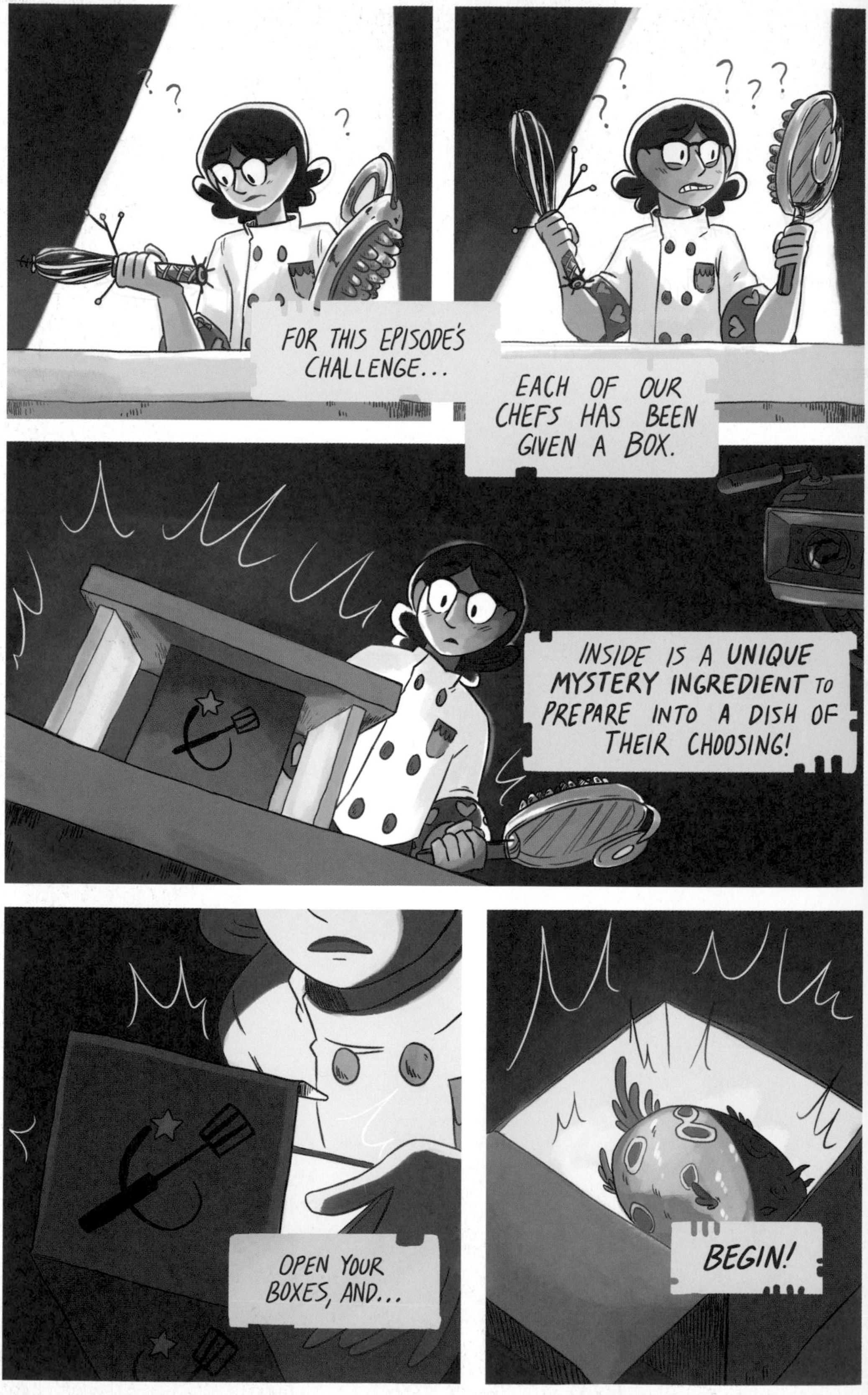
FOR THIS EPISODE'S CHALLENGE...
EACH OF OUR CHEFS HAS BEEN GIVEN A BOX.
INSIDE IS A UNIQUE MYSTERY INGREDIENT TO PREPARE INTO A DISH OF THEIR CHOOSING!
OPEN YOUR BOXES, AND...
BEGIN!

CHAPTER TWO

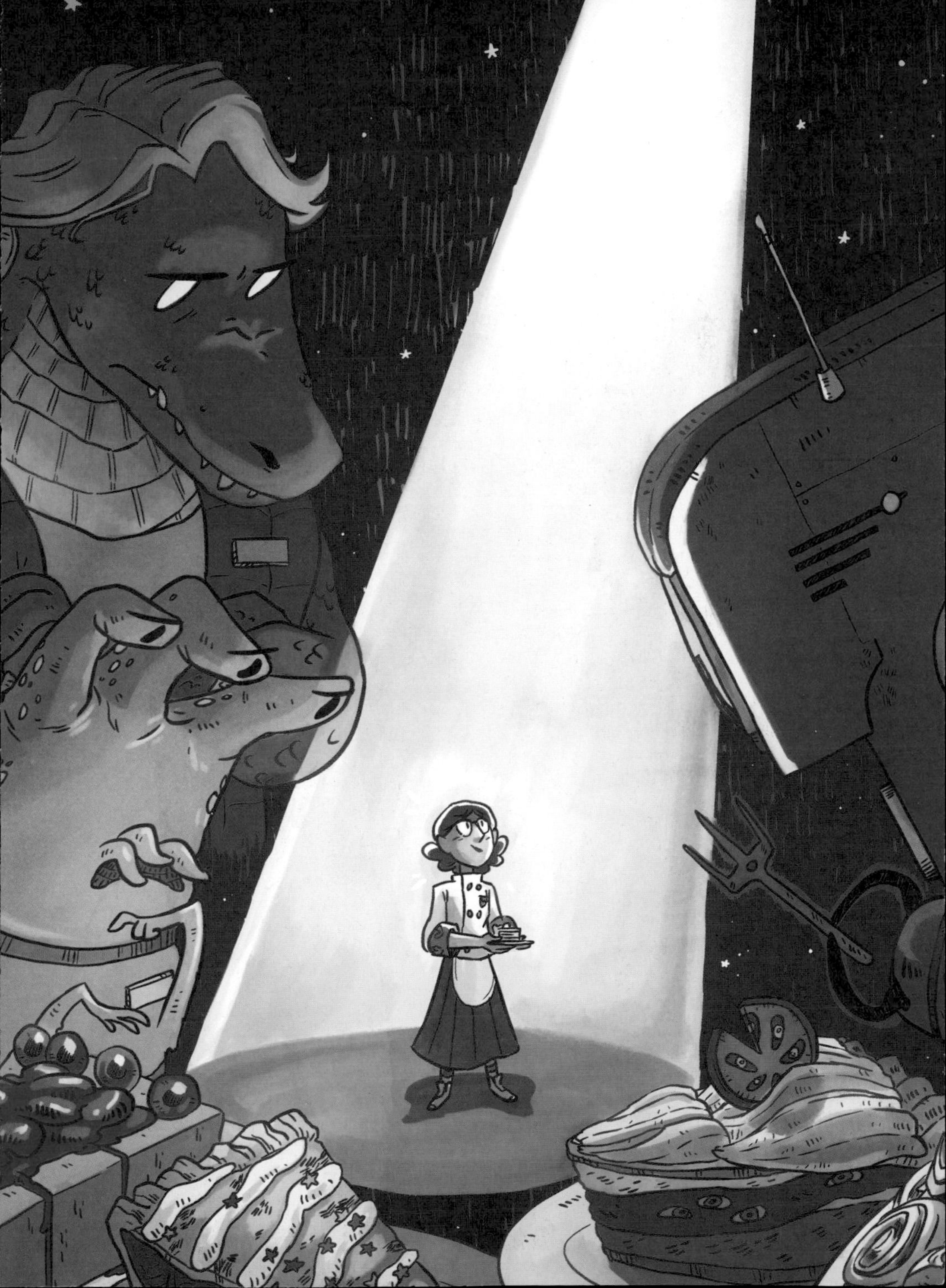

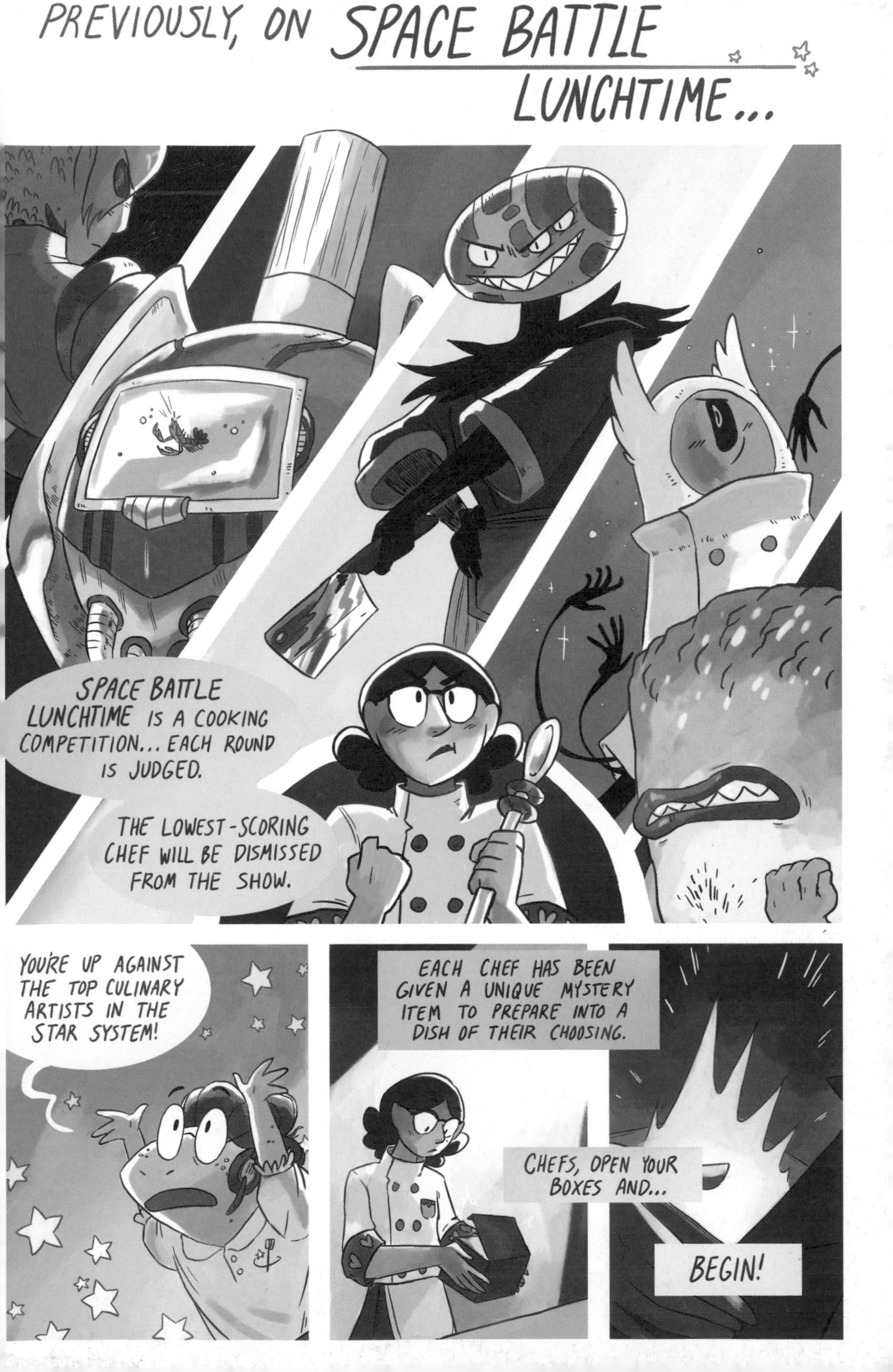
PREVIOUSLY, ON SPACE BATTLE LUNCHTIME...
SPACE BATTLE LUNCHTIME IS A COOKING COMPETITION... EACH ROUND IS JUDGED.
THE LOWEST-SCORING CHEF WILL BE DISMISSED FROM THE SHOW.
YOU'RE UP AGAINST THE TOP CULINARY ARTISTS IN THE STAR SYSTEM!
EACH CHEF HAS BEEN GIVEN A UNIQUE MYSTERY ITEM TO PREPARE INTO A DISH OF THEIR CHOOSING.
CHEFS, OPEN YOUR BOXES AND...
BEGIN!

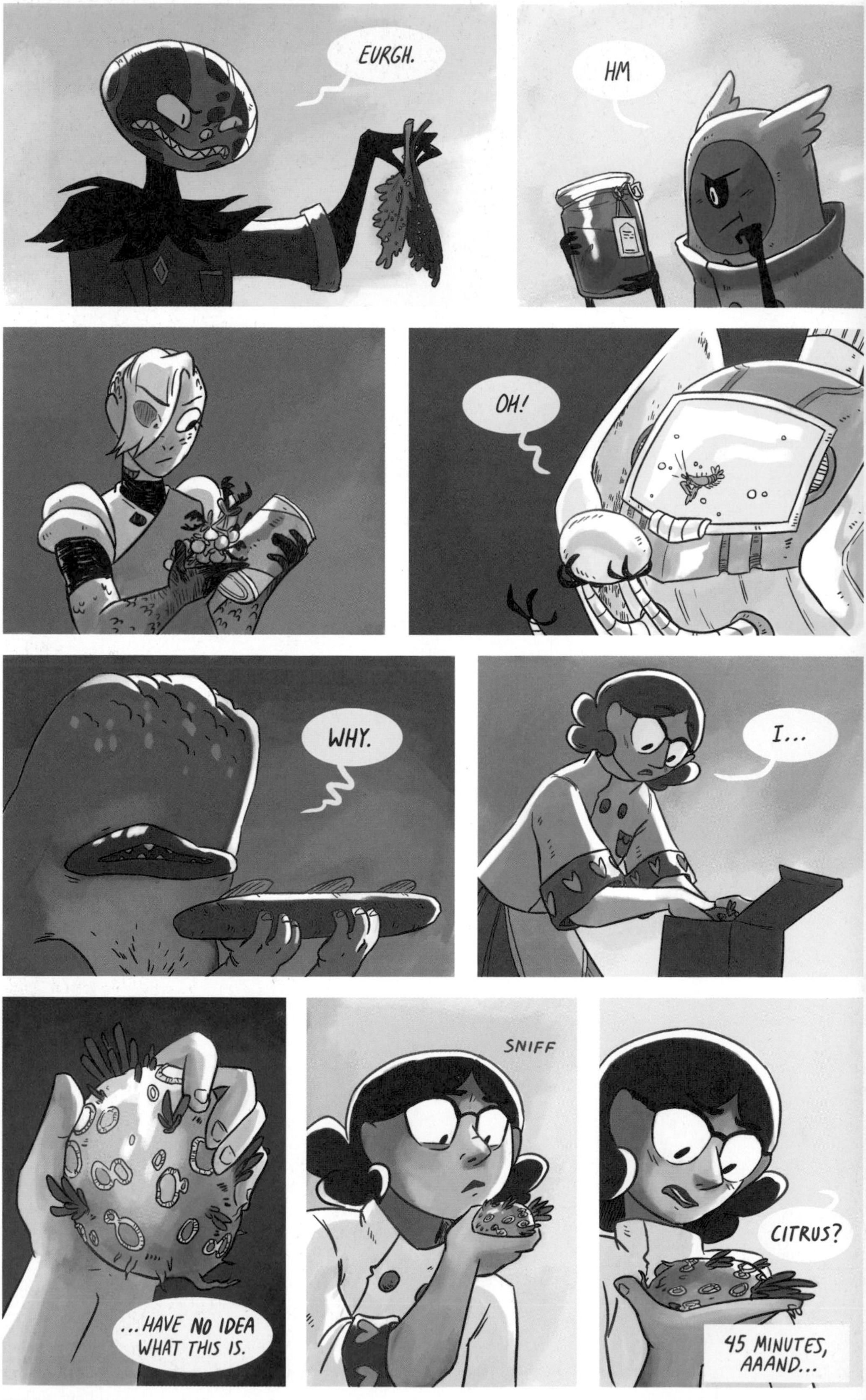
EURGH.
HM
OH!
WHY.
I...
SNIFF
...HAVE NO IDEA WHAT THIS IS.
CITRUS?
45 MINUTES, AAAND...

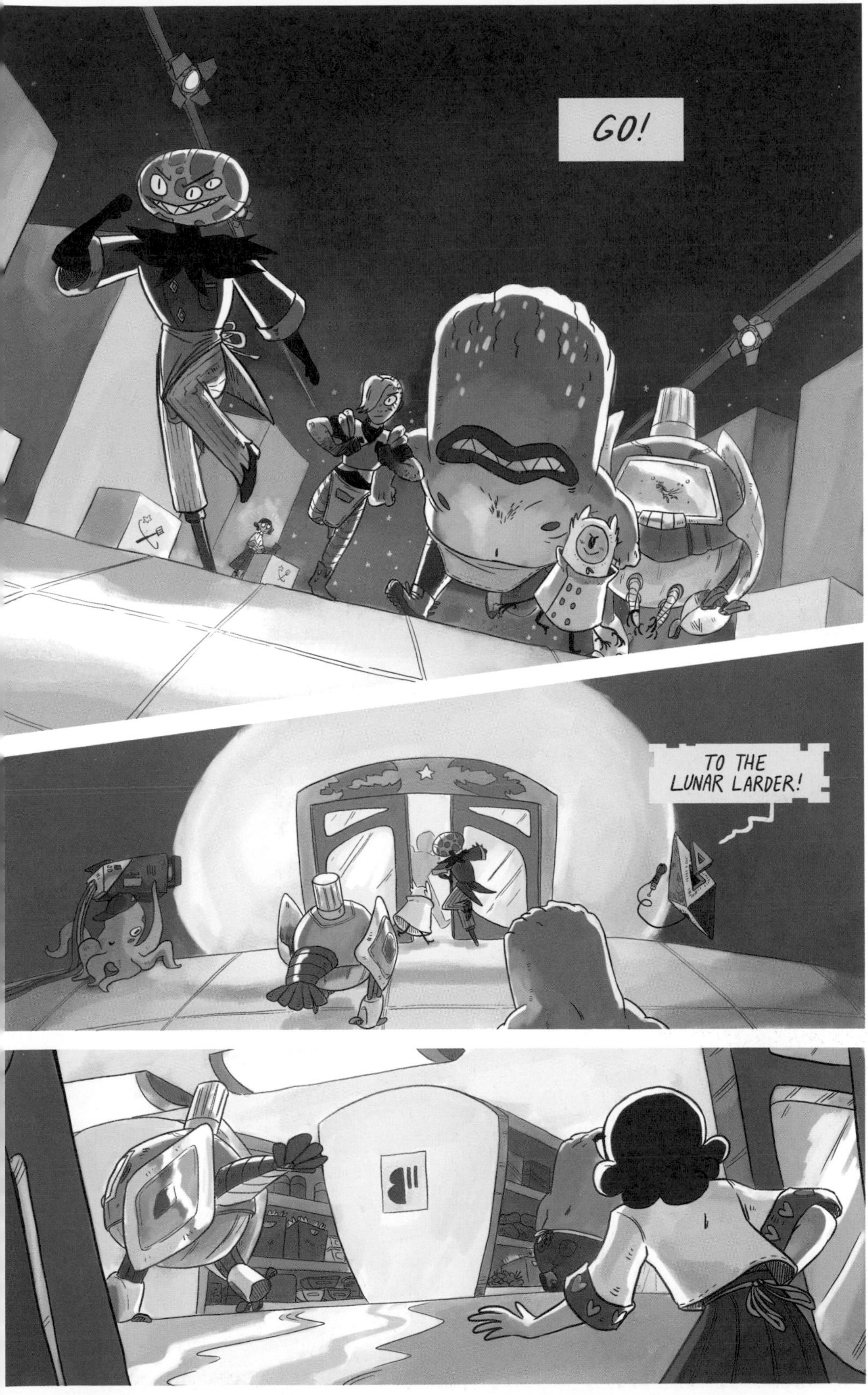
GO!
TO THE LUNAR LARDER!

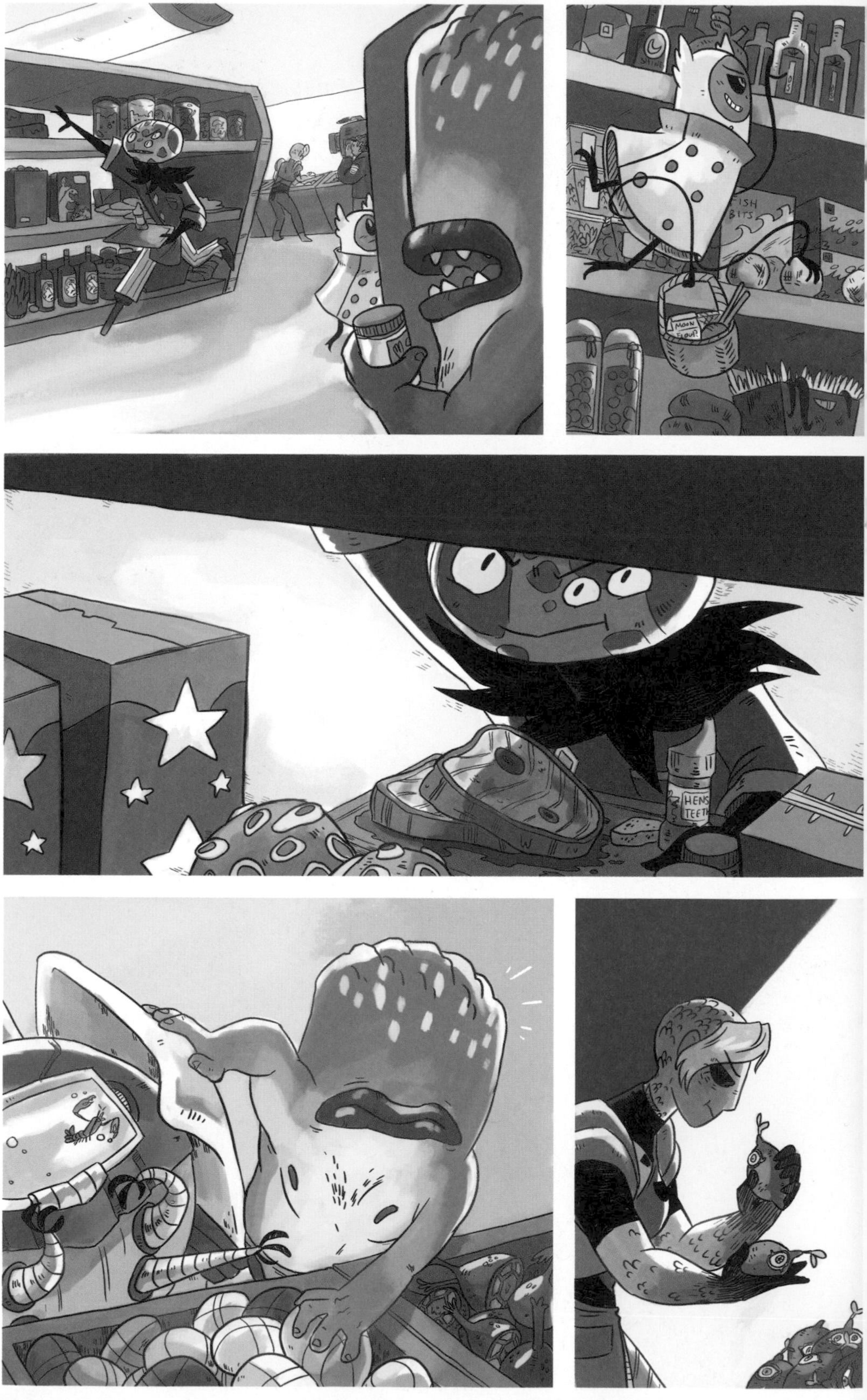
FISH BITS
HENS TEETH

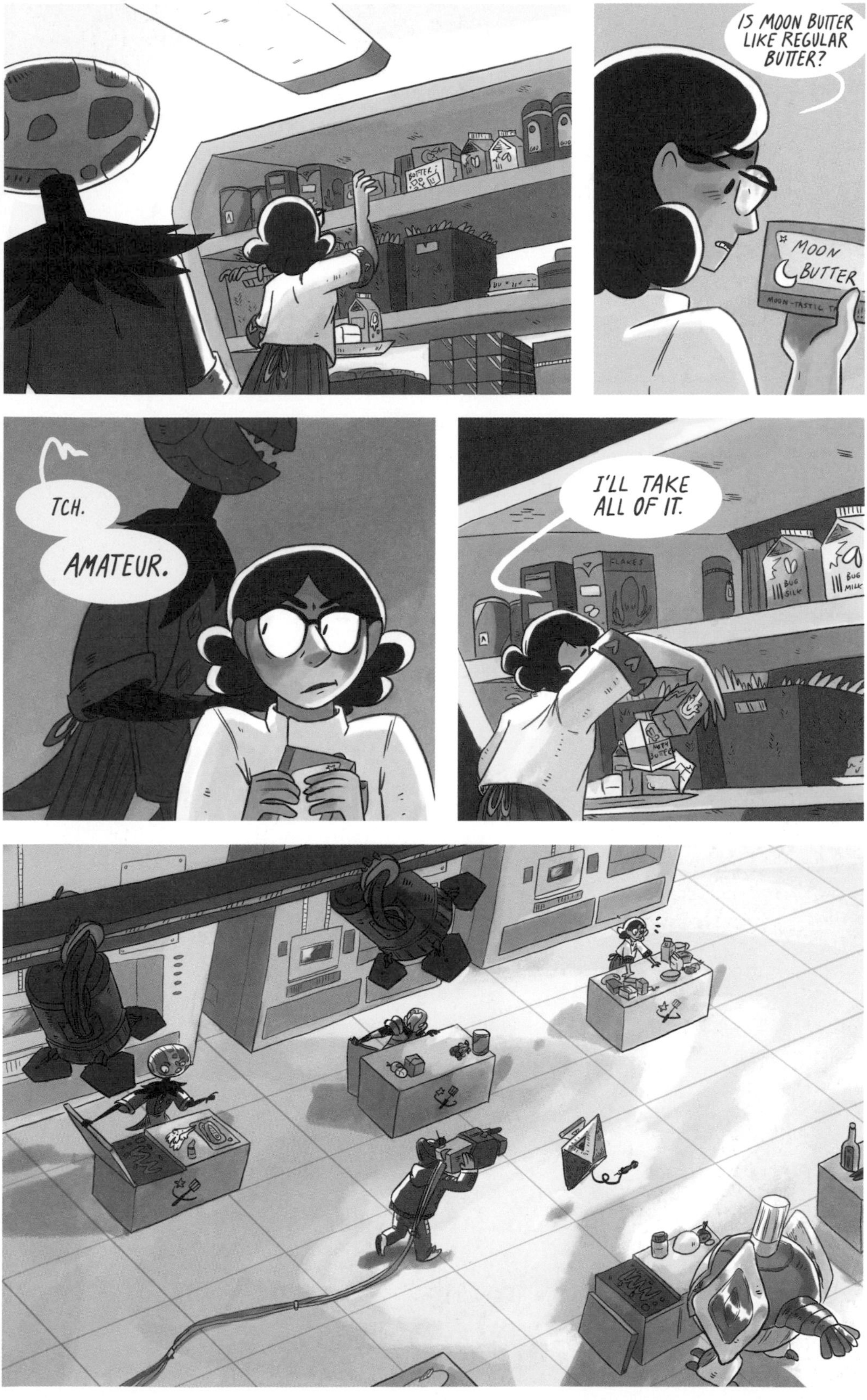
IS MOON BUTTER LIKE REGULAR BUTTER?
MOON BUTTER
TCH.
AMATEUR.
I'LL TAKE ALL OF IT.
BUG SILK
BUG MILK
FLAKES

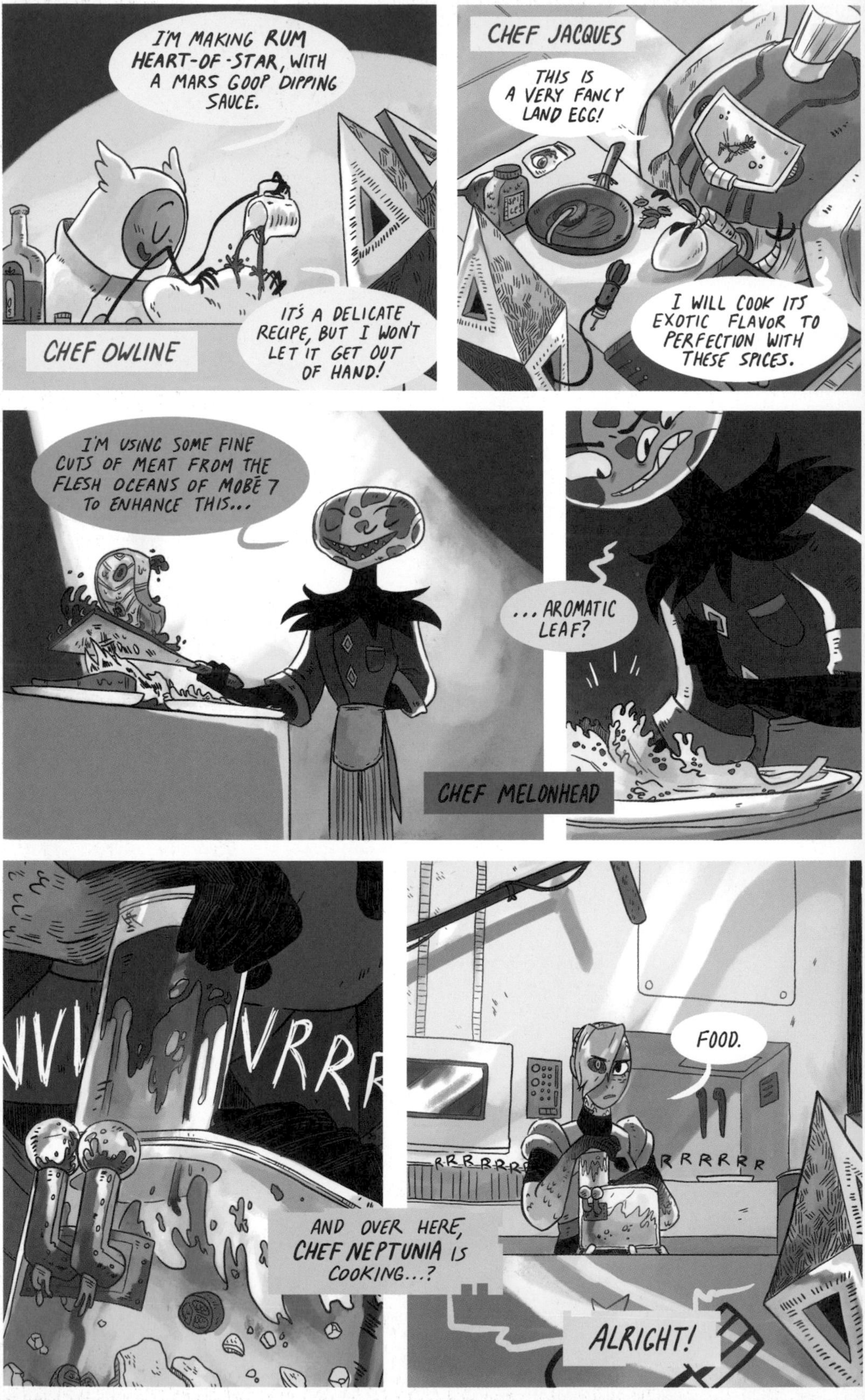
I'M MAKING RUM HEART-OF-STAR, WITH A MARS GOOP DIPPING SAUCE.
CHEF OWLINE
IT'S A DELICATE RECIPE, BUT I WON'T LET IT GET OUT OF HAND!
CHEF JACQUES
THIS IS A VERY FANCY LAND EGG!
I WILL COOK ITS EXOTIC FLAVOR TO PERFECTION WITH THESE SPICES.
I'M USING SOME FINE CUTS OF MEAT FROM THE FLESH OCEANS OF MOBĒ 7 TO ENHANCE THIS...
...AROMATIC LEAF?
CHEF MELONHEAD
VRRR
AND OVER HERE, CHEF NEPTUNIA IS COOKING...?
FOOD.
RRRRRRR
RRRRRR
ALRIGHT!

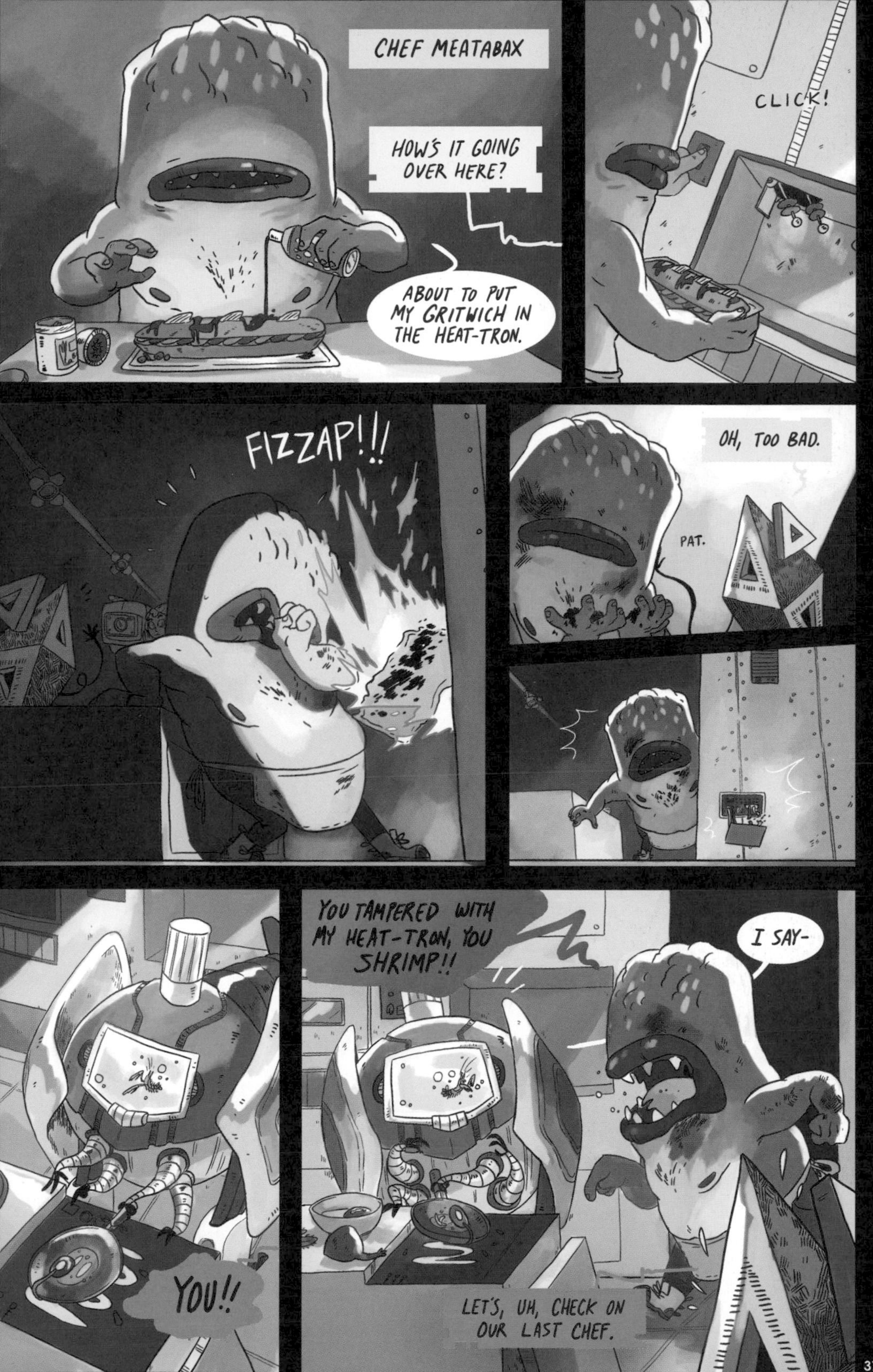
CHEF MEATABAX
HOW'S IT GOING OVER HERE?
ABOUT TO PUT MY GRITWICH IN THE HEAT-TRON.
CLICK!
FIZZAP!!!
OH, TOO BAD.
PAT.
YOU!!
YOU TAMPERED WITH MY HEAT-TRON, YOU SHRIMP!!
I SAY-
LET'S, UH, CHECK ON OUR LAST CHEF.

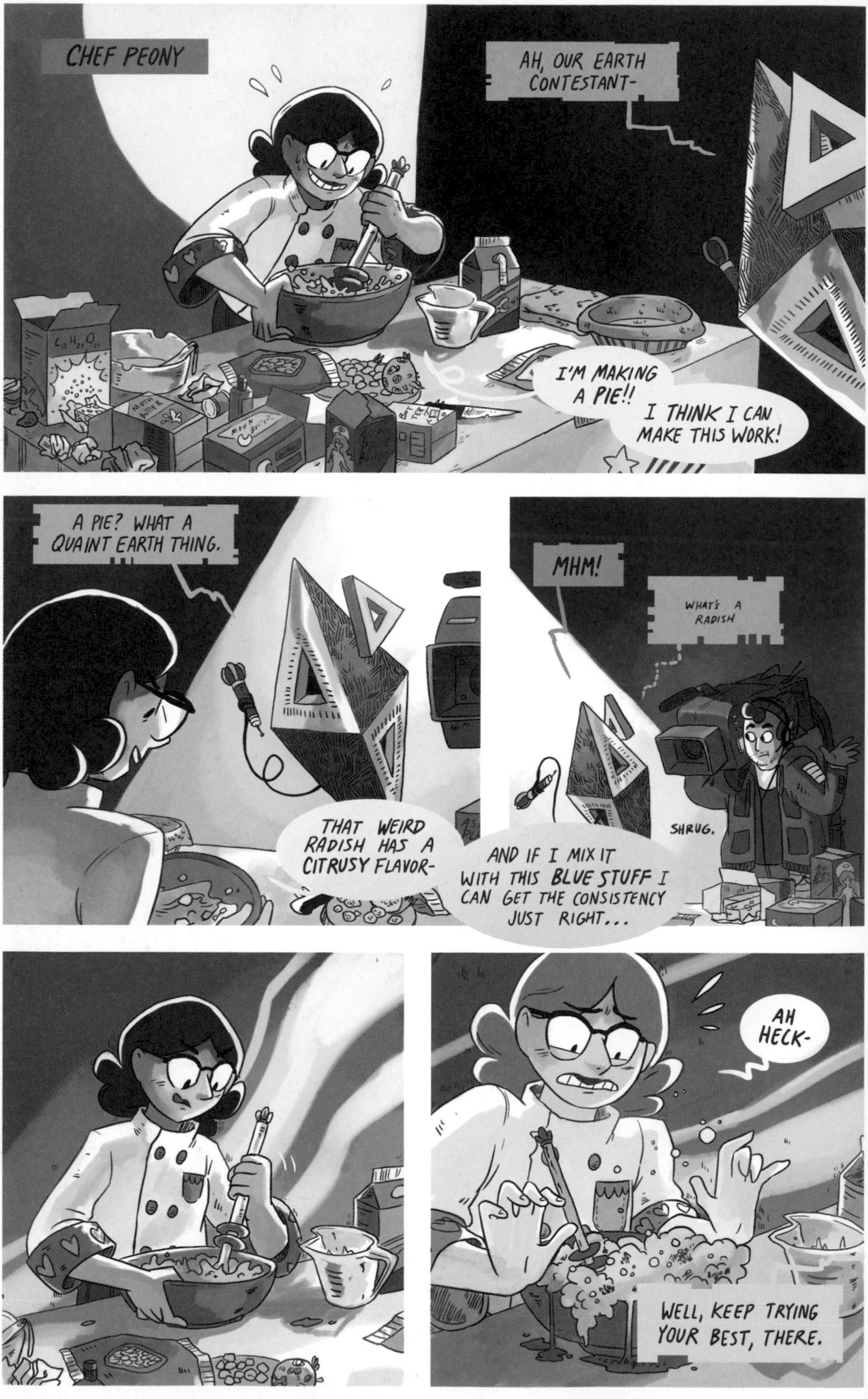
CHEF PEONY
AH, OUR EARTH CONTESTANT-
I'M MAKING A PIE!!
I THINK I CAN MAKE THIS WORK!
A PIE? WHAT A QUAINT EARTH THING.
MHM!
WHAT'S A RADISH
THAT WEIRD RADISH HAS A CITRUSY FLAVOR-
AND IF I MIX IT WITH THIS BLUE STUFF I CAN GET THE CONSISTENCY JUST RIGHT...
SHRUG.
AH HECK-
WELL, KEEP TRYING YOUR BEST, THERE.

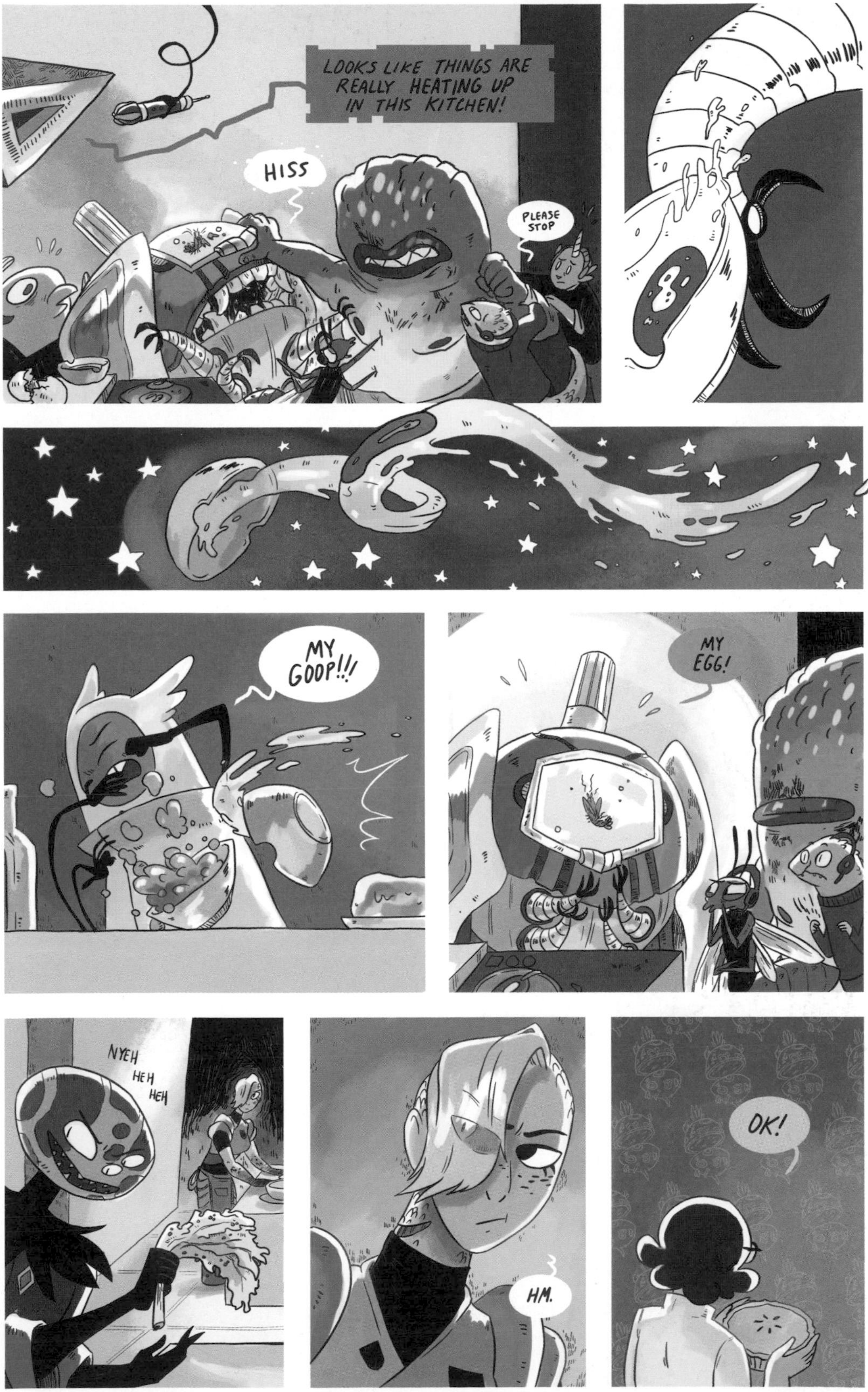
LOOKS LIKE THINGS ARE REALLY HEATING UP IN THIS KITCHEN!
HISS
PLEASE STOP
MY GOOP!!!
MY EGG!
NYEH HEH HEH
HM.
OK!

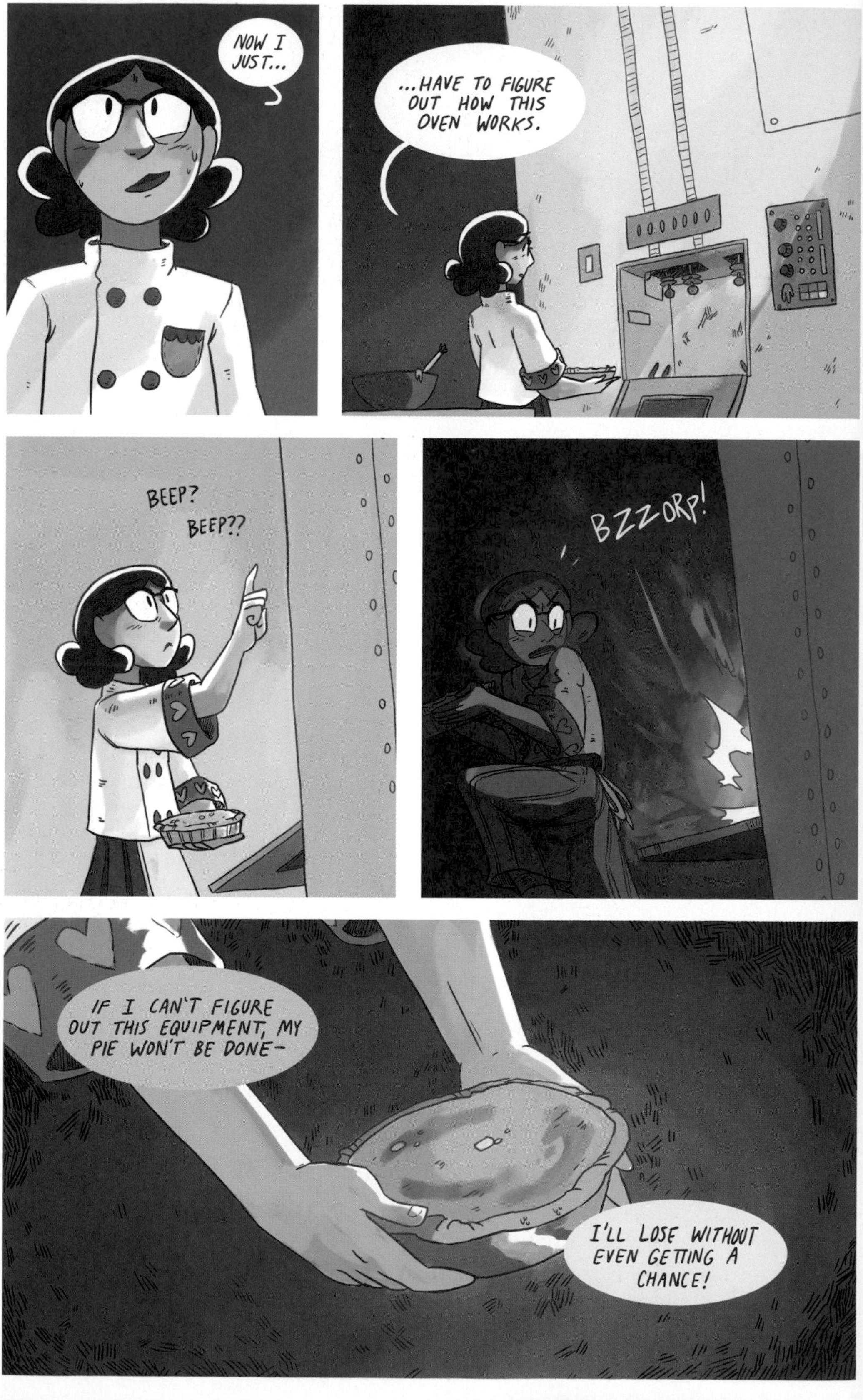
NOW I JUST...
...HAVE TO FIGURE OUT HOW THIS OVEN WORKS.
BEEP?
BEEP??
BZZ-ORP!
IF I CAN'T FIGURE OUT THIS EQUIPMENT, MY PIE WON'T BE DONE-
I'LL LOSE WITHOUT EVEN GETTING A CHANCE!

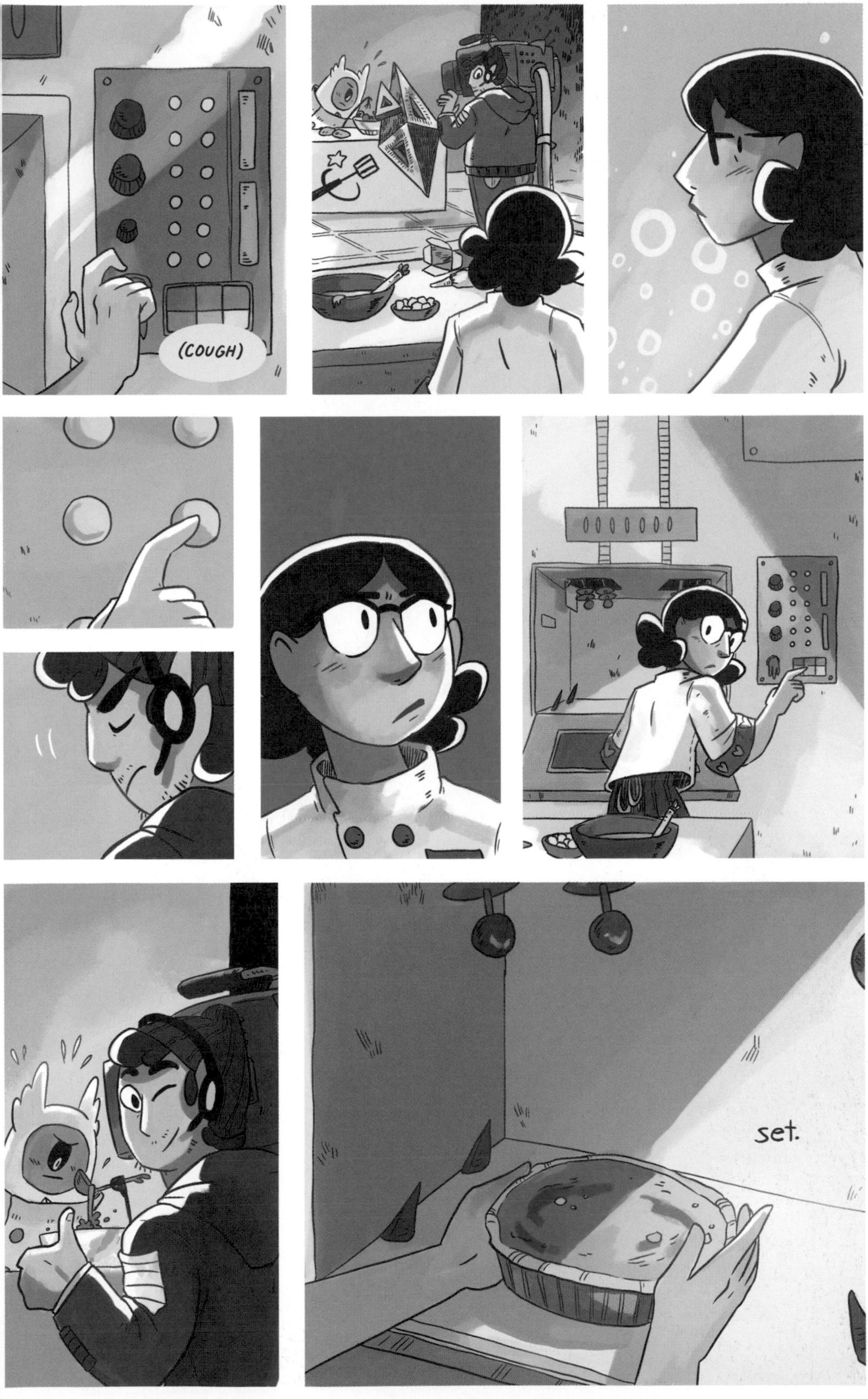
(COUGH)
set.

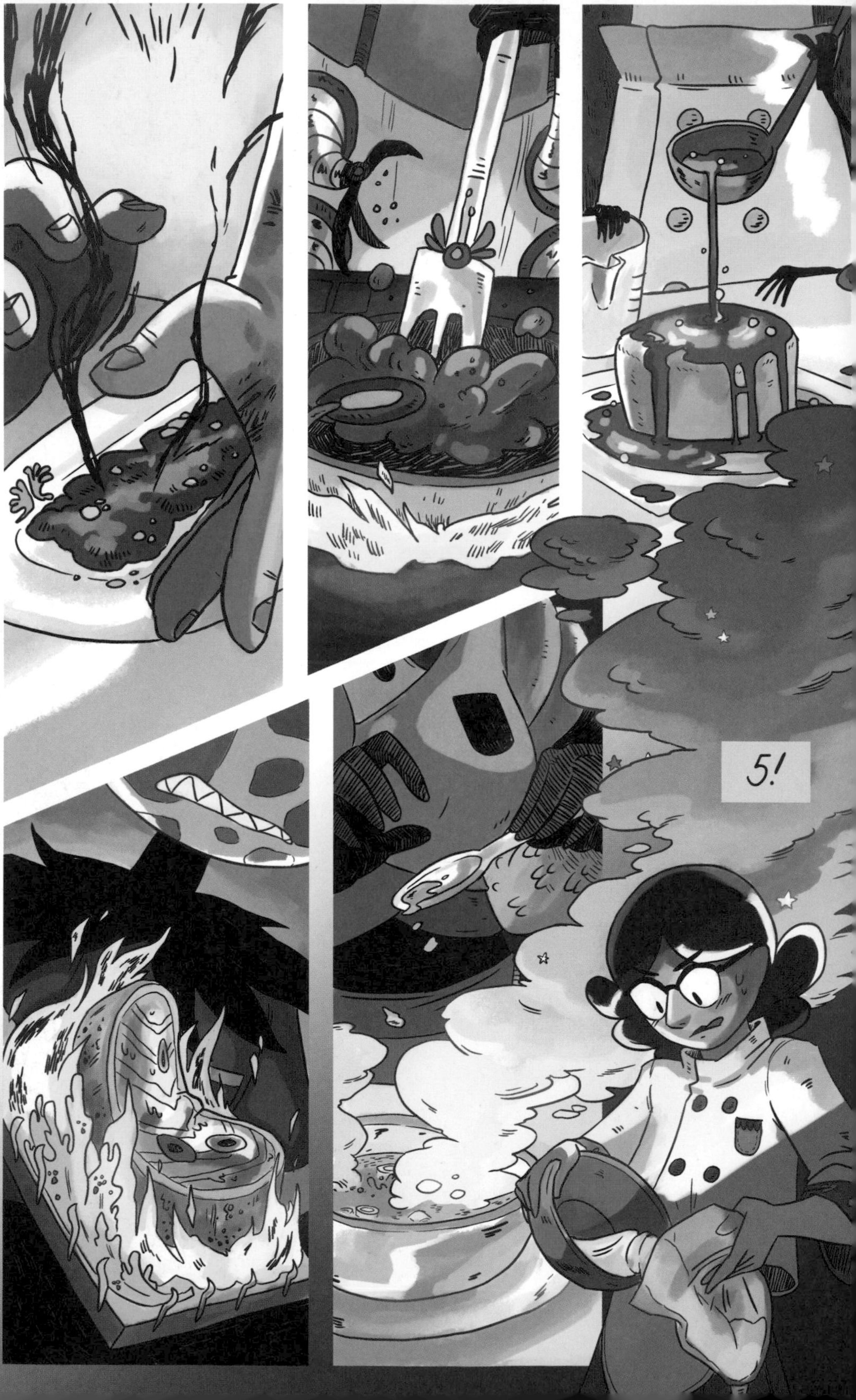
5!

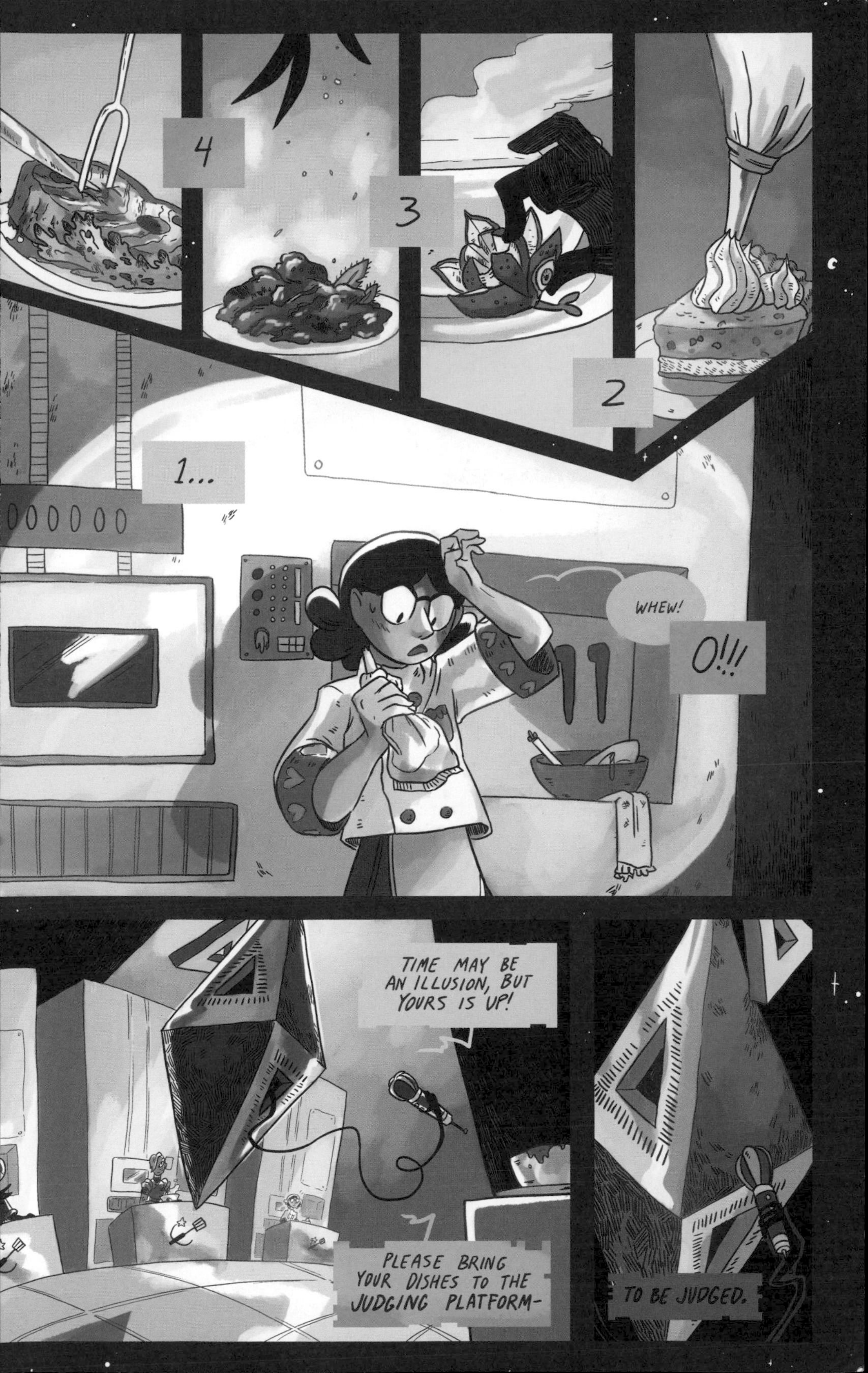
4
3
2
1...
WHEW!
0!!!
TIME MAY BE AN ILLUSION, BUT YOURS IS UP!
PLEASE BRING YOUR DISHES TO THE JUDGING PLATFORM-
TO BE JUDGED.

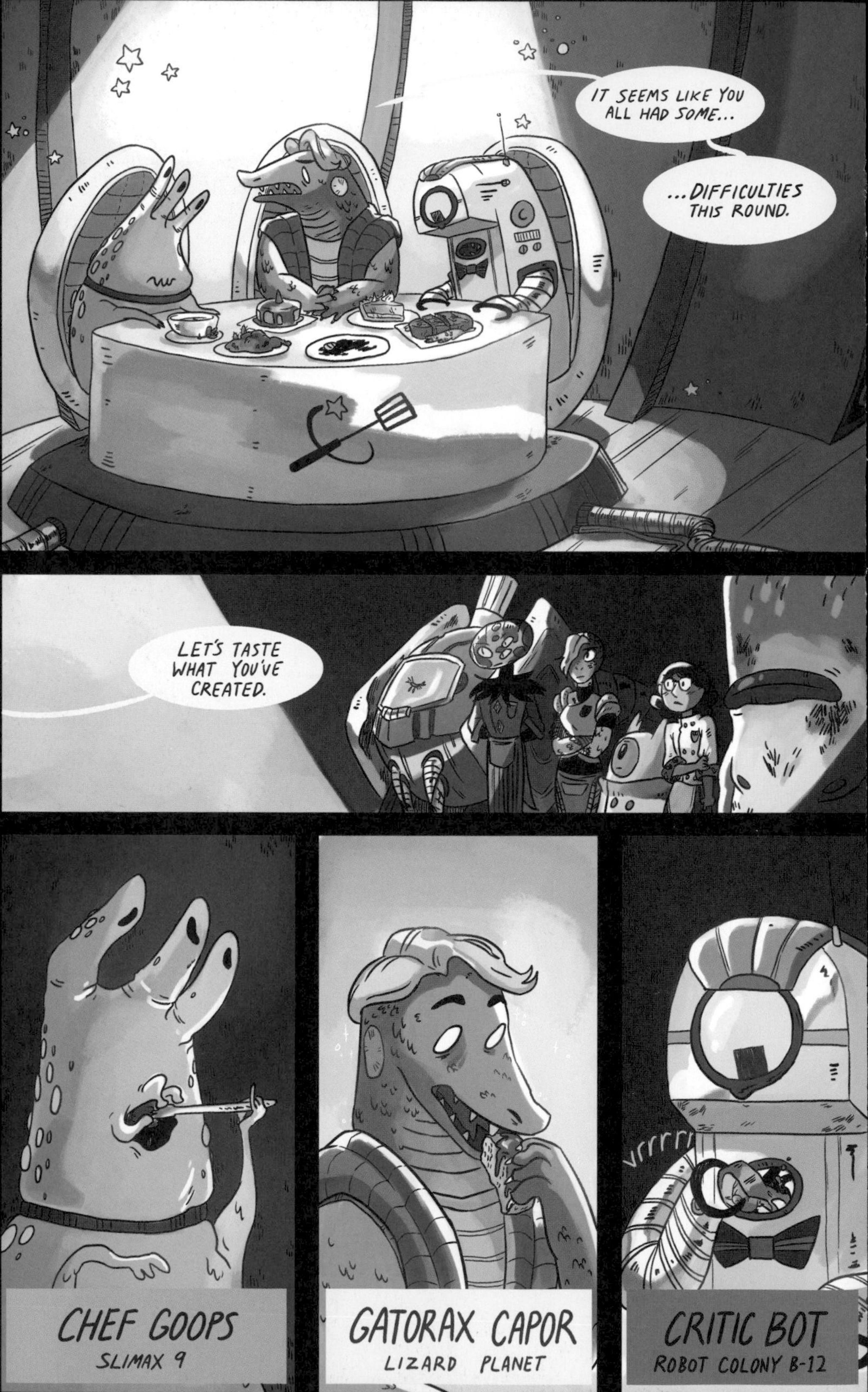
IT SEEMS LIKE YOU ALL HAD SOME...
...DIFFICULTIES THIS ROUND.
LET'S TASTE WHAT YOU'VE CREATED.
CHEF GOOPS
SLIMAX 9
GATORAX CAPOR
LIZARD PLANET
vrrrrr
CRITIC BOT
ROBOT COLONY B-12

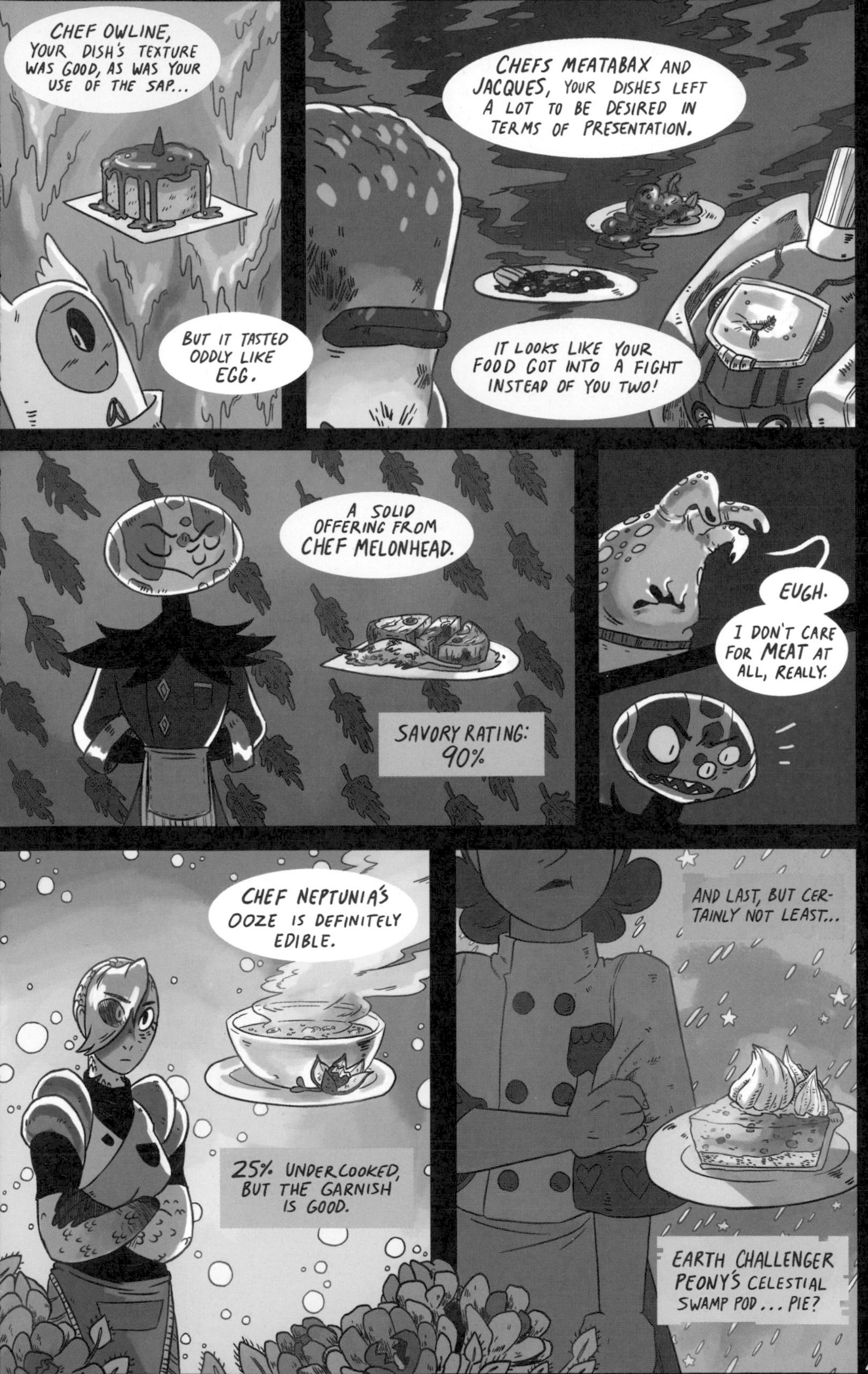

CHEF OWLINE, YOUR DISH'S TEXTURE WAS GOOD, AS WAS YOUR USE OF THE SAP...
BUT IT TASTED ODDLY LIKE EGG.
CHEFS MEATABAX AND JACQUES, YOUR DISHES LEFT A LOT TO BE DESIRED IN TERMS OF PRESENTATION.
IT LOOKS LIKE YOUR FOOD GOT INTO A FIGHT INSTEAD OF YOU TWO!
A SOLID OFFERING FROM CHEF MELONHEAD.
SAVORY RATING: 90%
EUGH.
I DON'T CARE FOR MEAT AT ALL, REALLY.
CHEF NEPTUNIA'S OOZE IS DEFINITELY EDIBLE.
25% UNDERCOOKED, BUT THE GARNISH IS GOOD.
AND LAST, BUT CERTAINLY NOT LEAST...
EARTH CHALLENGER PEONY'S CELESTIAL SWAMP POD... PIE?

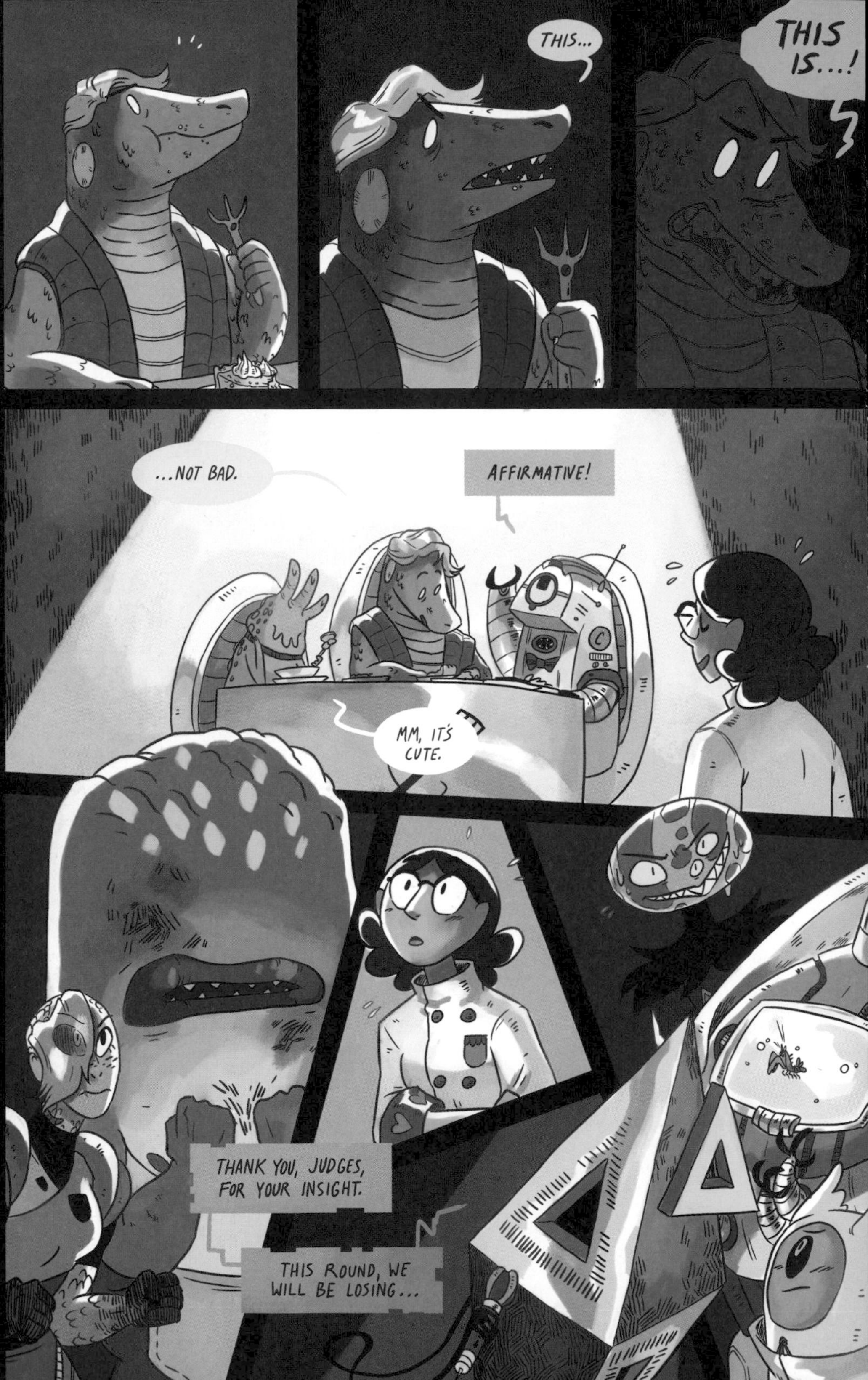
THIS...
THIS IS...!
...NOT BAD.
AFFIRMATIVE!
MM, IT'S CUTE.
THANK YOU, JUDGES, FOR YOUR INSIGHT.
THIS ROUND, WE WILL BE LOSING...

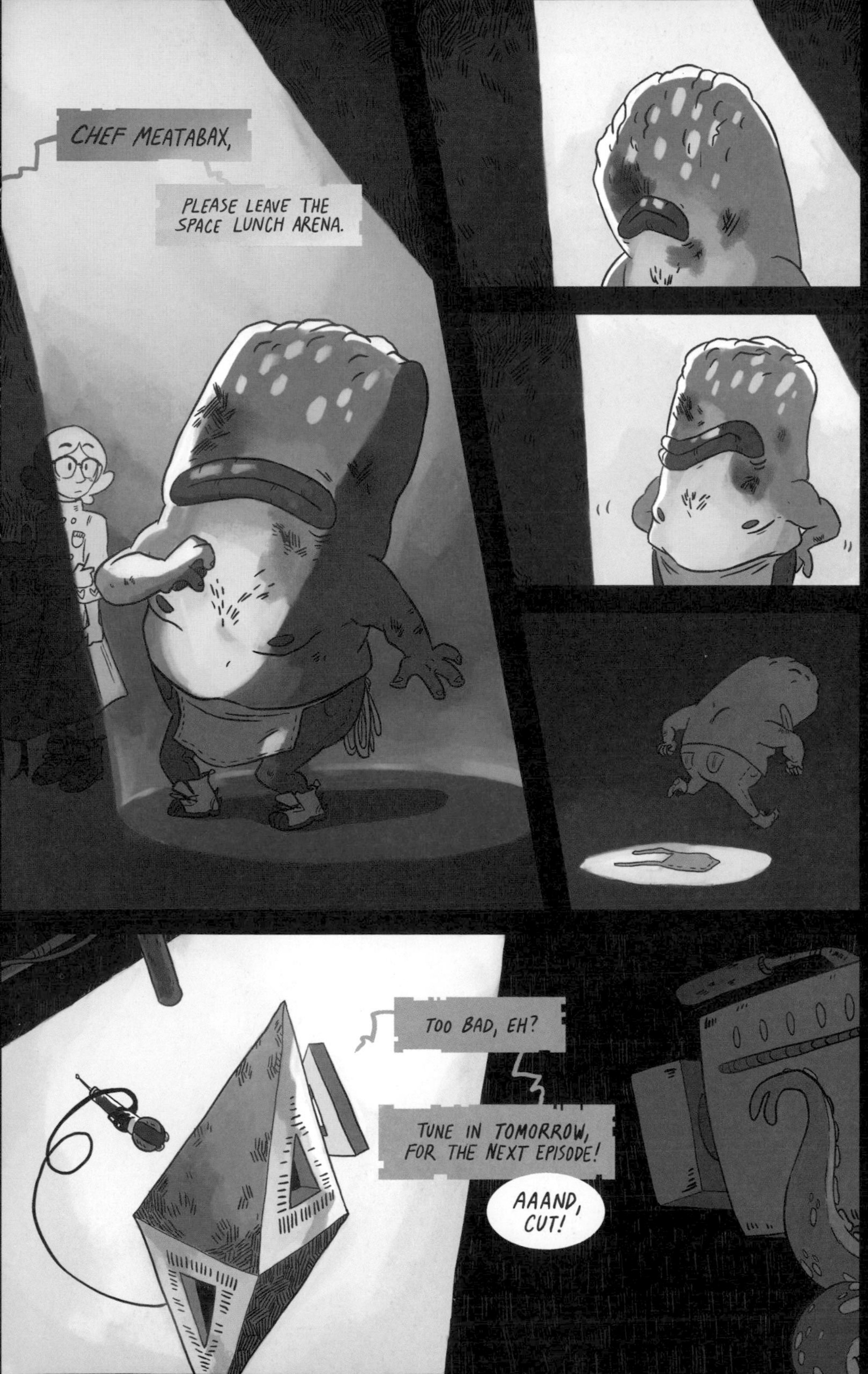
CHEF MEATABAX,
PLEASE LEAVE THE SPACE LUNCH ARENA.
TOO BAD, EH?
TUNE IN TOMORROW, FOR THE NEXT EPISODE!
AAAND, CUT!

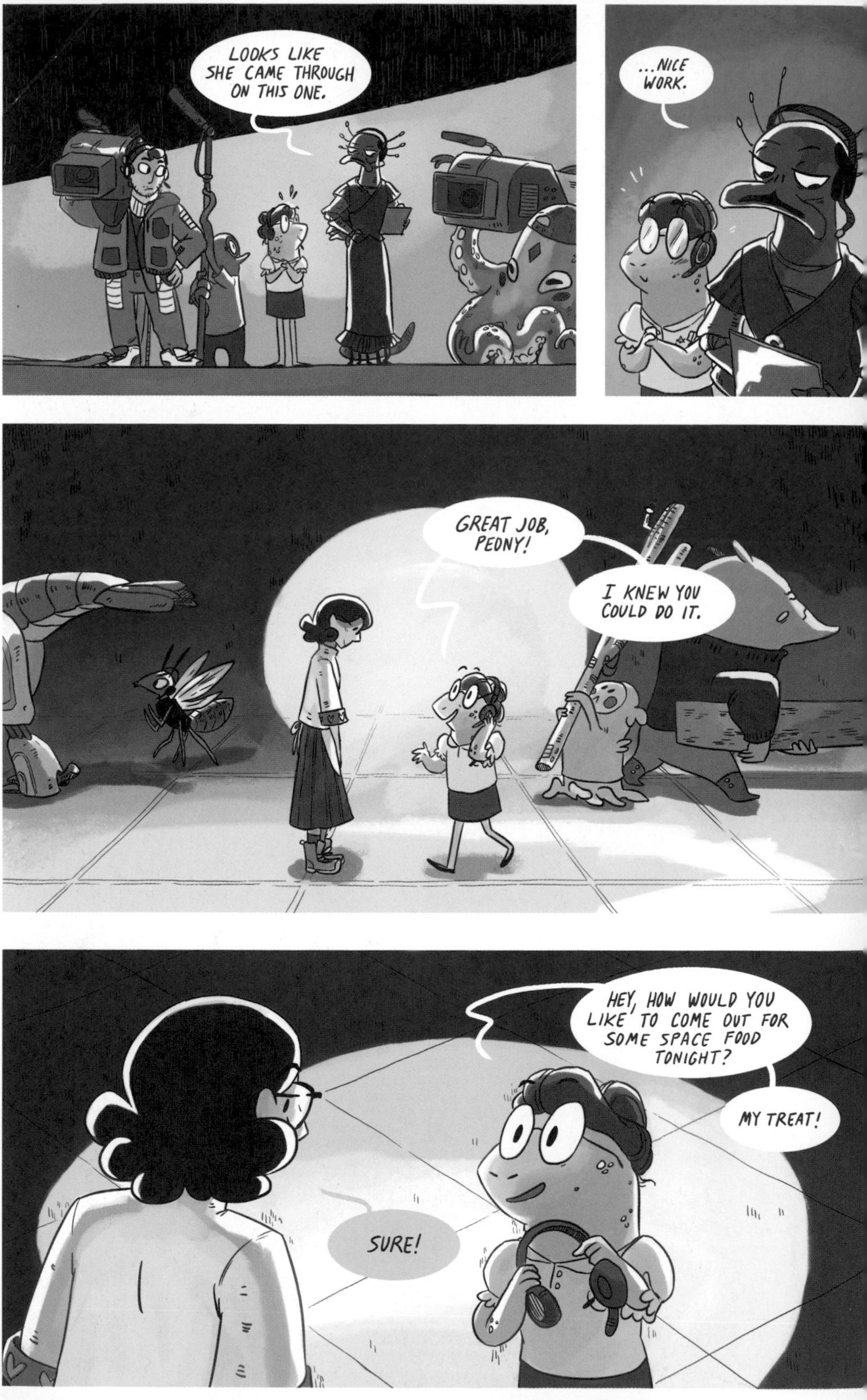
LOOKS LIKE SHE CAME THROUGH ON THIS ONE.
...NICE WORK.
GREAT JOB, PEONY!
I KNEW YOU COULD DO IT.
HEY, HOW WOULD YOU LIKE TO COME OUT FOR SOME SPACE FOOD TONIGHT?
MY TREAT!
SURE!

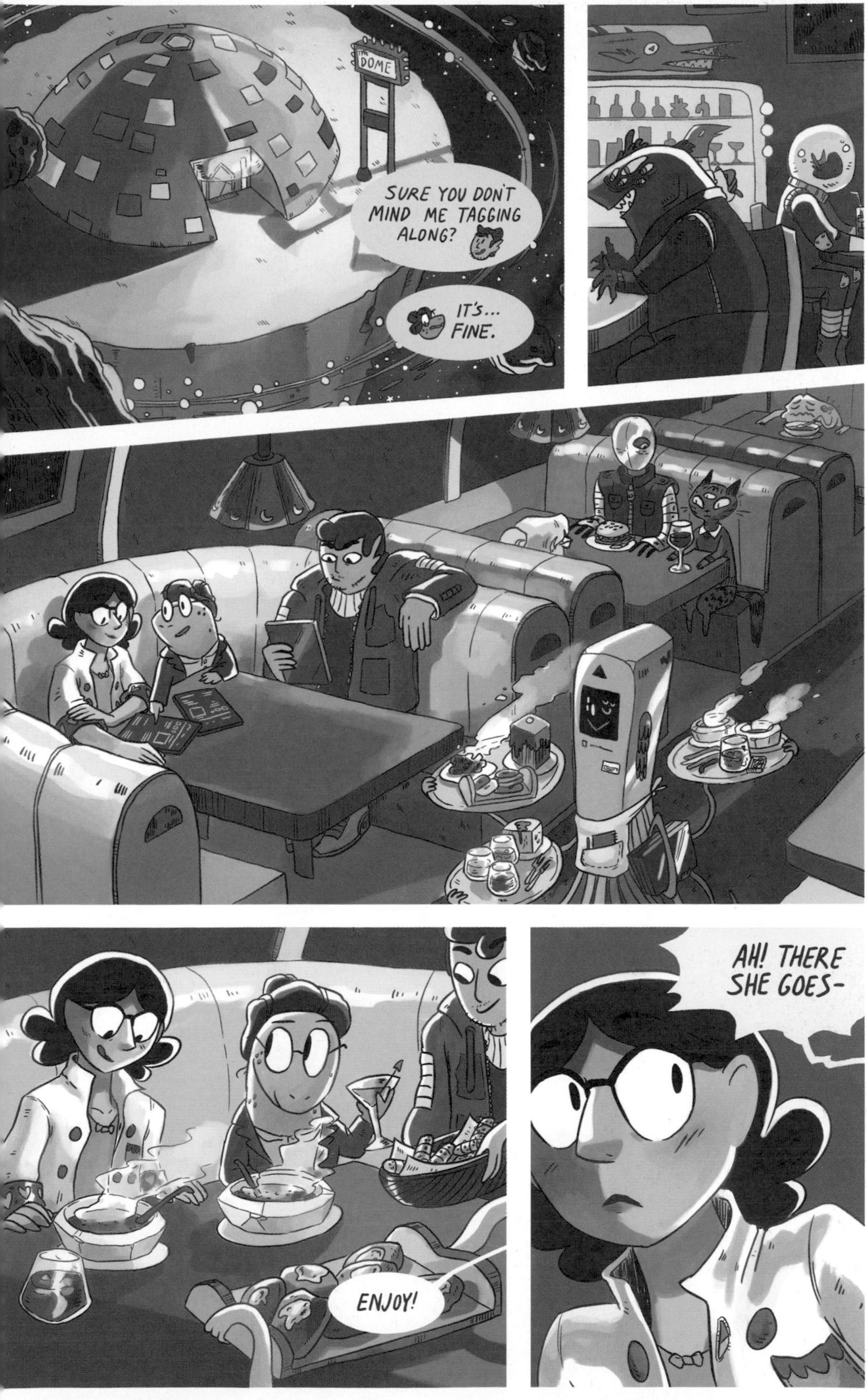
THE DOME
SURE YOU DON'T MIND ME TAGGING ALONG?
IT'S... FINE.
ENJOY!
AH! THERE SHE GOES-

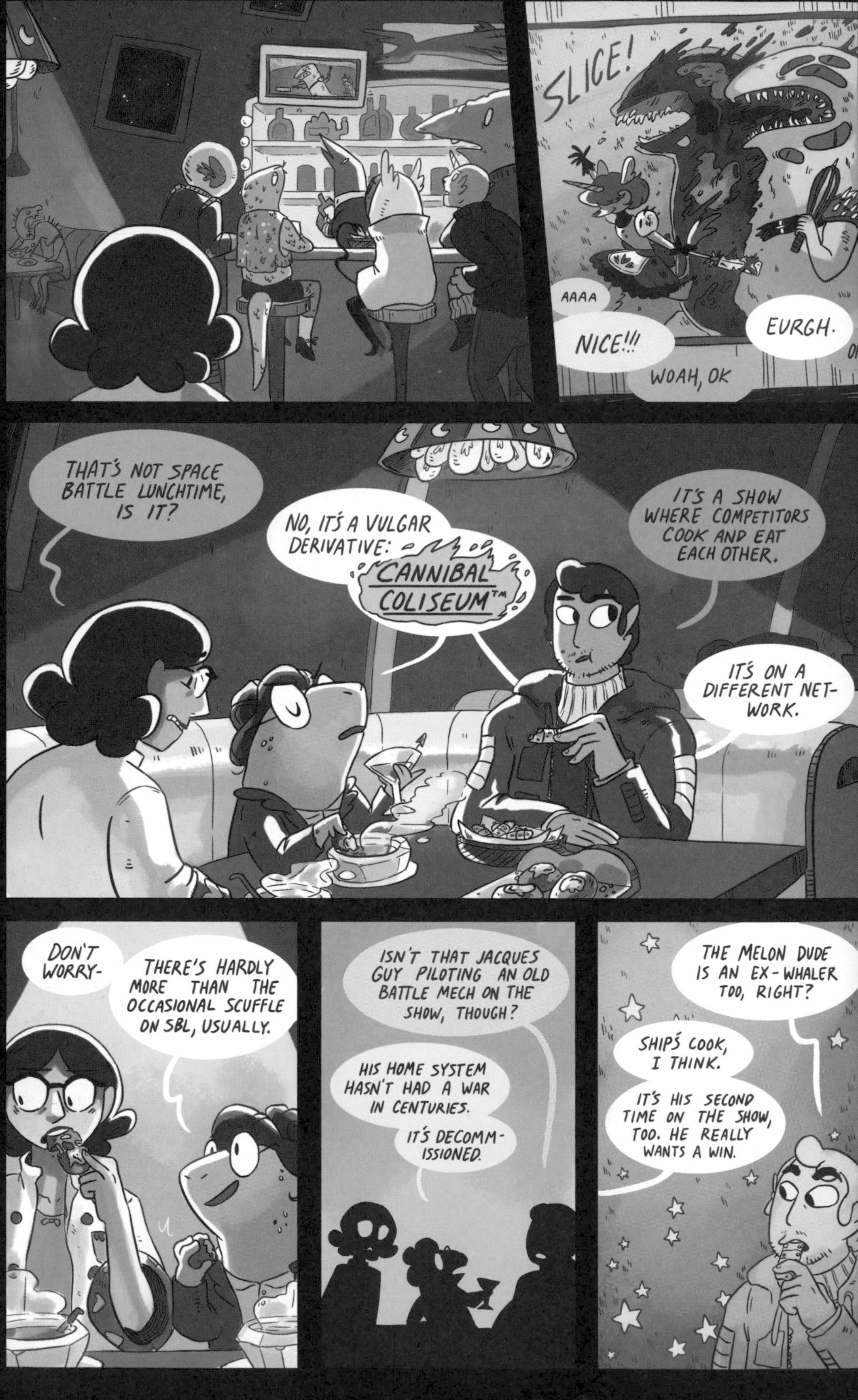
SLICE!
AAAA
NICE!!!
EURGH.
WOAH, OK
THAT'S NOT SPACE BATTLE LUNCHTIME, IS IT?
NO, IT'S A VULGAR DERIVATIVE:
CANNIBAL COLISEUM™
IT'S A SHOW WHERE COMPETITORS COOK AND EAT EACH OTHER.
IT'S ON A DIFFERENT NET-WORK.
DON'T WORRY-
THERE'S HARDLY MORE THAN THE OCCASIONAL SCUFFLE ON SBL, USUALLY.
ISN'T THAT JACQUES GUY PILOTING AN OLD BATTLE MECH ON THE SHOW, THOUGH?
HIS HOME SYSTEM HASN'T HAD A WAR IN CENTURIES.
IT'S DECOMM-ISSIONED.
THE MELON DUDE IS AN EX-WHALER TOO, RIGHT?
SHIP'S COOK, I THINK.
IT'S HIS SECOND TIME ON THE SHOW, TOO. HE REALLY WANTS A WIN.

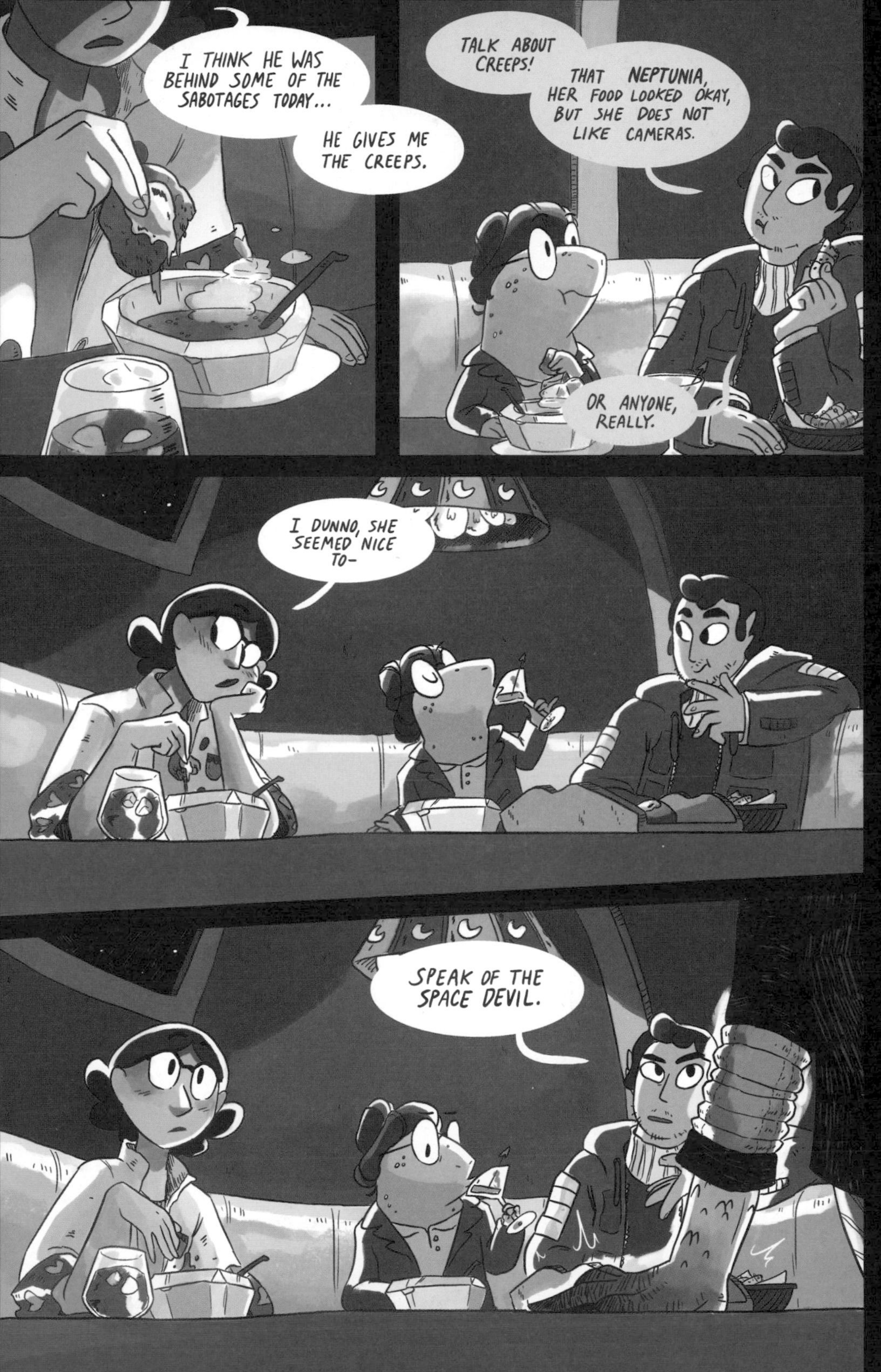
I THINK HE WAS BEHIND SOME OF THE SABOTAGES TODAY...
HE GIVES ME THE CREEPS.
TALK ABOUT CREEPS!
THAT NEPTUNIA, HER FOOD LOOKED OKAY, BUT SHE DOES NOT LIKE CAMERAS.
OR ANYONE, REALLY.
I DUNNO, SHE SEEMED NICE TO-
SPEAK OF THE SPACE DEVIL.

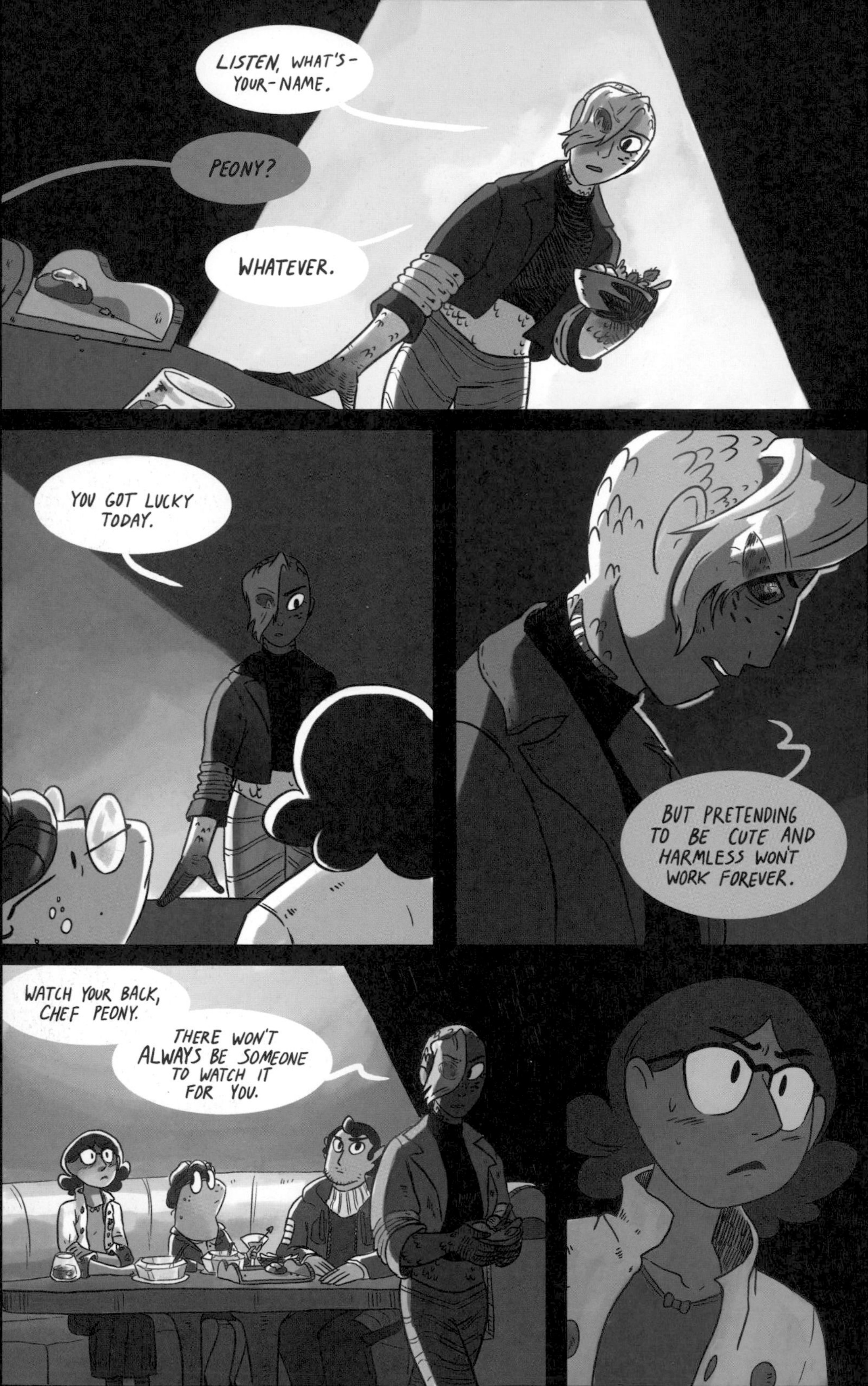
LISTEN, WHAT'S-YOUR-NAME.
PEONY?
WHATEVER.
YOU GOT LUCKY TODAY.
BUT PRETENDING TO BE CUTE AND HARMLESS WON'T WORK FOREVER.
WATCH YOUR BACK, CHEF PEONY.
THERE WON'T ALWAYS BE SOMEONE TO WATCH IT FOR YOU.

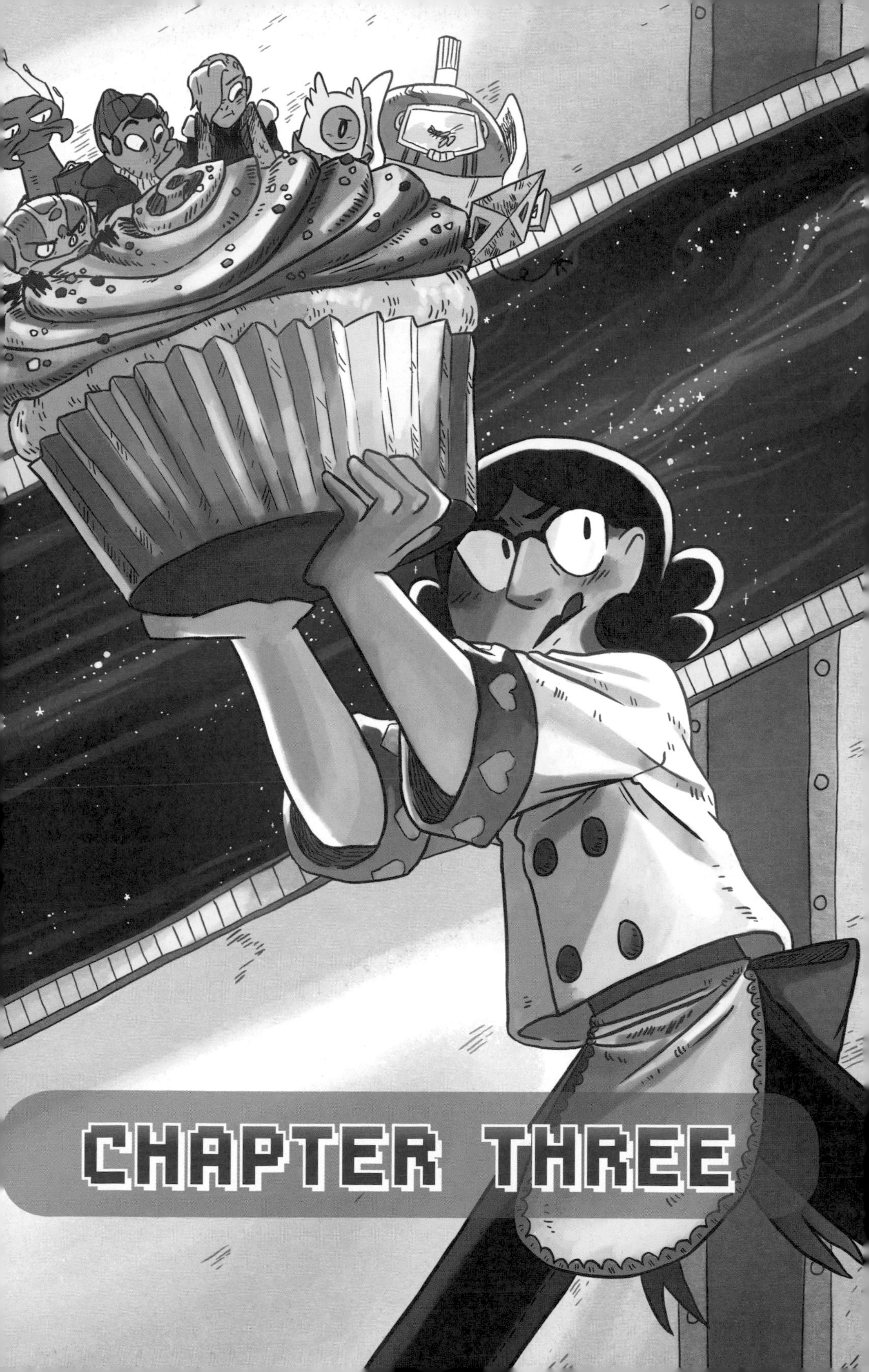

CHAPTER THREE

PREVIOUSLY, ON SPACE BATTLE LUNCHTIME...

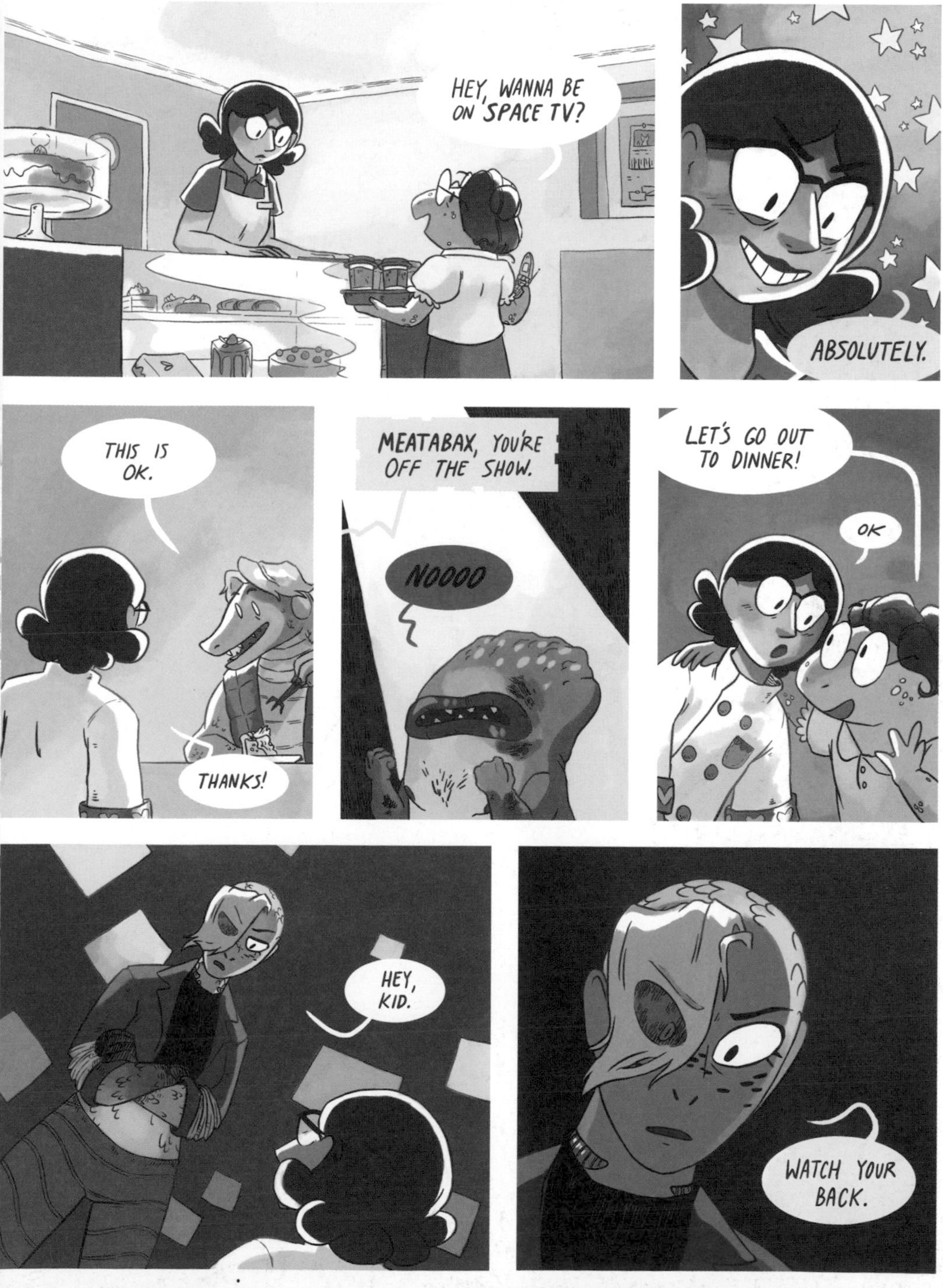

HEY, WANNA BE ON SPACE TV?
ABSOLUTELY.
THIS IS OK.
THANKS!
MEATABAX, YOU'RE OFF THE SHOW.
NOOOO
LET'S GO OUT TO DINNER!
OK
HEY, KID.
WATCH YOUR BACK.

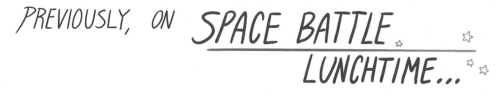

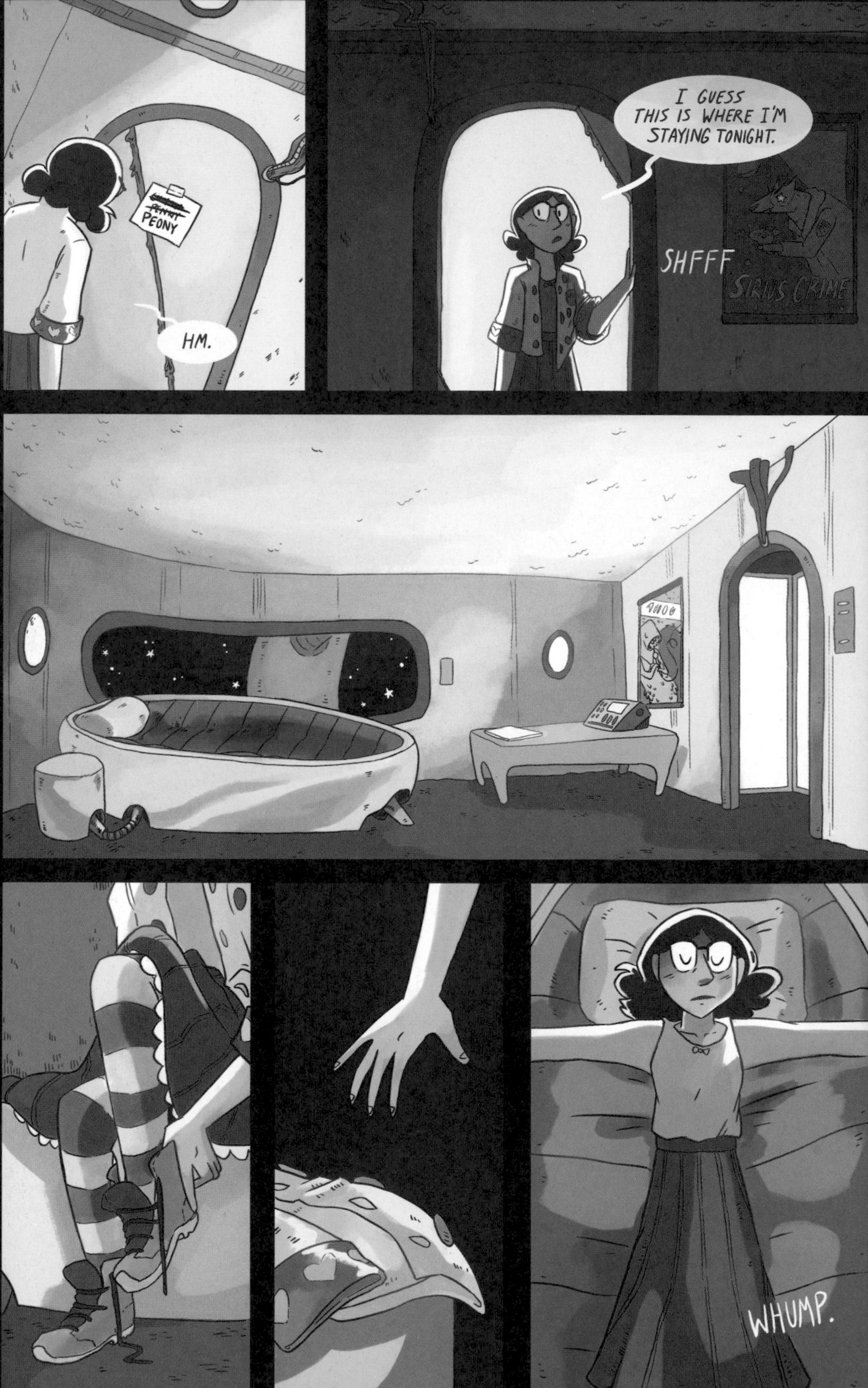
PEONY
HM.
I GUESS THIS IS WHERE I'M STAYING TONIGHT.
SHFFF
SIRIUS CRIME
WHUMP.

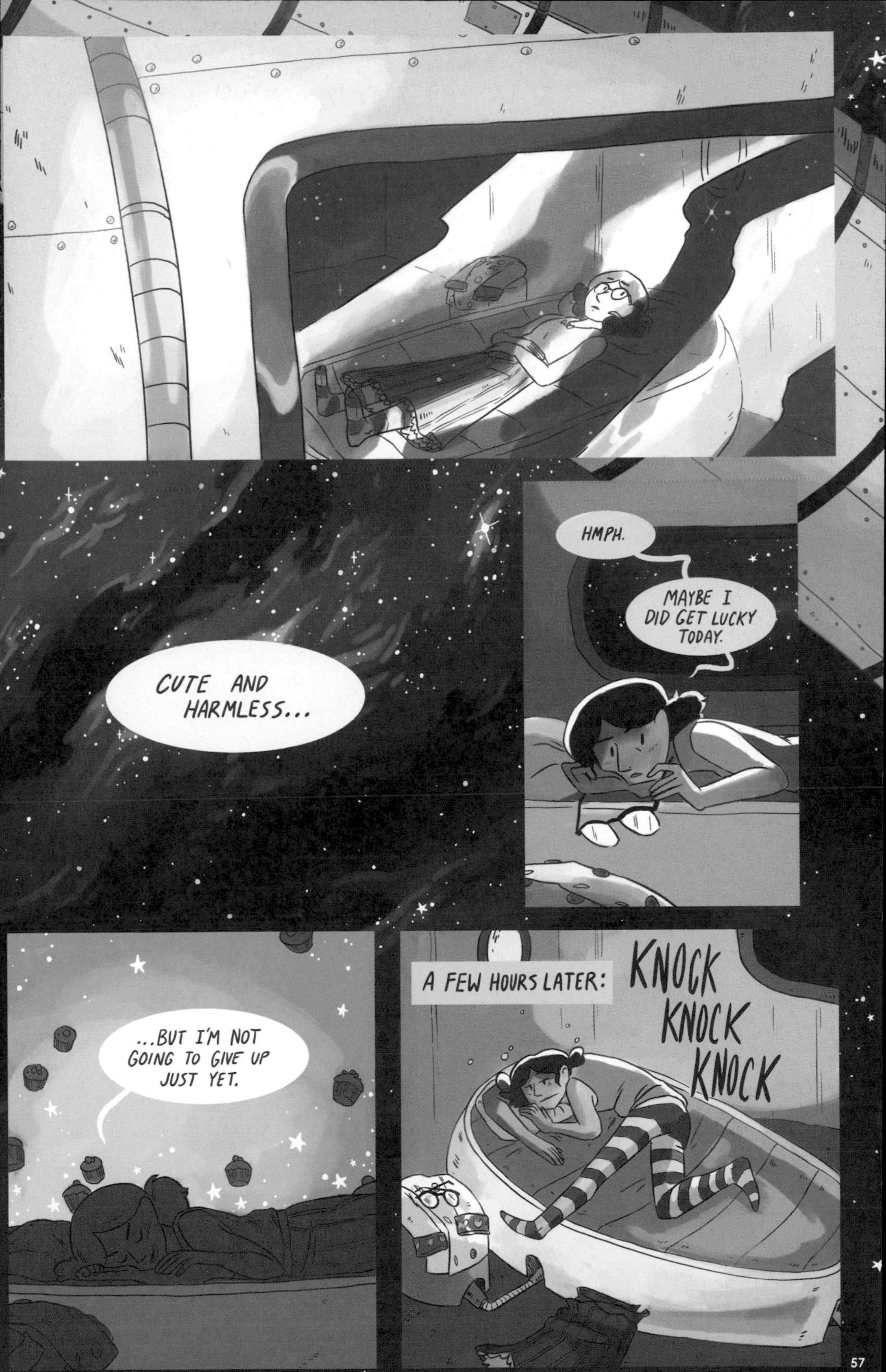
CUTE AND HARMLESS...
HMPH.
MAYBE I DID GET LUCKY TODAY.
...BUT I'M NOT GOING TO GIVE UP JUST YET.
A FEW HOURS LATER:
KNOCK KNOCK KNOCK

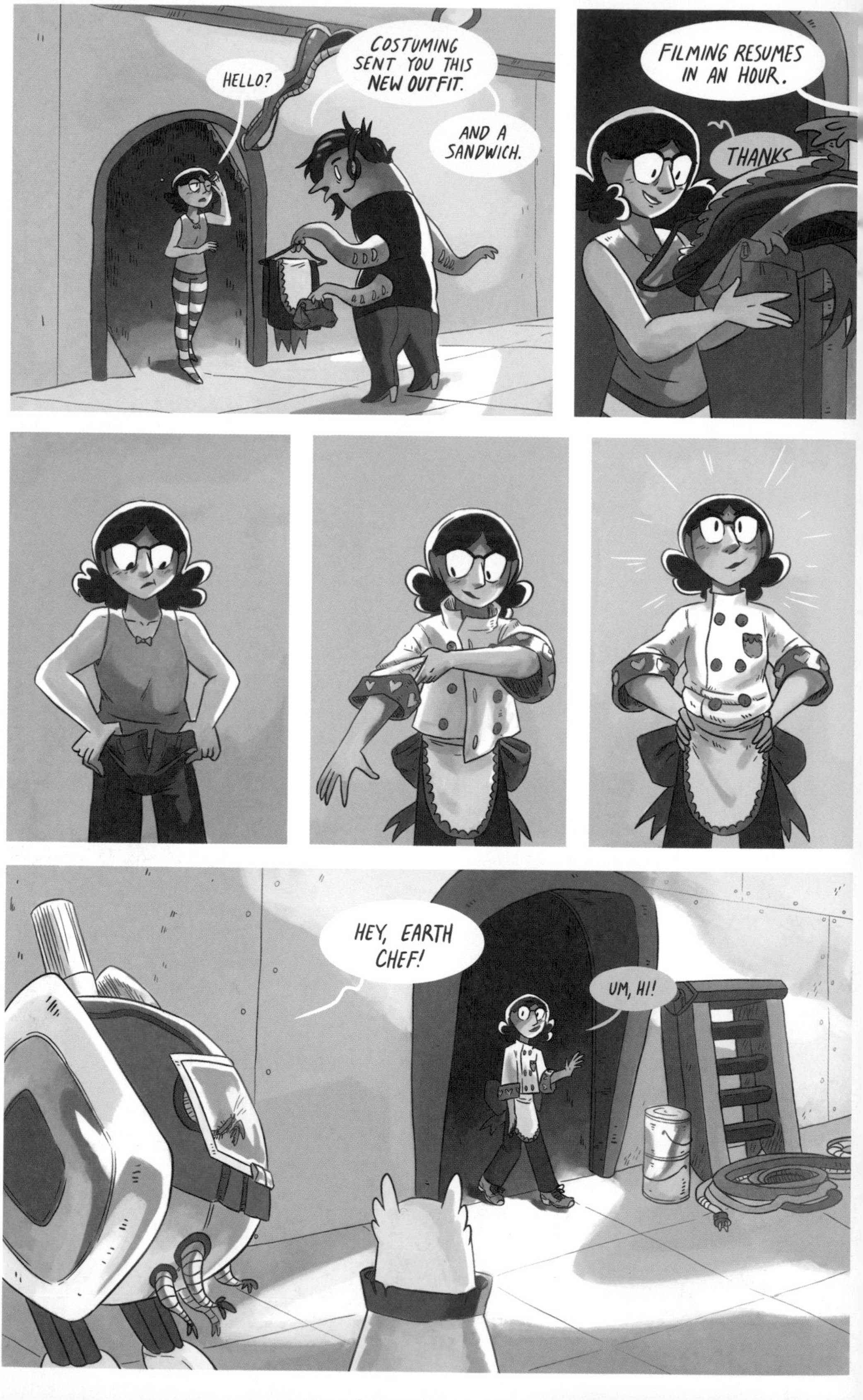
HELLO?
COSTUMING SENT YOU THIS NEW OUTFIT.
AND A SANDWICH.
FILMING RESUMES IN AN HOUR.
THANKS
HEY, EARTH CHEF!
UM, HI!

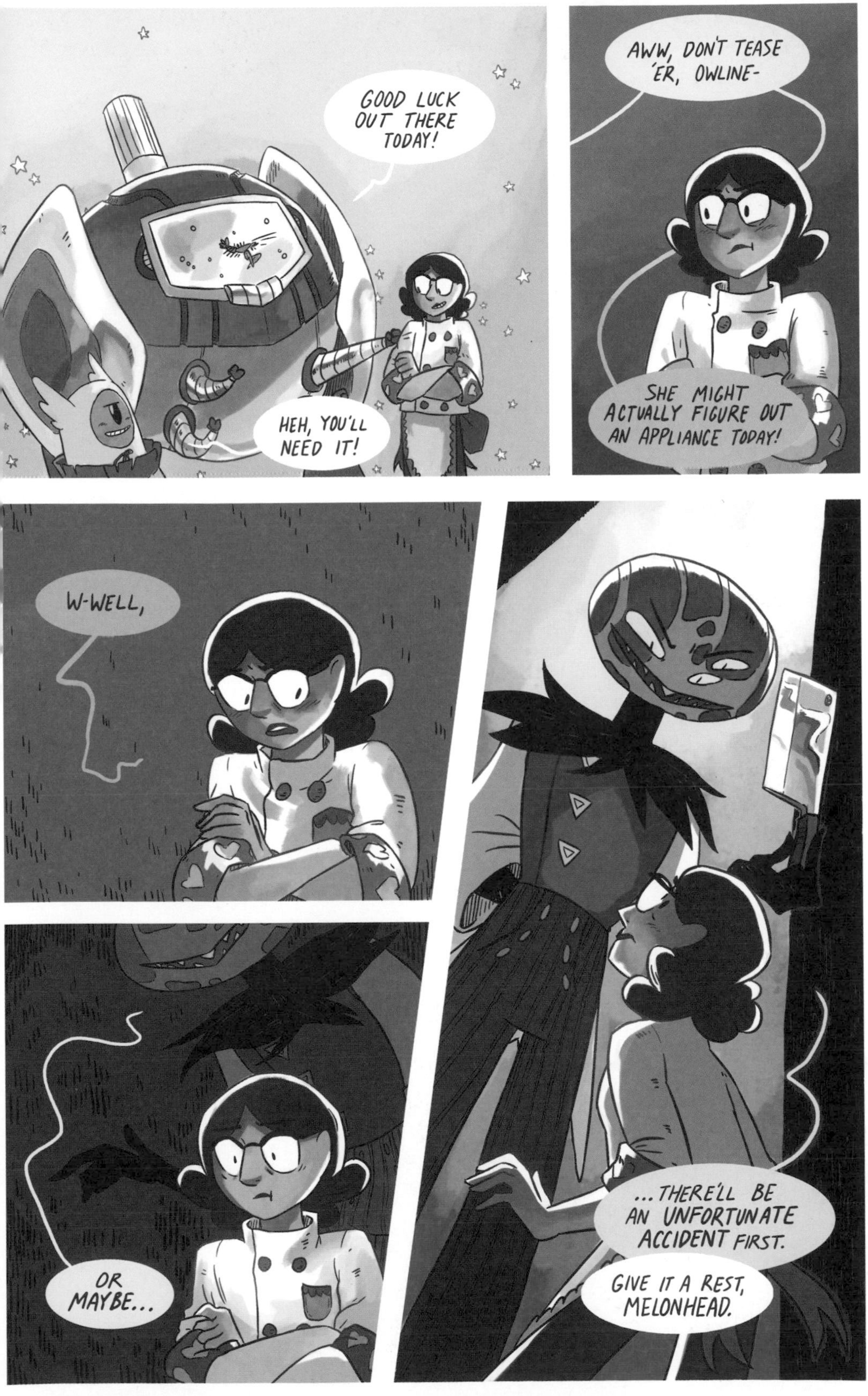
GOOD LUCK OUT THERE TODAY!
HEH, YOU'LL NEED IT!
AWW, DON'T TEASE 'ER, OWLINE-
SHE MIGHT ACTUALLY FIGURE OUT AN APPLIANCE TODAY!
W-WELL,
OR MAYBE...
...THERE'LL BE AN UNFORTUNATE ACCIDENT FIRST.
GIVE IT A REST, MELONHEAD.

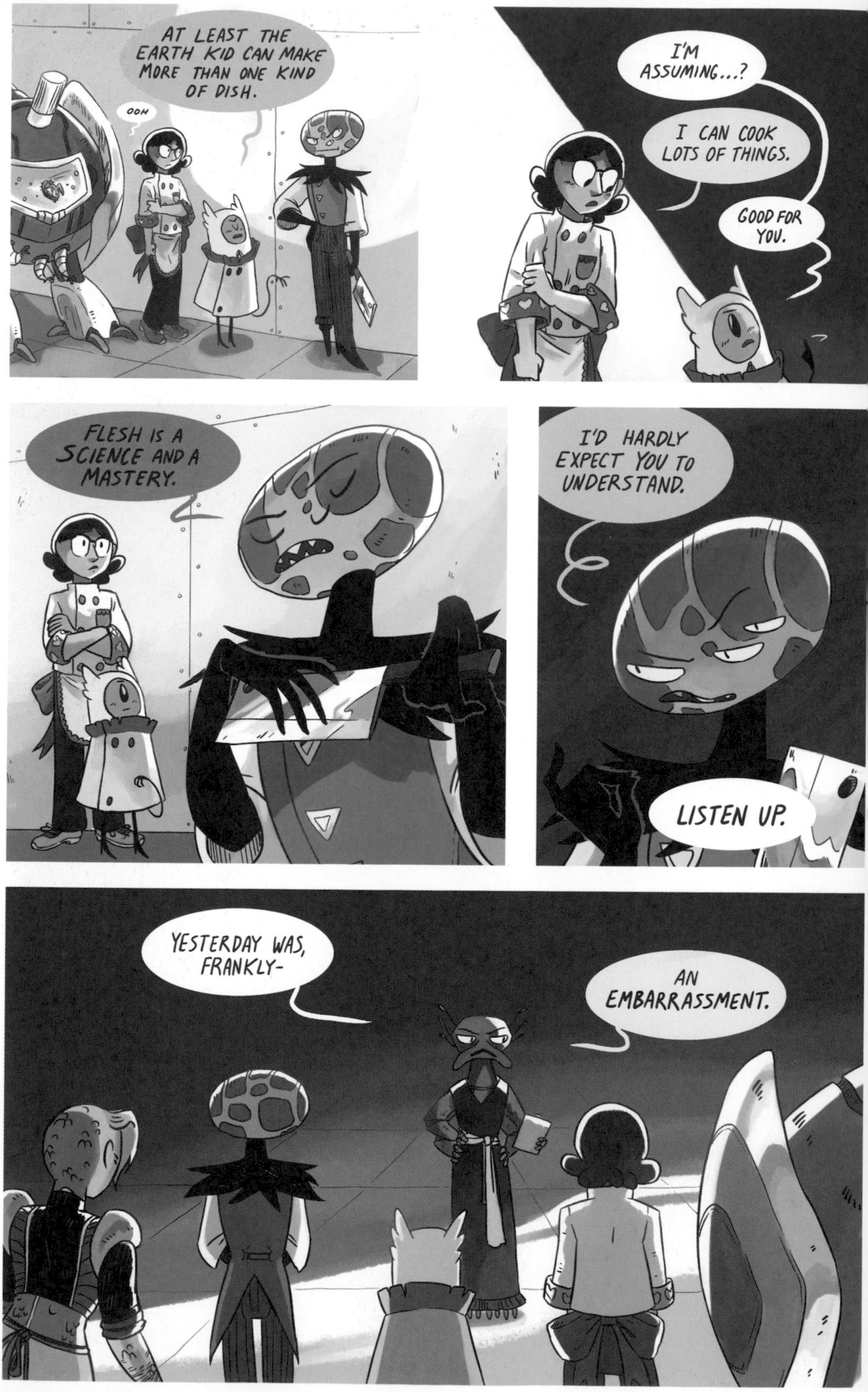
AT LEAST THE EARTH KID CAN MAKE MORE THAN ONE KIND OF DISH.
OOH
I'M ASSUMING...?
I CAN COOK LOTS OF THINGS.
GOOD FOR YOU.
FLESH IS A SCIENCE AND A MASTERY.
I'D HARDLY EXPECT YOU TO UNDERSTAND.
LISTEN UP.
YESTERDAY WAS, FRANKLY-
AN EMBARRASSMENT.

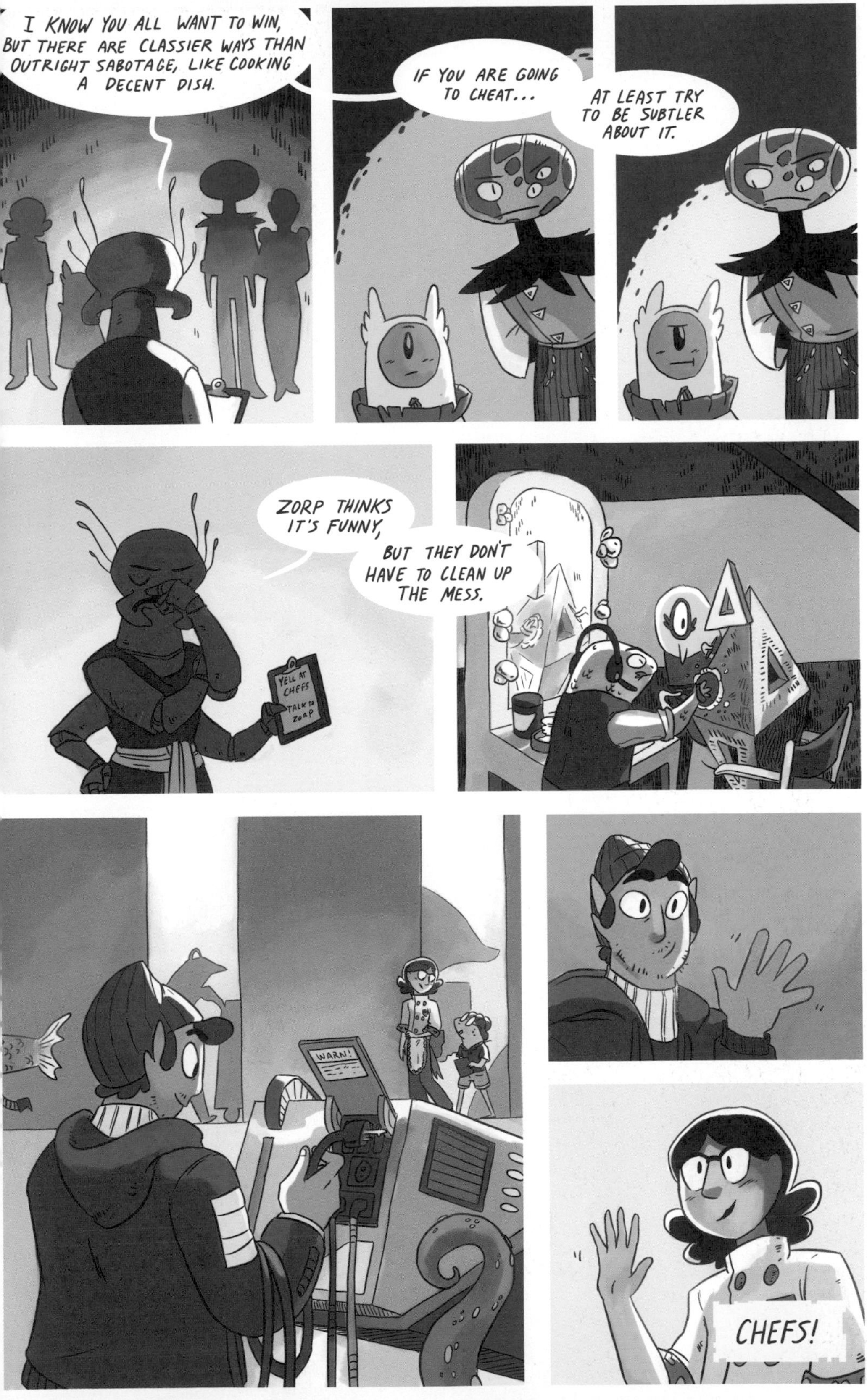
I KNOW YOU ALL WANT TO WIN, BUT THERE ARE CLASSIER WAYS THAN OUTRIGHT SABOTAGE, LIKE COOKING A DECENT DISH.
IF YOU ARE GOING TO CHEAT...
AT LEAST TRY TO BE SUBTLER ABOUT IT.
ZORP THINKS IT'S FUNNY,
BUT THEY DON'T HAVE TO CLEAN UP THE MESS.
YELL AT CHEFS
TALK TO ZORP
WARN!
CHEFS!

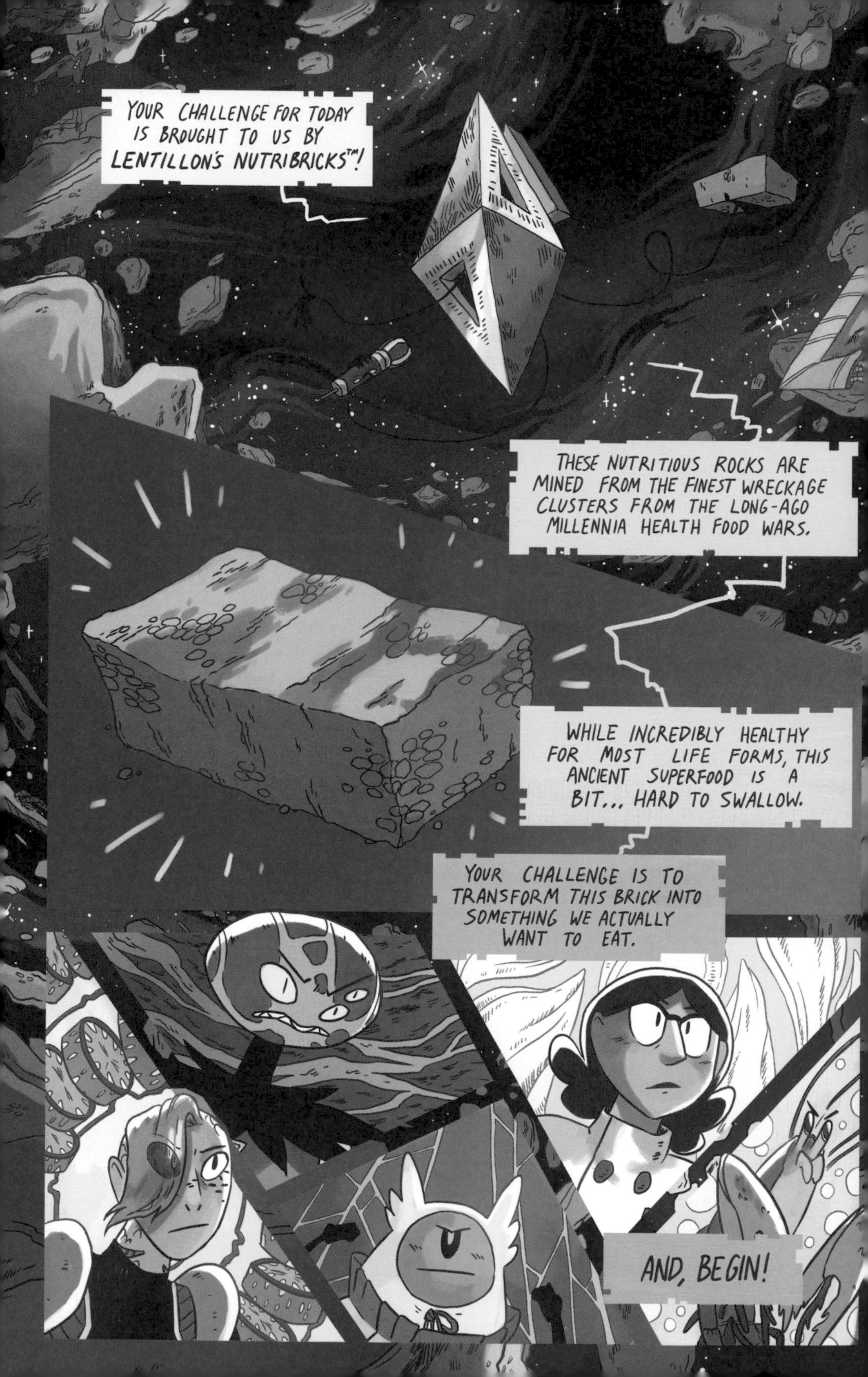
YOUR CHALLENGE FOR TODAY IS BROUGHT TO US BY LENTILLON'S NUTRIBRICKS™!
THESE NUTRITIOUS ROCKS ARE MINED FROM THE FINEST WRECKAGE CLUSTERS FROM THE LONG-AGO MILLENNIA HEALTH FOOD WARS.
WHILE INCREDIBLY HEALTHY FOR MOST LIFE FORMS, THIS ANCIENT SUPERFOOD IS A BIT... HARD TO SWALLOW.
YOUR CHALLENGE IS TO TRANSFORM THIS BRICK INTO SOMETHING WE ACTUALLY WANT TO EAT.
AND, BEGIN!

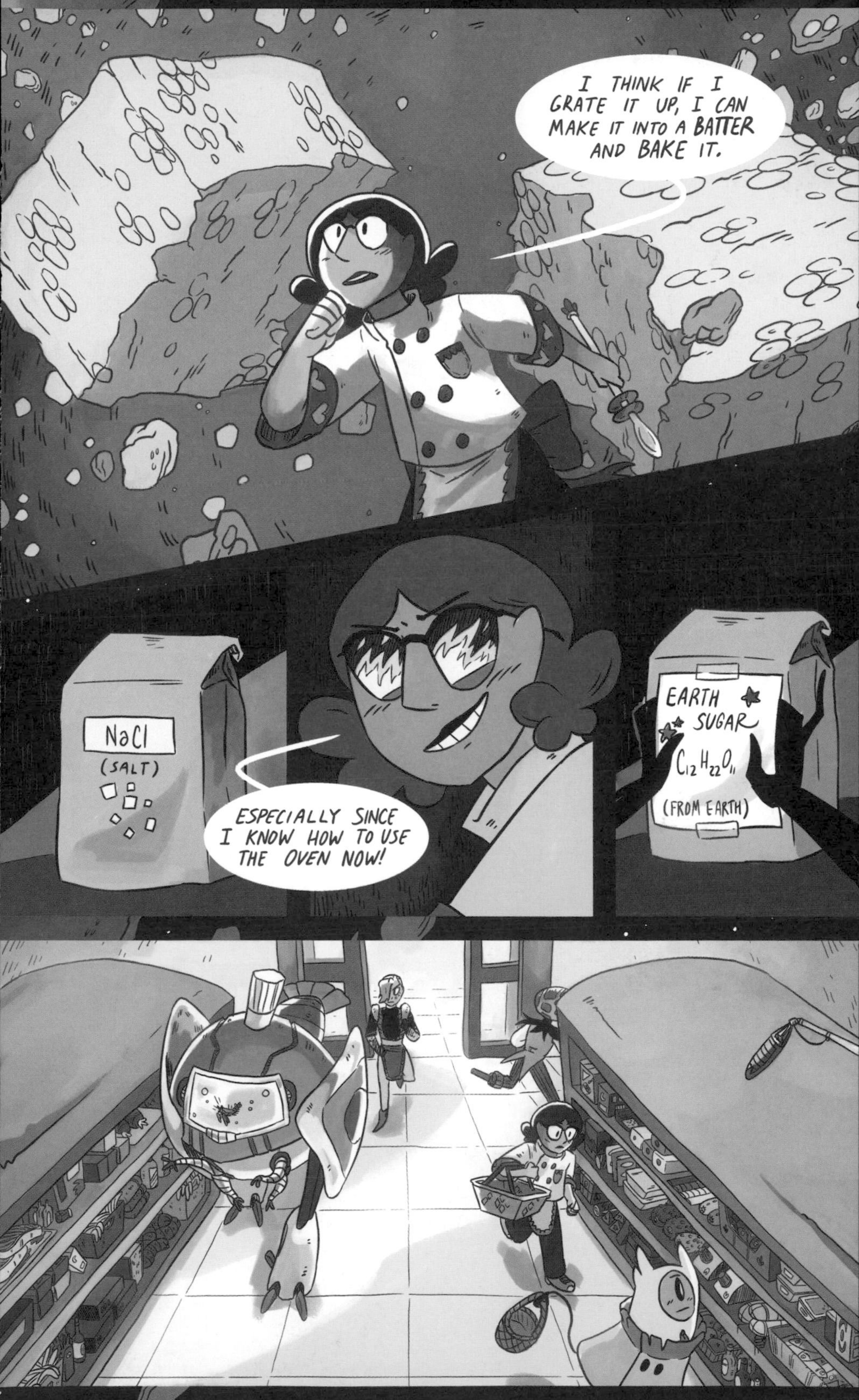
I THINK IF I GRATE IT UP, I CAN MAKE IT INTO A BATTER AND BAKE IT.
NaCl
(SALT)
ESPECIALLY SINCE I KNOW HOW TO USE THE OVEN NOW!
EARTH SUGAR
$C_{12}H_{22}O_{11}$
(FROM EARTH)

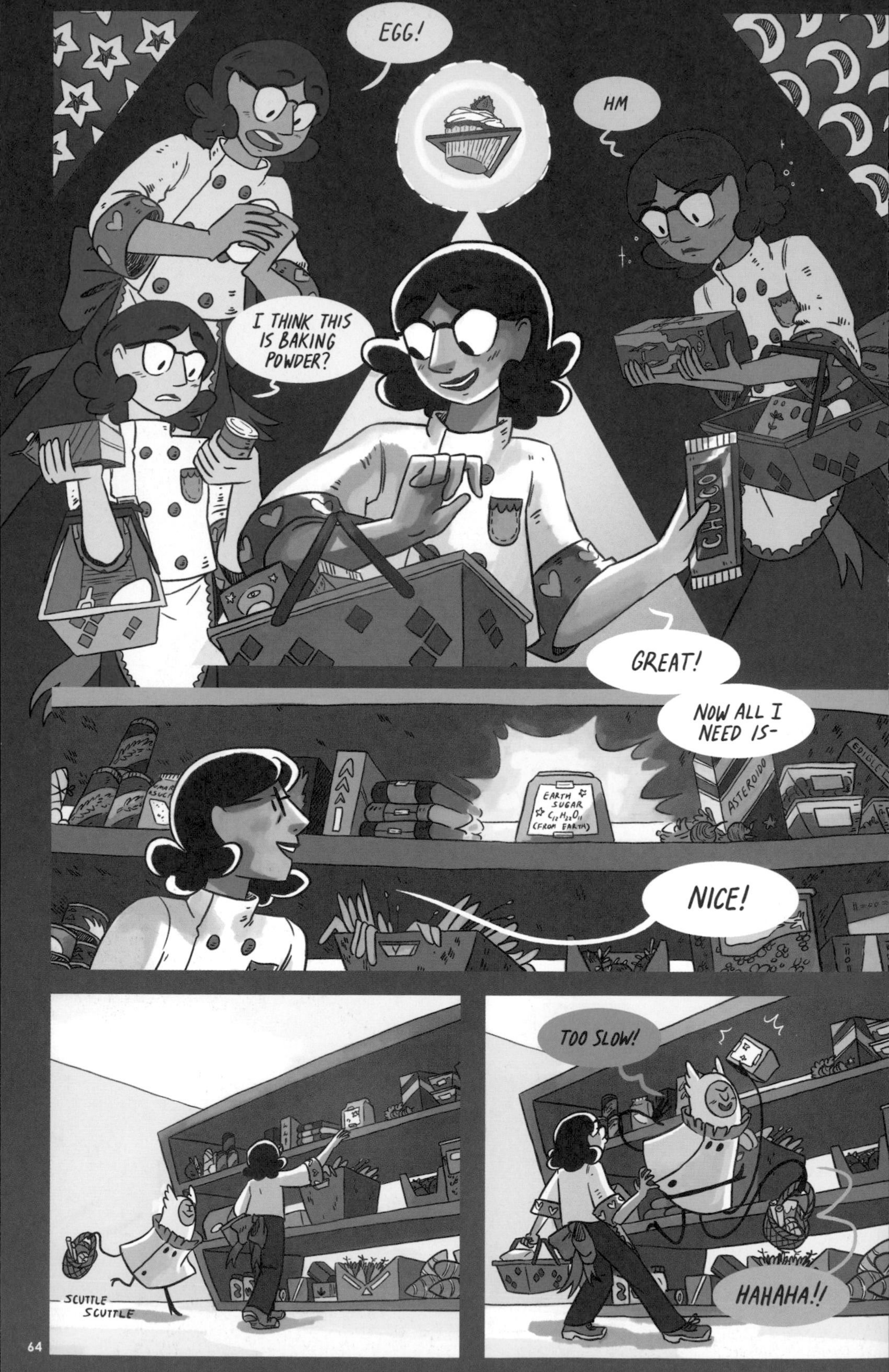
EGG!
HM
I THINK THIS IS BAKING POWDER?
CHOCO
GREAT!
NOW ALL I NEED IS-
ASTEROIDO
EARTH SUGAR $C_{12}H_{22}O_{11}$ (FROM EARTH)
NICE!
SCUTTLE SCUTTLE
TOO SLOW!
HAHAHA!!

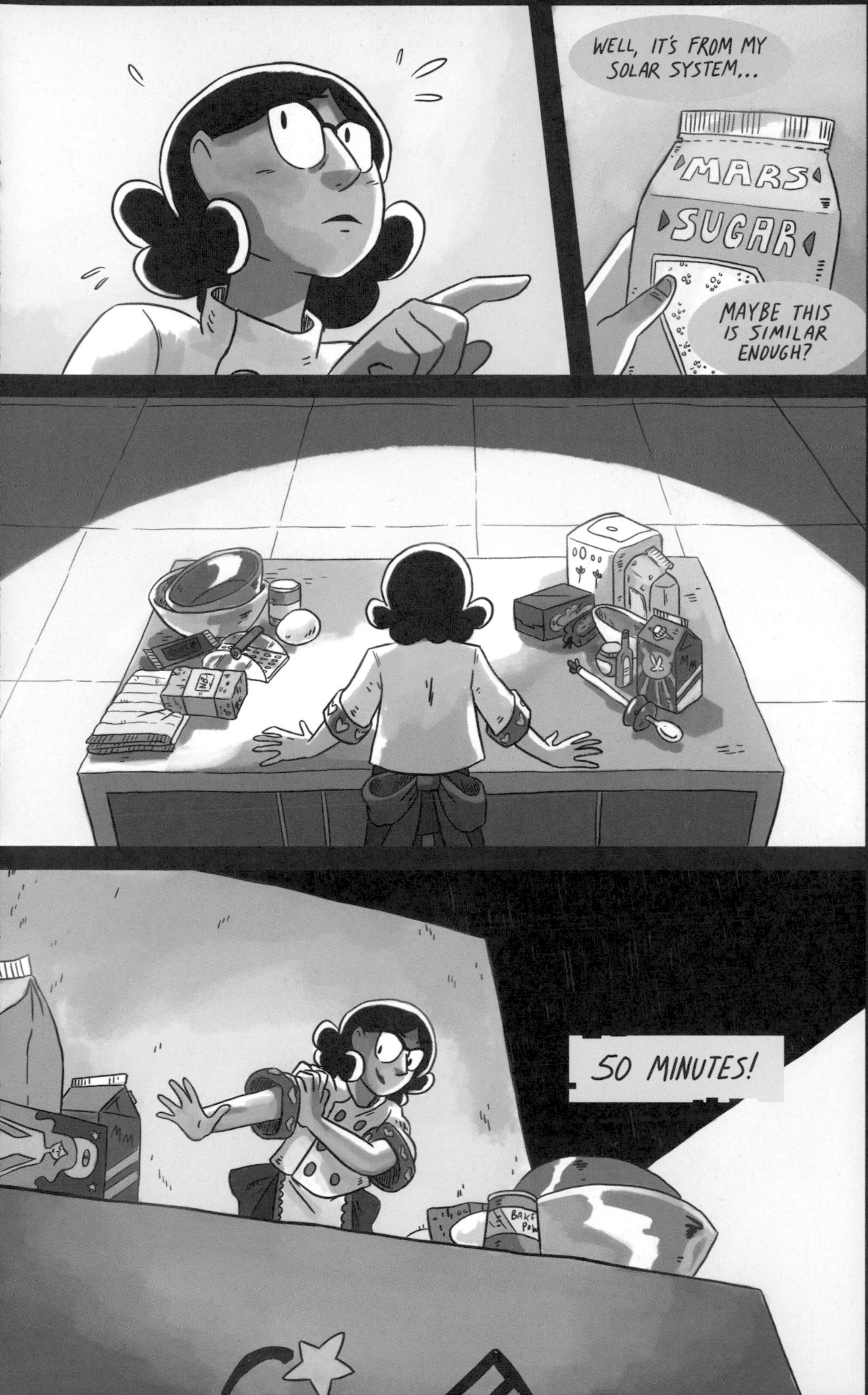
WELL, IT'S FROM MY SOLAR SYSTEM...
MARS
SUGAR
MAYBE THIS IS SIMILAR ENOUGH?
50 MINUTES!

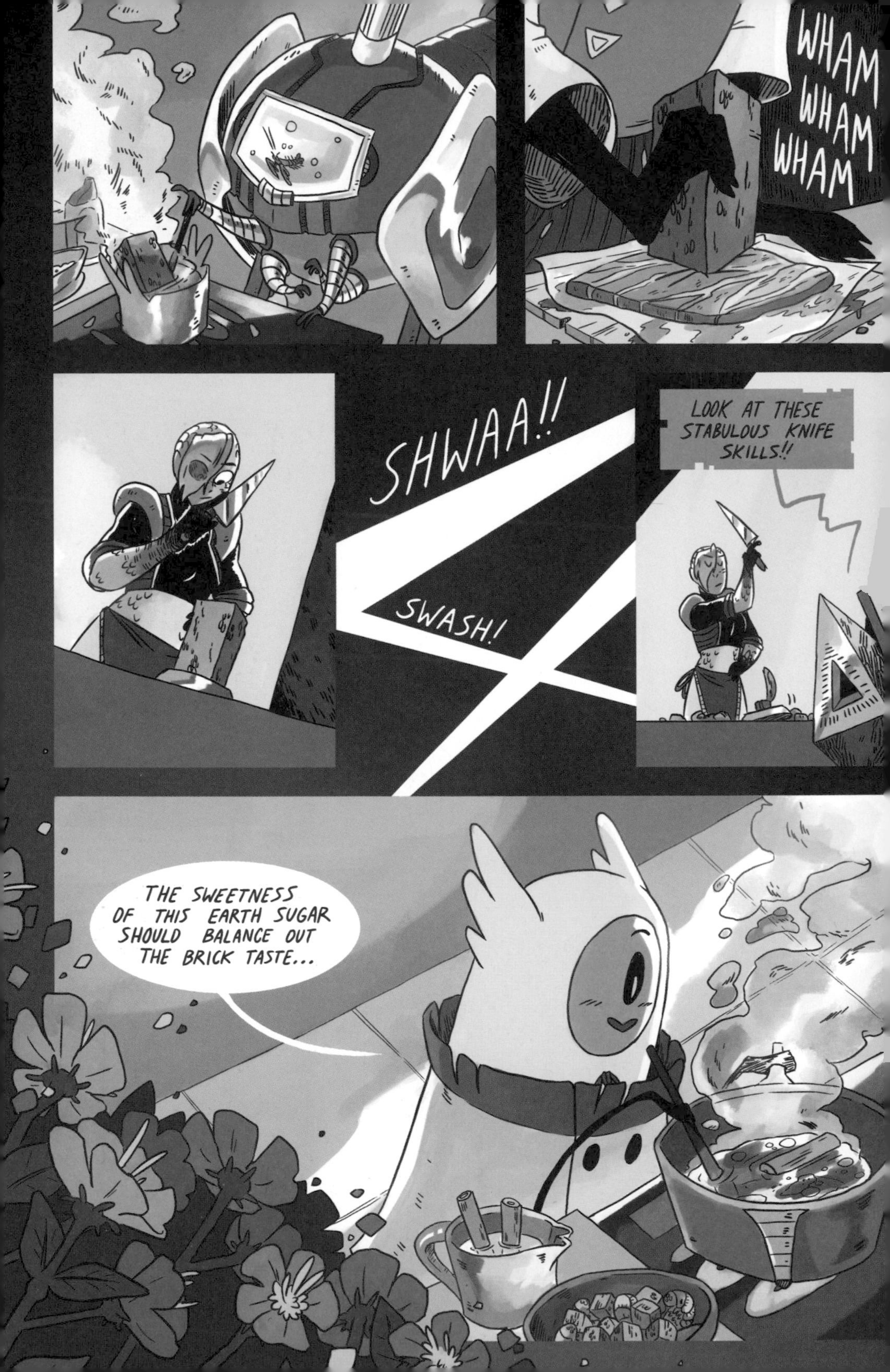
WHAM
WHAM
WHAM
SHWAA!!
SWASH!
LOOK AT THESE STABULOUS KNIFE SKILLS!!
THE SWEETNESS OF THIS EARTH SUGAR SHOULD BALANCE OUT THE BRICK TASTE...

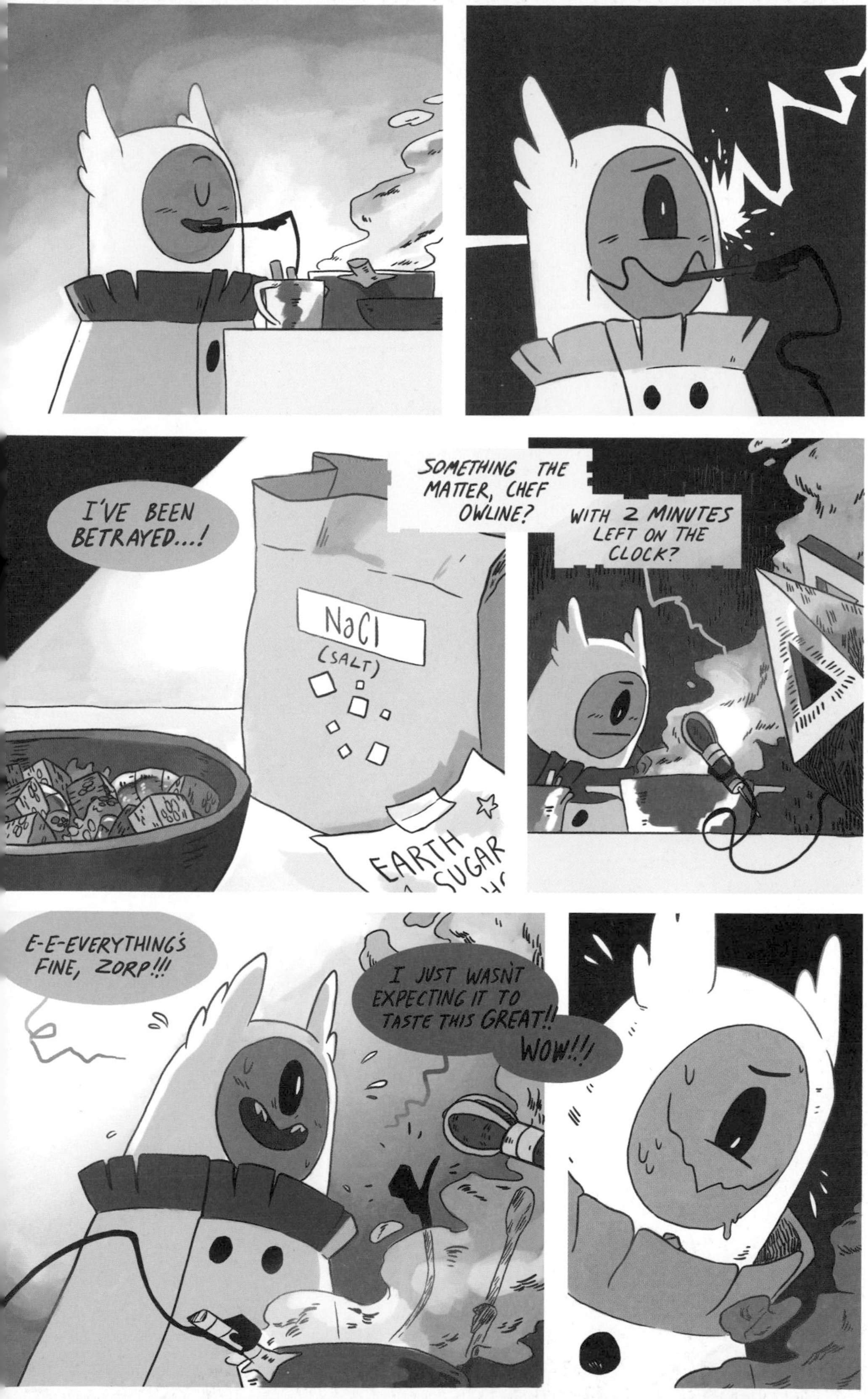
I'VE BEEN BETRAYED...!
NaCl
(SALT)
EARTH SUGAR
SOMETHING THE MATTER, CHEF OWLINE?
WITH 2 MINUTES LEFT ON THE CLOCK?
E-E-EVERYTHING'S FINE, ZORP!!!
I JUST WASN'T EXPECTING IT TO TASTE THIS GREAT!!
WOW!!!

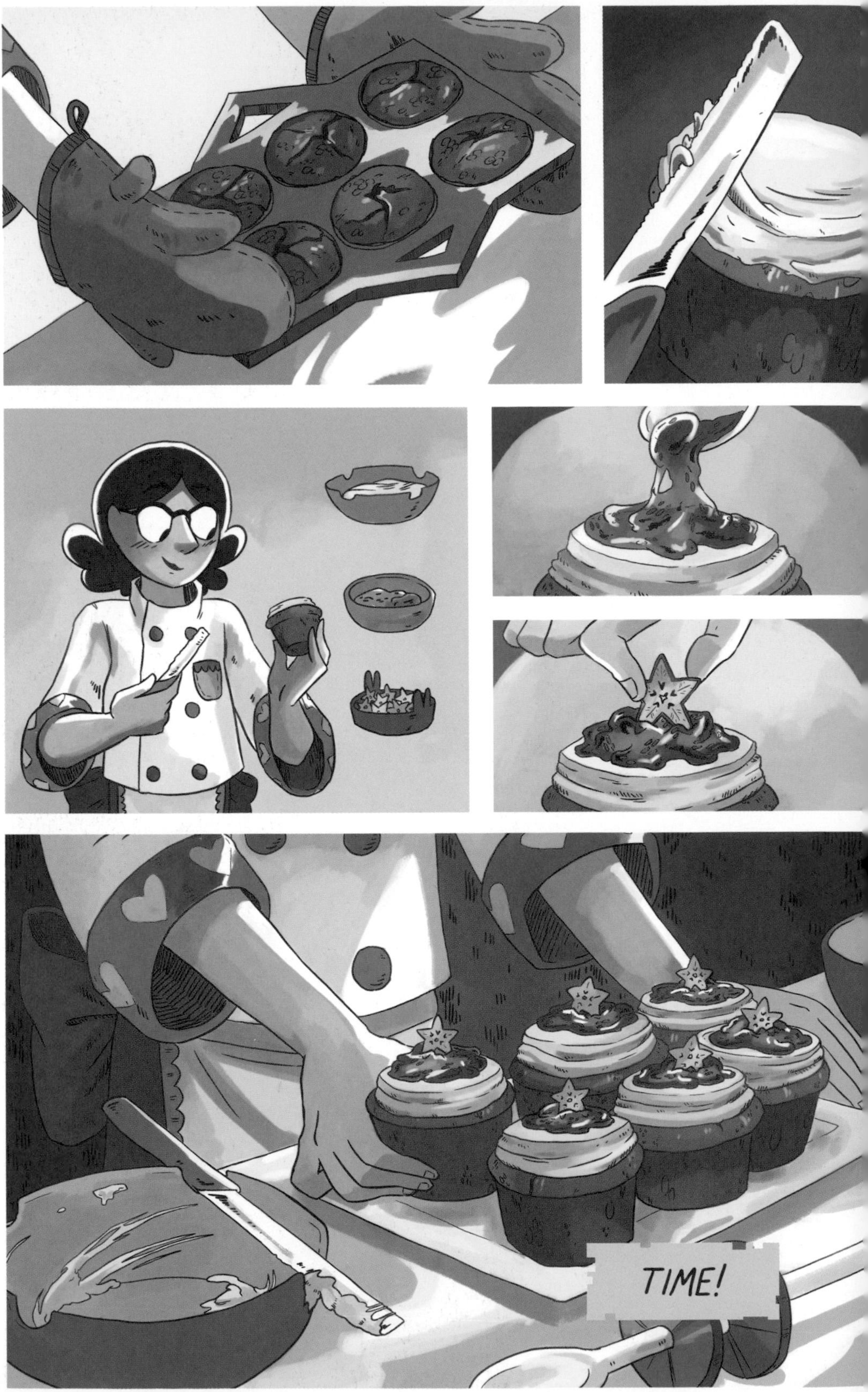
TIME!

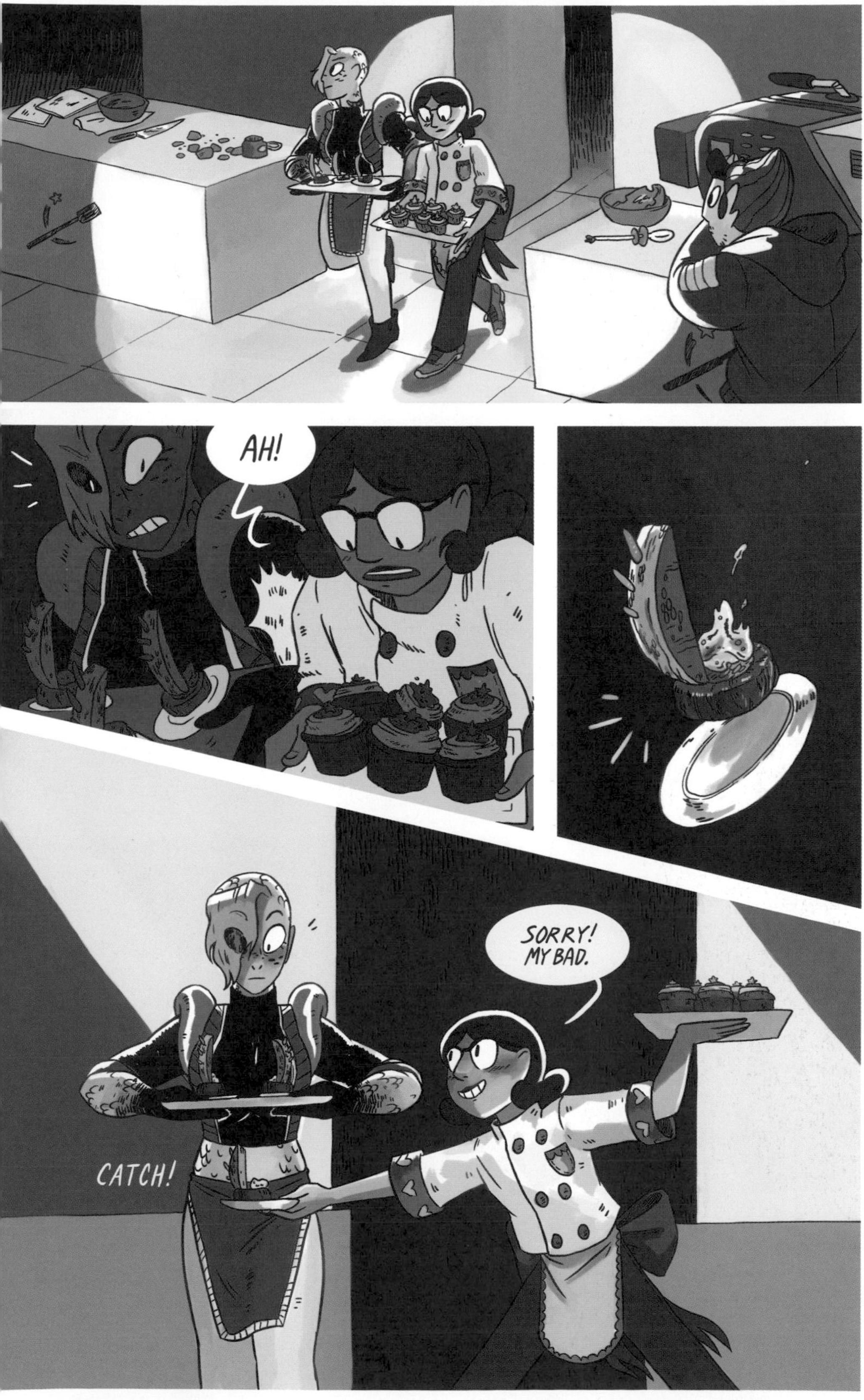
AH!
SORRY!
MY BAD.
CATCH!

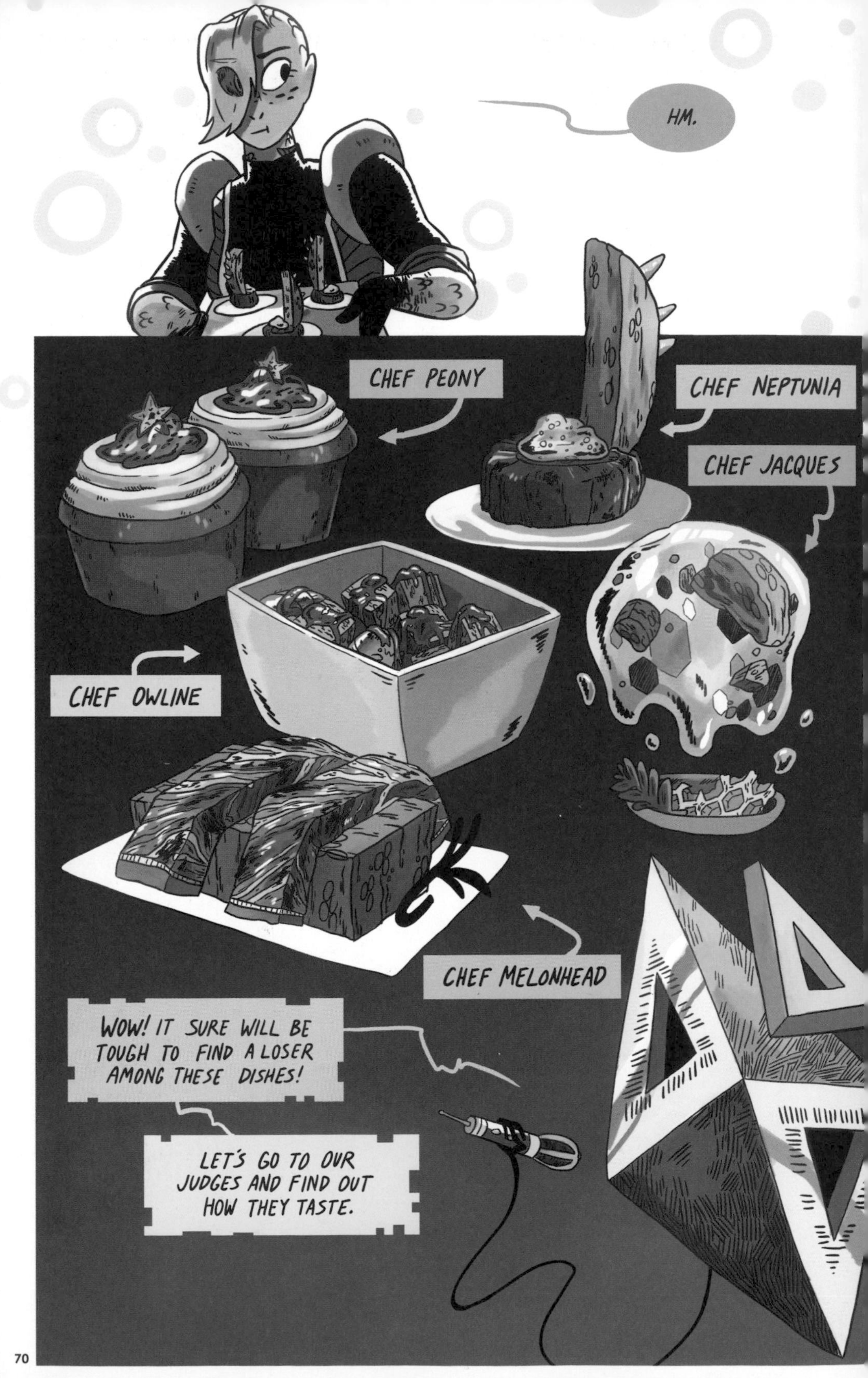
HM.
CHEF PEONY
CHEF NEPTUNIA
CHEF JACQUES
CHEF OWLINE
CHEF MELONHEAD
WOW! IT SURE WILL BE TOUGH TO FIND A LOSER AMONG THESE DISHES!
LET'S GO TO OUR JUDGES AND FIND OUT HOW THEY TASTE.

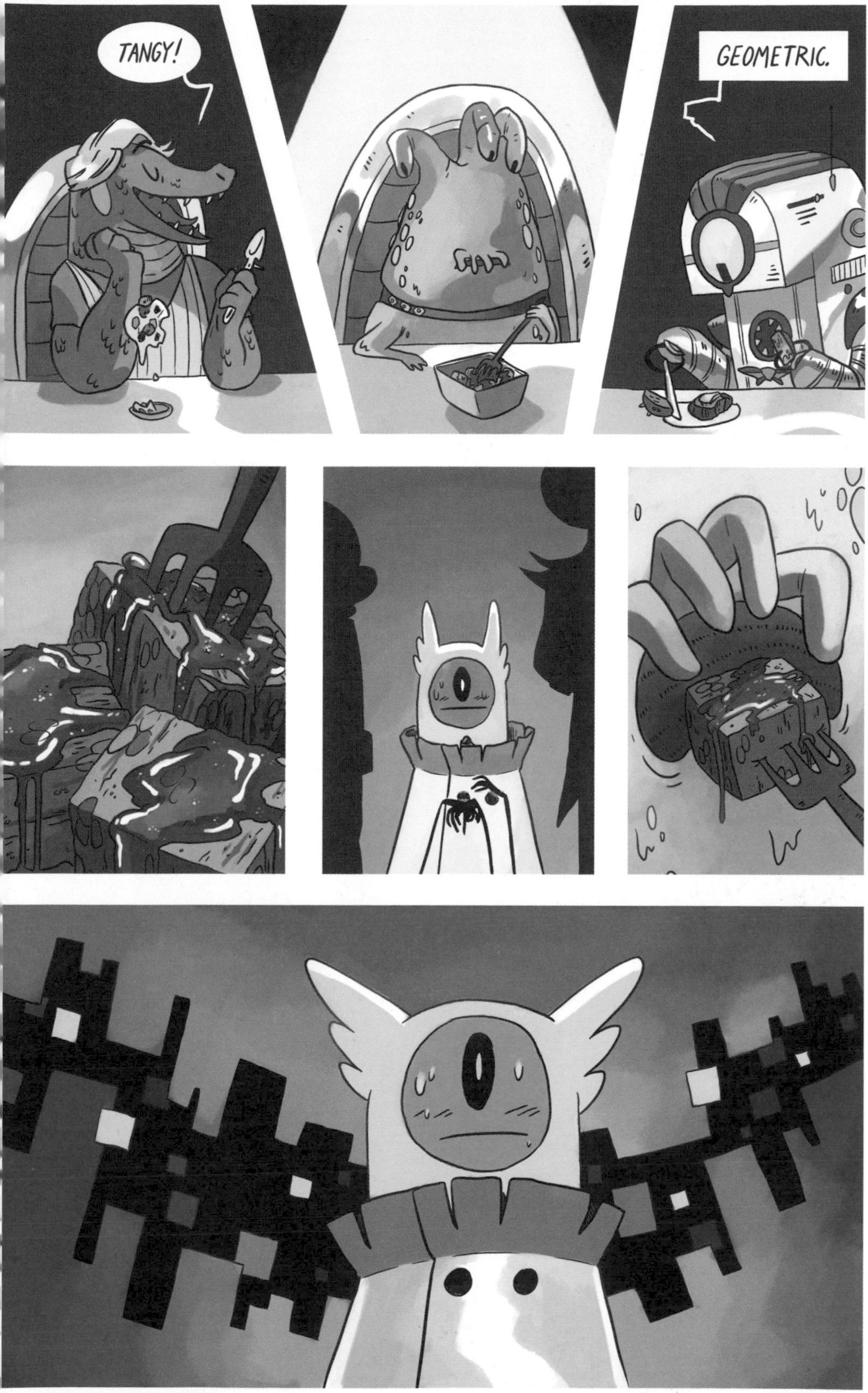
TANGY!
GEOMETRIC.

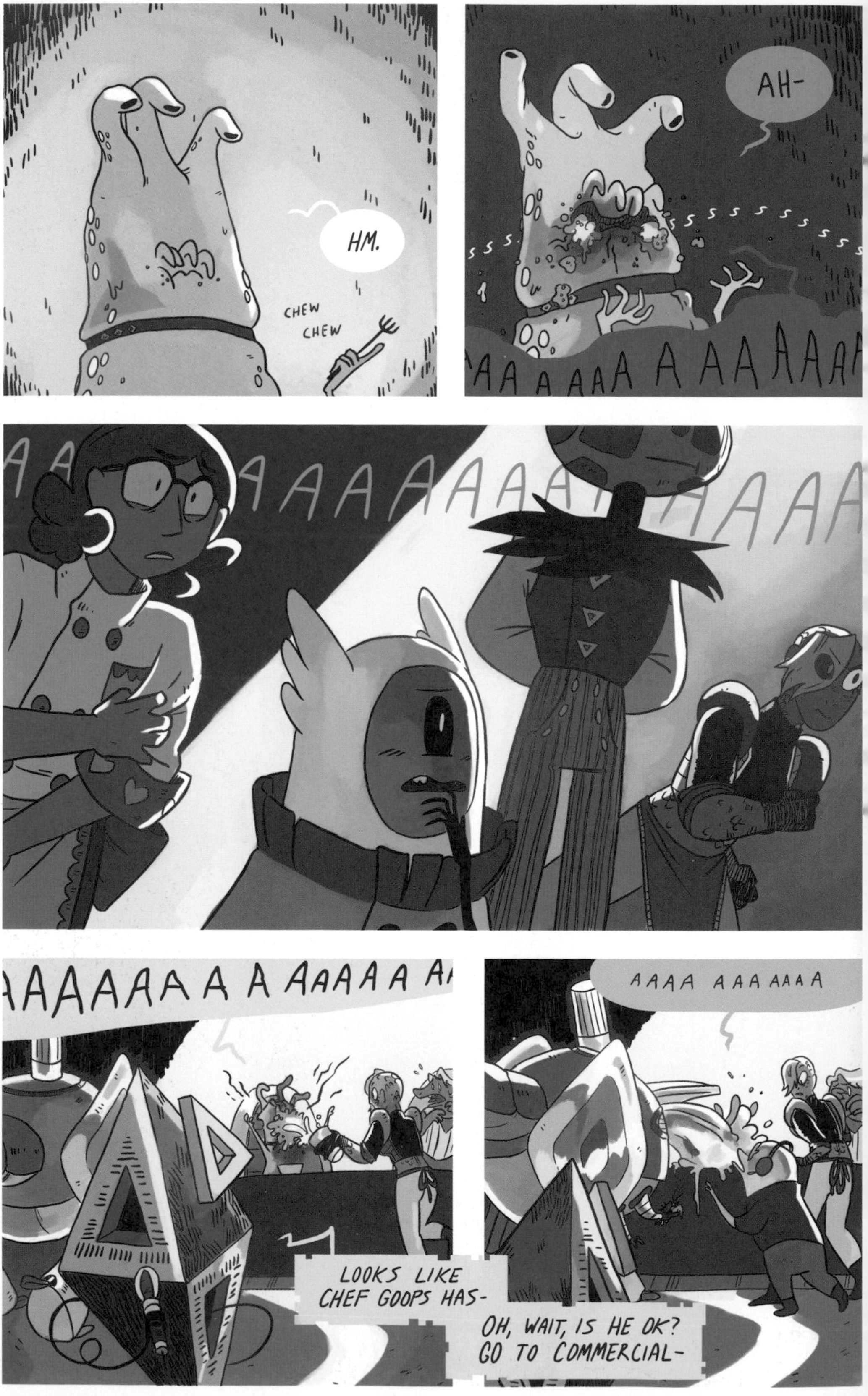
HM.
CHEW CHEW
AH-
SSSSSSS
AAAAAAAAAAA
AAAAAAAAAAAA
AAAAAAAAAAAA
AAAA AAAAAAA
LOOKS LIKE CHEF GOOPS HAS-
OH, WAIT, IS HE OK? GO TO COMMERCIAL-

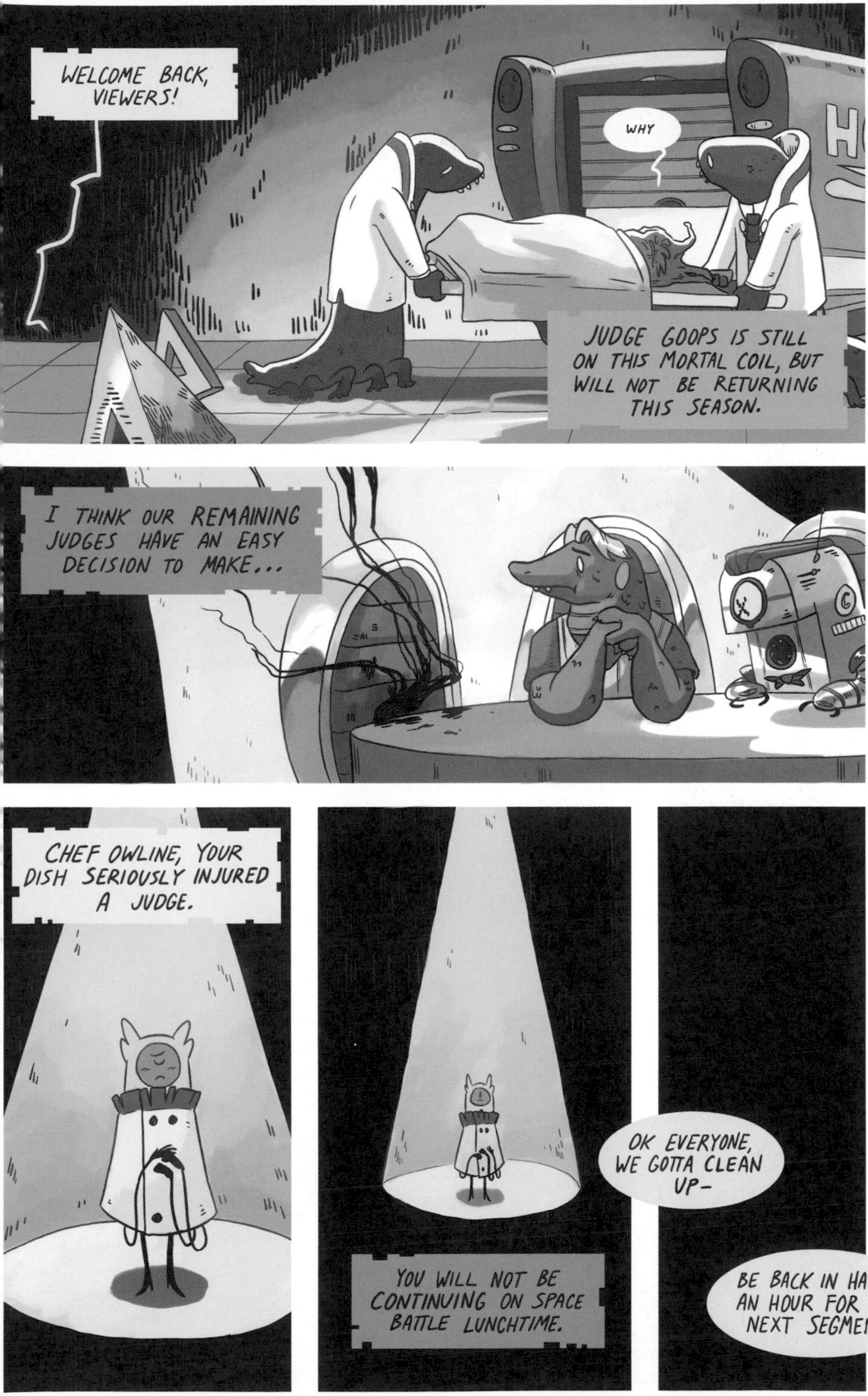
WELCOME BACK, VIEWERS!
WHY
JUDGE GOOPS IS STILL ON THIS MORTAL COIL, BUT WILL NOT BE RETURNING THIS SEASON.
I THINK OUR REMAINING JUDGES HAVE AN EASY DECISION TO MAKE...
CHEF OWLINE, YOUR DISH SERIOUSLY INJURED A JUDGE.
YOU WILL NOT BE CONTINUING ON SPACE BATTLE LUNCHTIME.
OK EVERYONE, WE GOTTA CLEAN UP-
BE BACK IN HALF AN HOUR FOR THE NEXT SEGMENT!

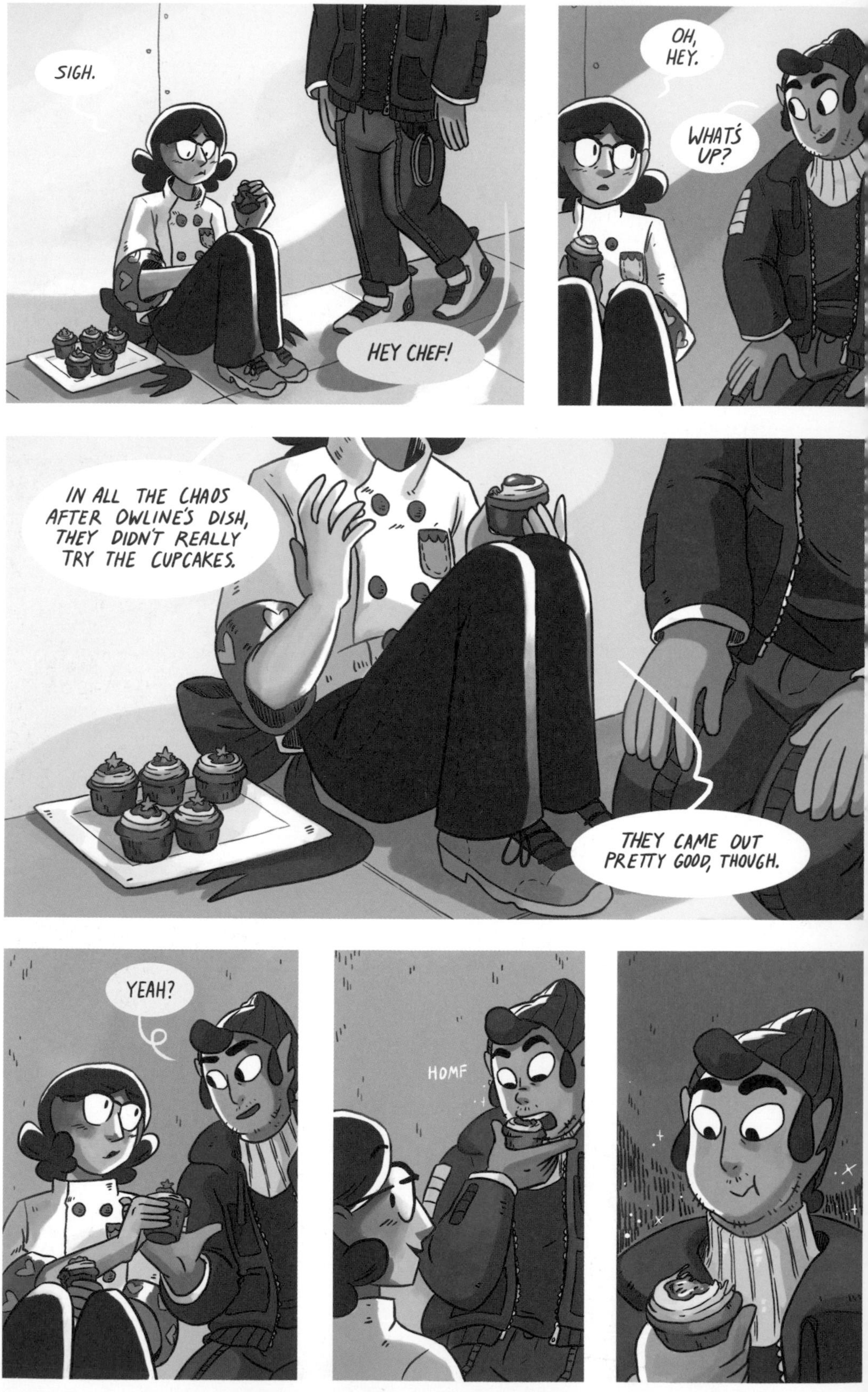
SIGH.
HEY CHEF!
OH, HEY.
WHAT'S UP?
IN ALL THE CHAOS AFTER OWLINE'S DISH, THEY DIDN'T REALLY TRY THE CUPCAKES.
THEY CAME OUT PRETTY GOOD, THOUGH.
YEAH?
HOMF

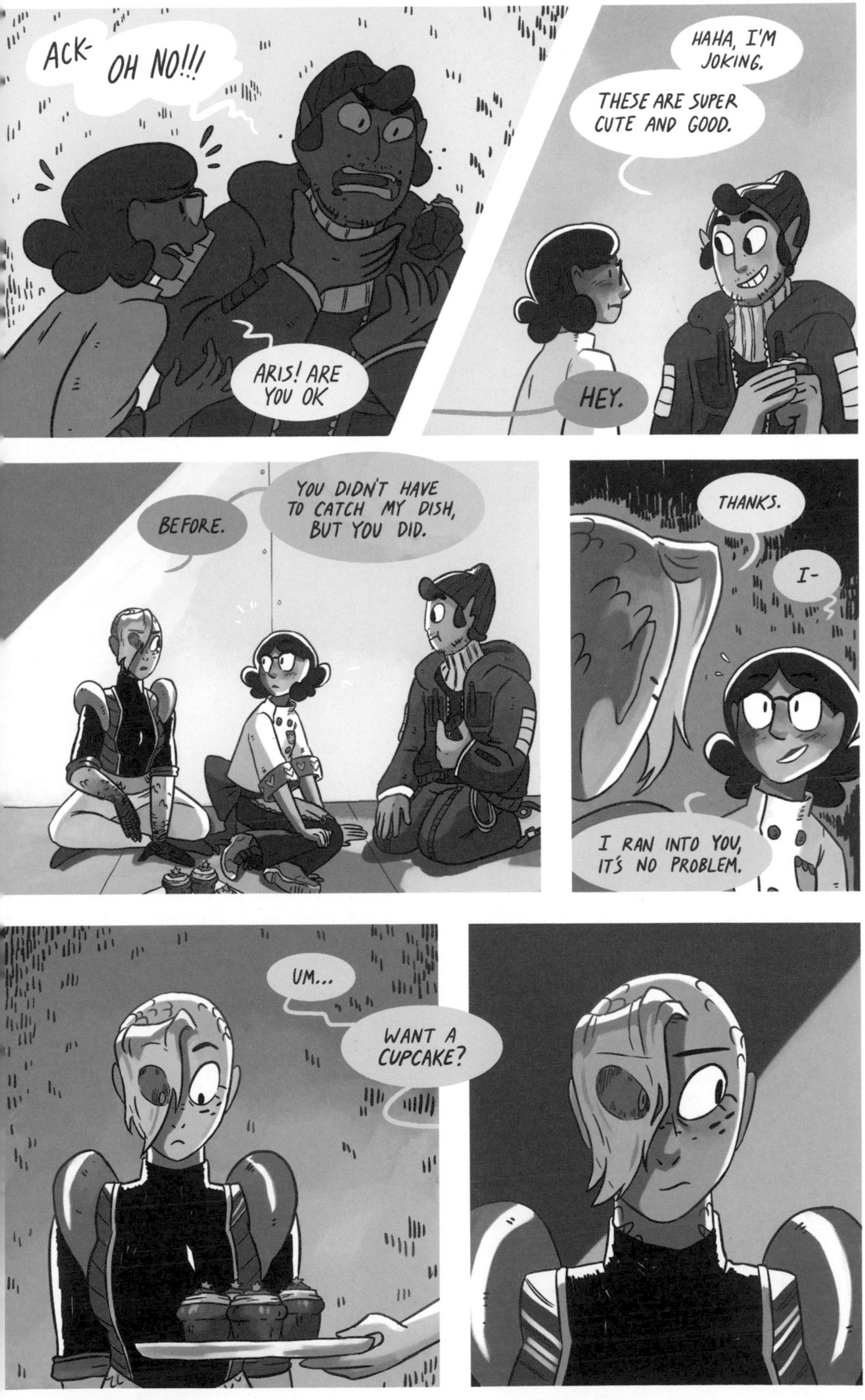
ACK-
OH NO!!!
ARIS! ARE YOU OK
HAHA, I'M JOKING.
THESE ARE SUPER CUTE AND GOOD.
HEY.
BEFORE.
YOU DIDN'T HAVE TO CATCH MY DISH, BUT YOU DID.
THANKS.
I-
I RAN INTO YOU, IT'S NO PROBLEM.
UM...
WANT A CUPCAKE?

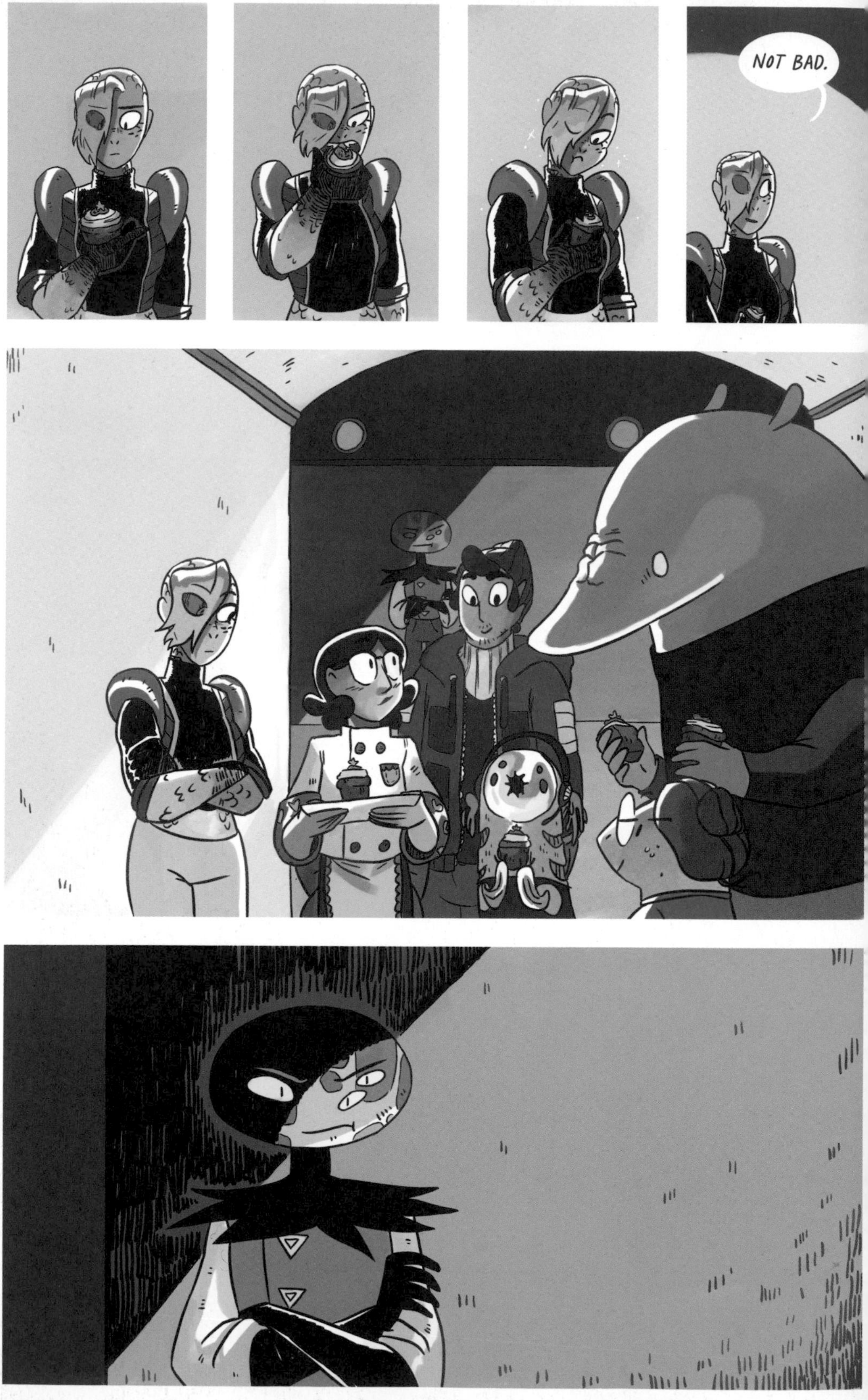
NOT BAD.

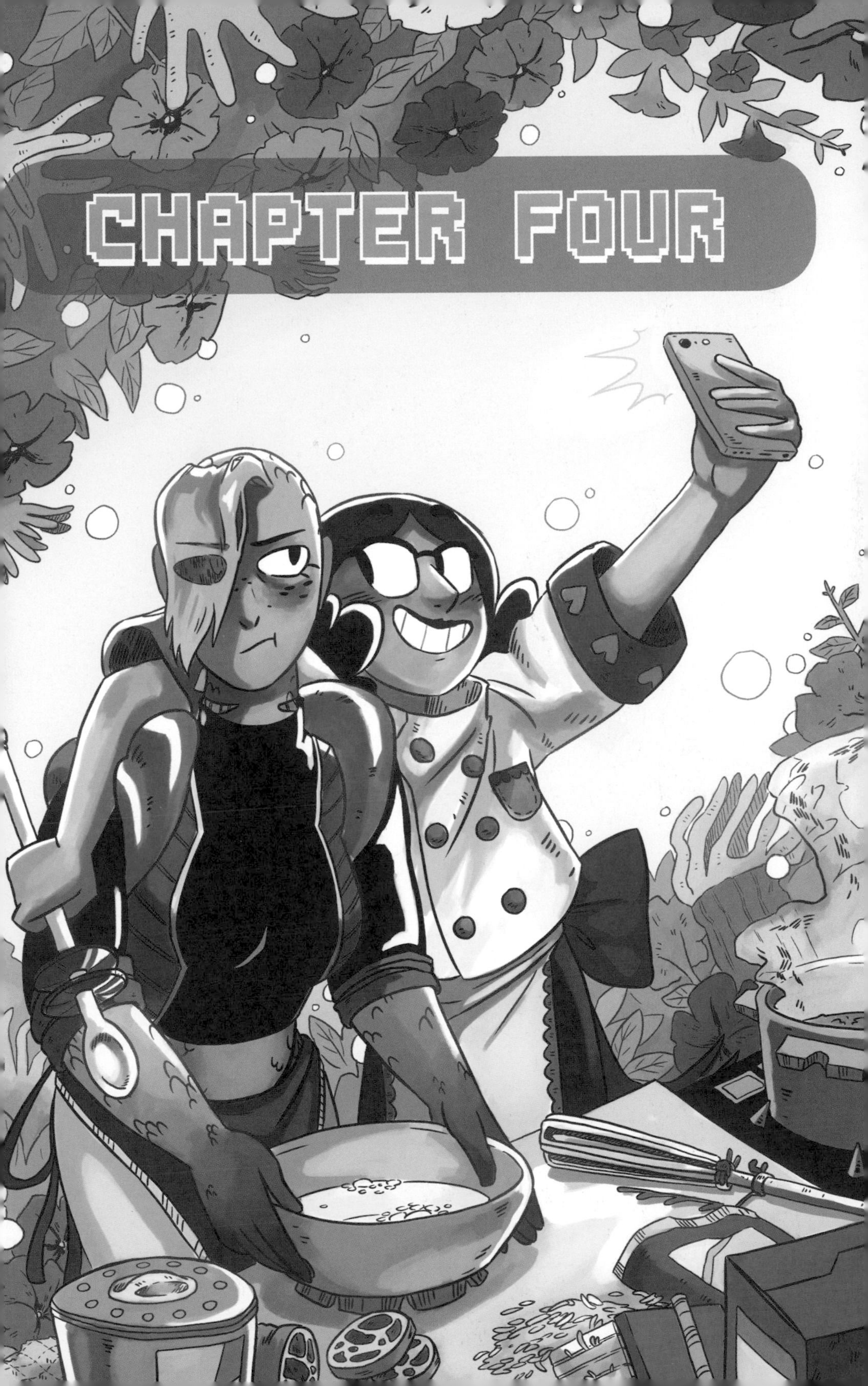
CHAPTER FOUR

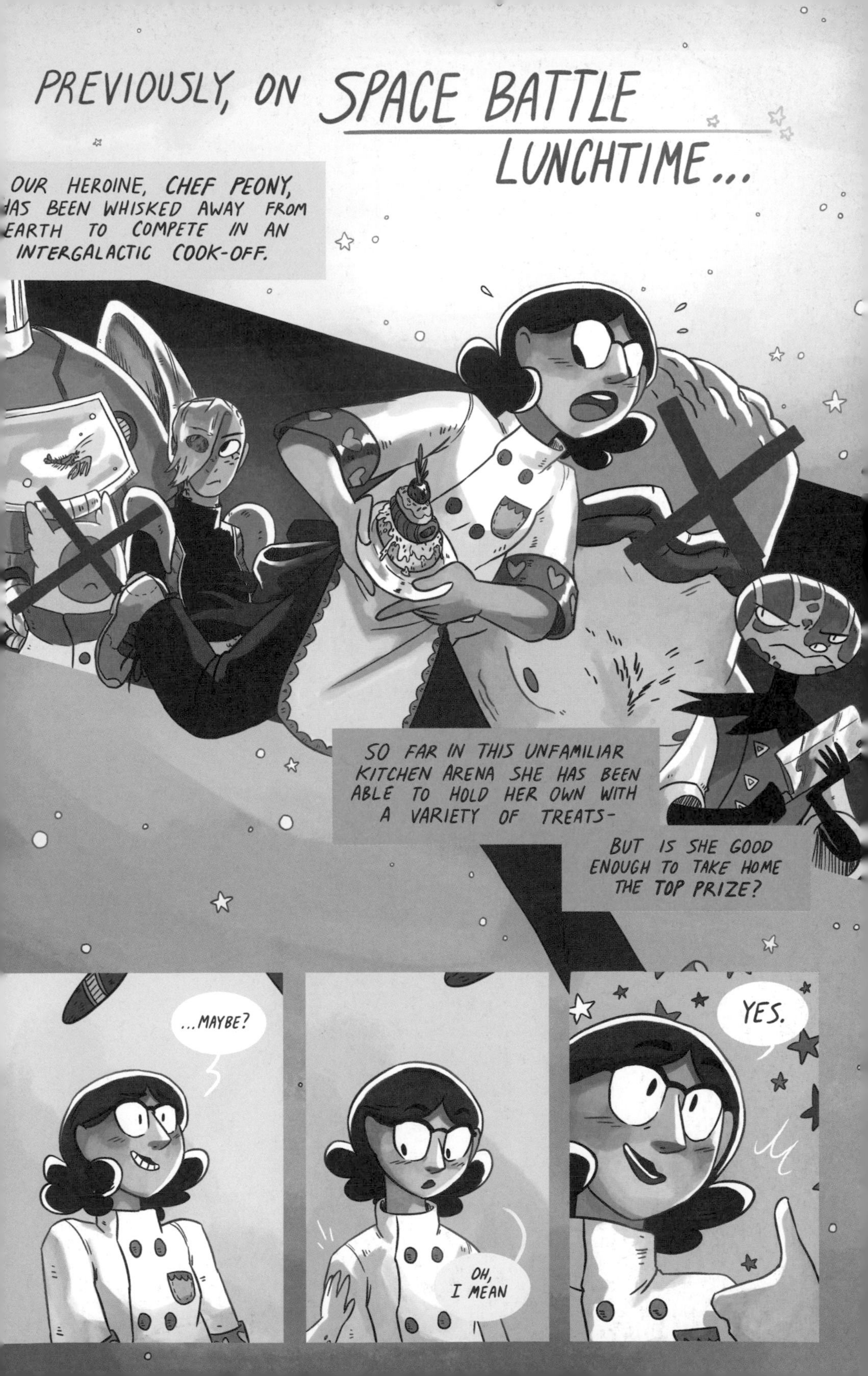

PREVIOUSLY, ON SPACE BATTLE LUNCHTIME...
OUR HEROINE, CHEF PEONY, HAS BEEN WHISKED AWAY FROM EARTH TO COMPETE IN AN INTERGALACTIC COOK-OFF.
SO FAR IN THIS UNFAMILIAR KITCHEN ARENA SHE HAS BEEN ABLE TO HOLD HER OWN WITH A VARIETY OF TREATS-
BUT IS SHE GOOD ENOUGH TO TAKE HOME THE TOP PRIZE?
...MAYBE?
OH, I MEAN
YES.

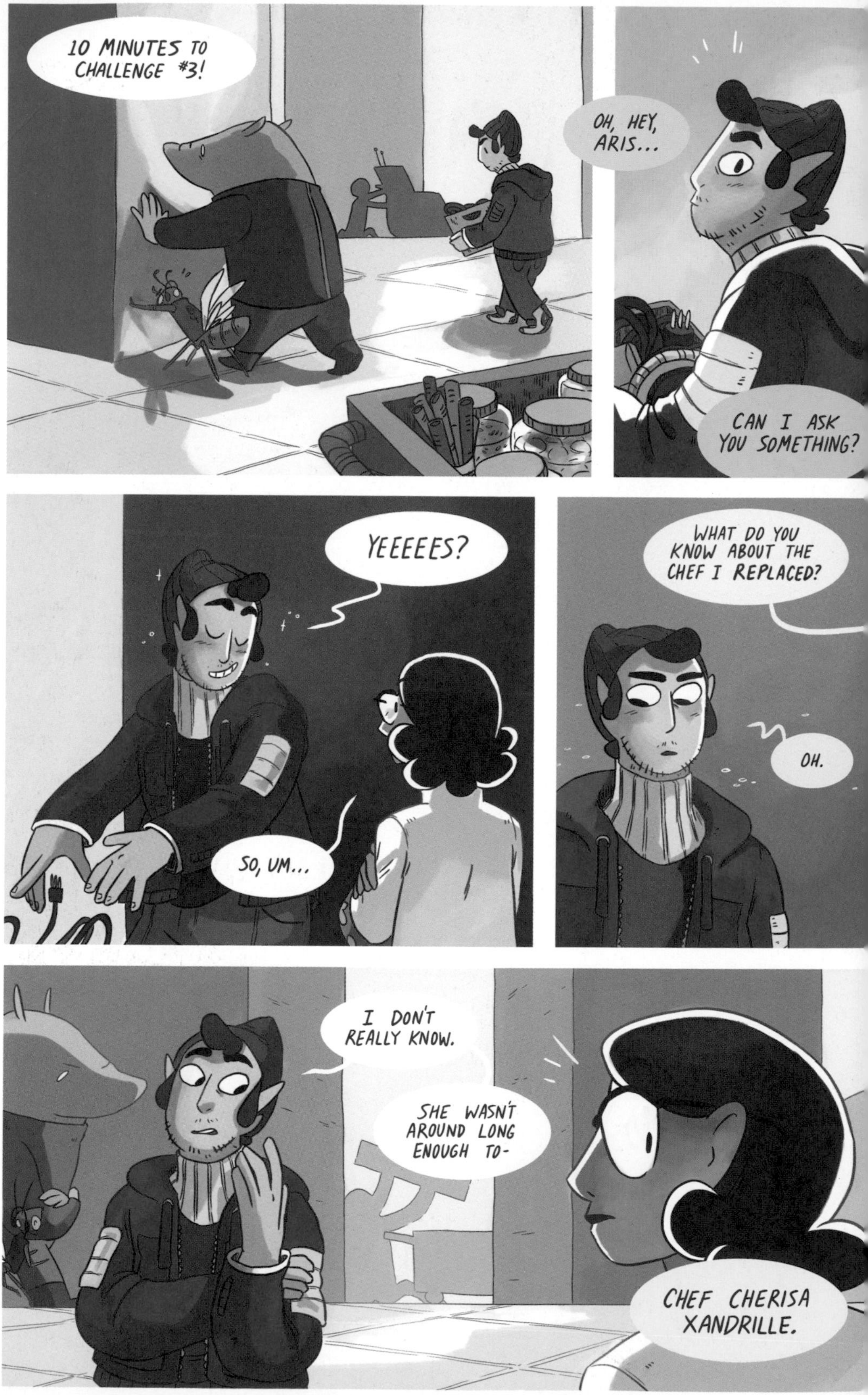
10 MINUTES TO CHALLENGE #3!
OH, HEY, ARIS...
CAN I ASK YOU SOMETHING?
YEEEEES?
SO, UM...
WHAT DO YOU KNOW ABOUT THE CHEF I REPLACED?
OH.
I DON'T REALLY KNOW.
SHE WASN'T AROUND LONG ENOUGH TO-
CHEF CHERISA XANDRILLE.

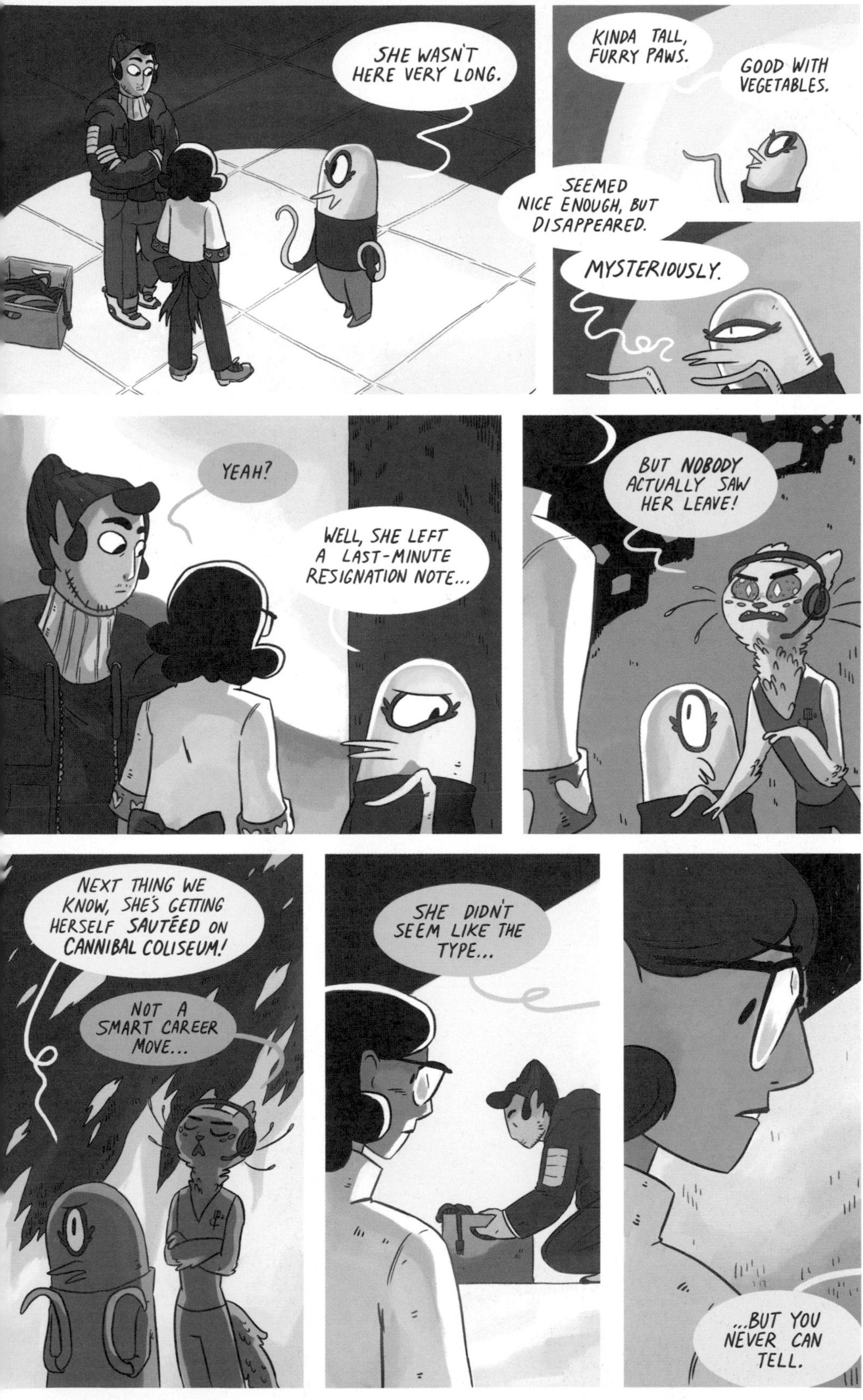

SHE WASN'T HERE VERY LONG.
KINDA TALL, FURRY PAWS.
GOOD WITH VEGETABLES.
SEEMED NICE ENOUGH, BUT DISAPPEARED.
MYSTERIOUSLY.
YEAH?
WELL, SHE LEFT A LAST-MINUTE RESIGNATION NOTE...
BUT NOBODY ACTUALLY SAW HER LEAVE!
NEXT THING WE KNOW, SHE'S GETTING HERSELF SAUTÉED ON CANNIBAL COLISEUM!
NOT A SMART CAREER MOVE...
SHE DIDN'T SEEM LIKE THE TYPE...
...BUT YOU NEVER CAN TELL.

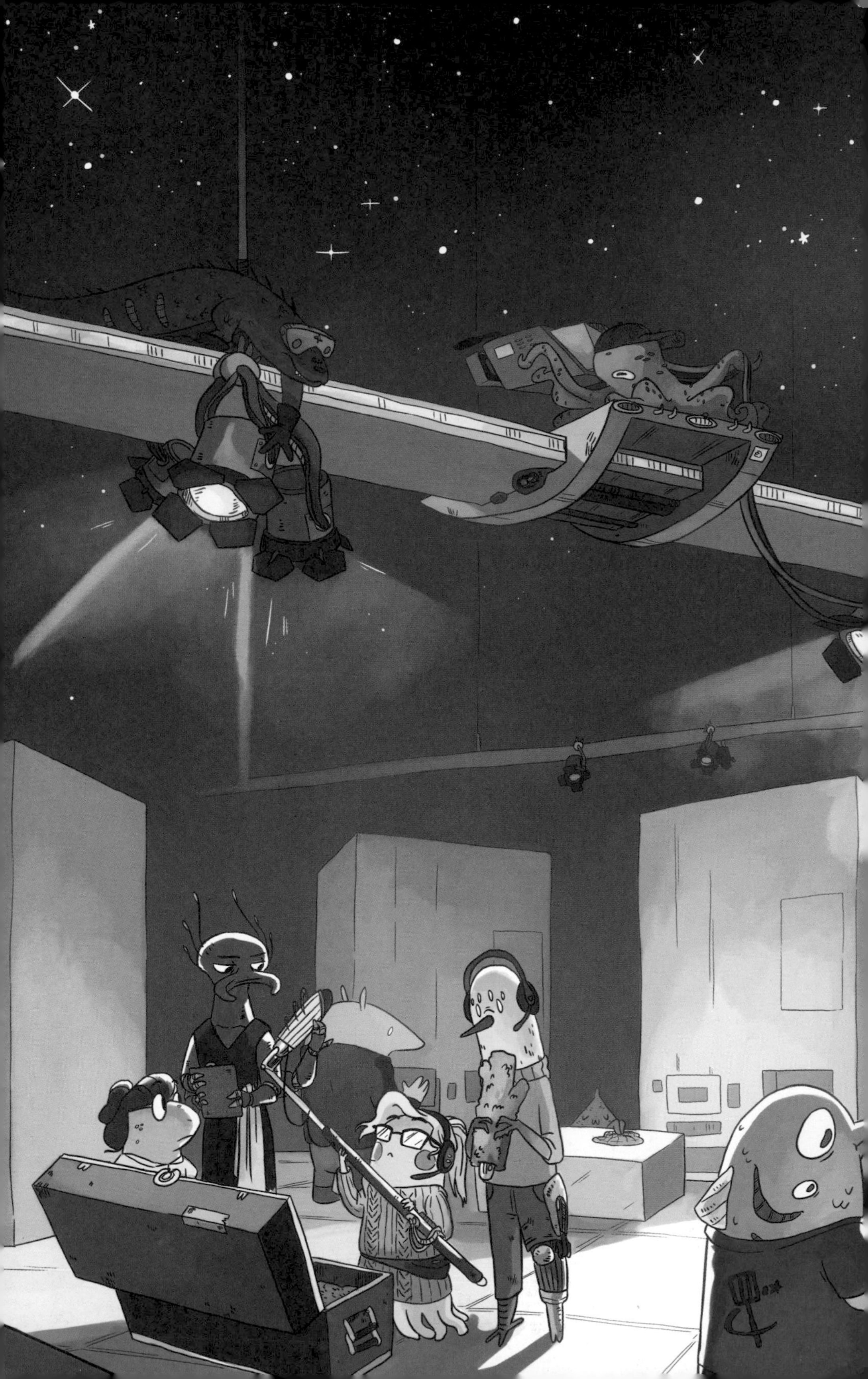

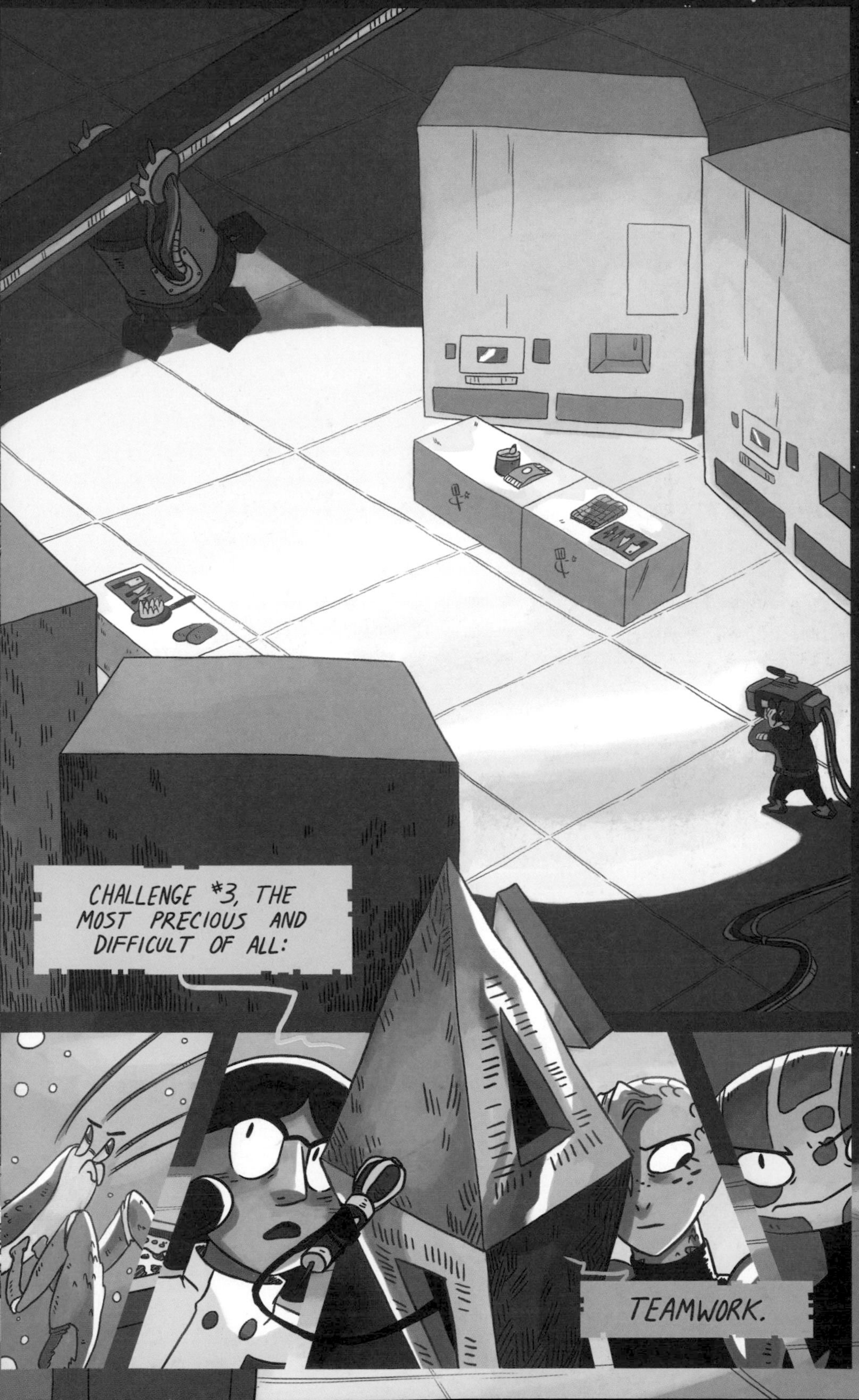
CHALLENGE #3, THE MOST PRECIOUS AND DIFFICULT OF ALL:
TEAMWORK.

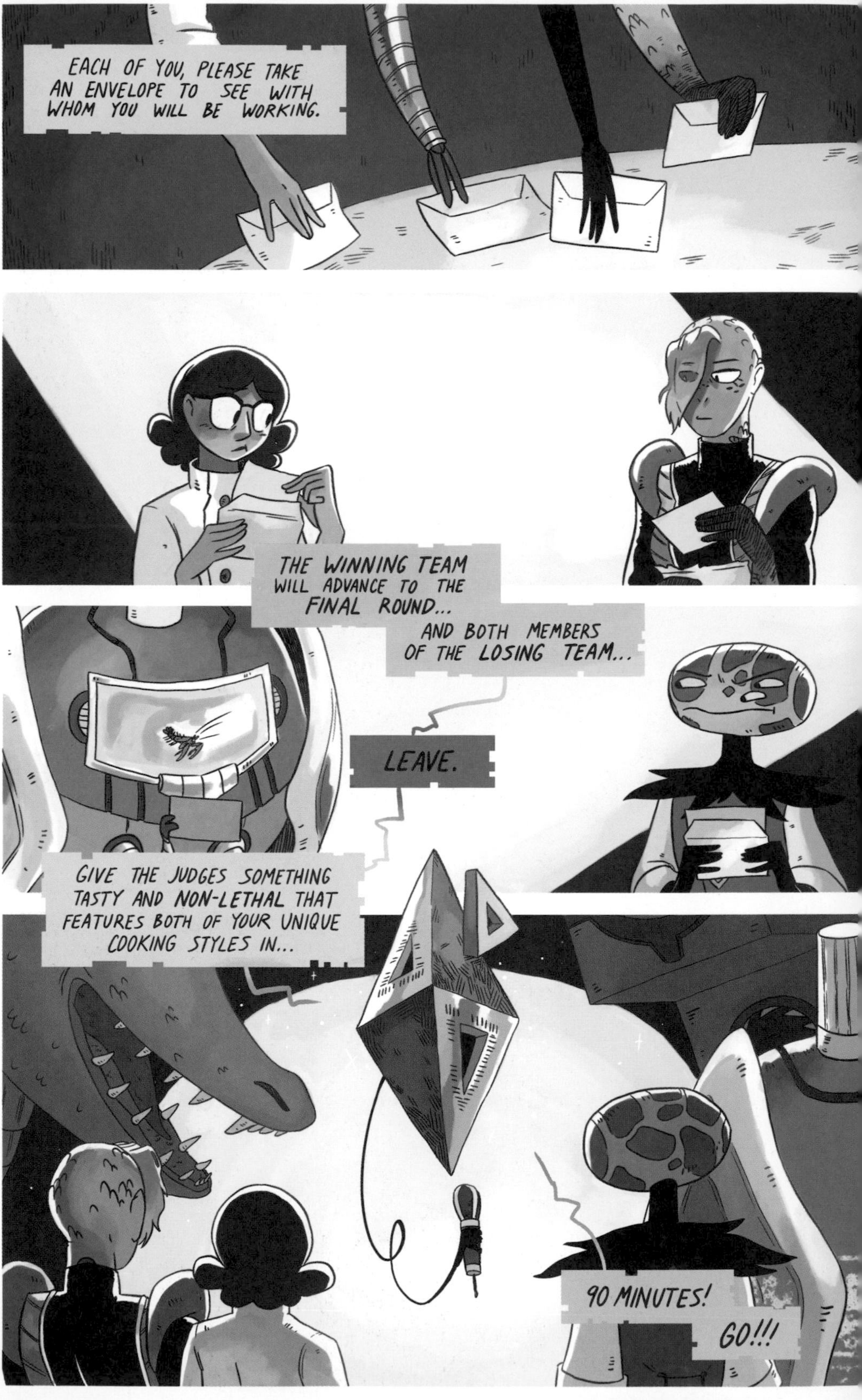
EACH OF YOU, PLEASE TAKE AN ENVELOPE TO SEE WITH WHOM YOU WILL BE WORKING.
THE WINNING TEAM WILL ADVANCE TO THE FINAL ROUND...
AND BOTH MEMBERS OF THE LOSING TEAM...
LEAVE.
GIVE THE JUDGES SOMETHING TASTY AND NON-LETHAL THAT FEATURES BOTH OF YOUR UNIQUE COOKING STYLES IN...
90 MINUTES!
GO!!!

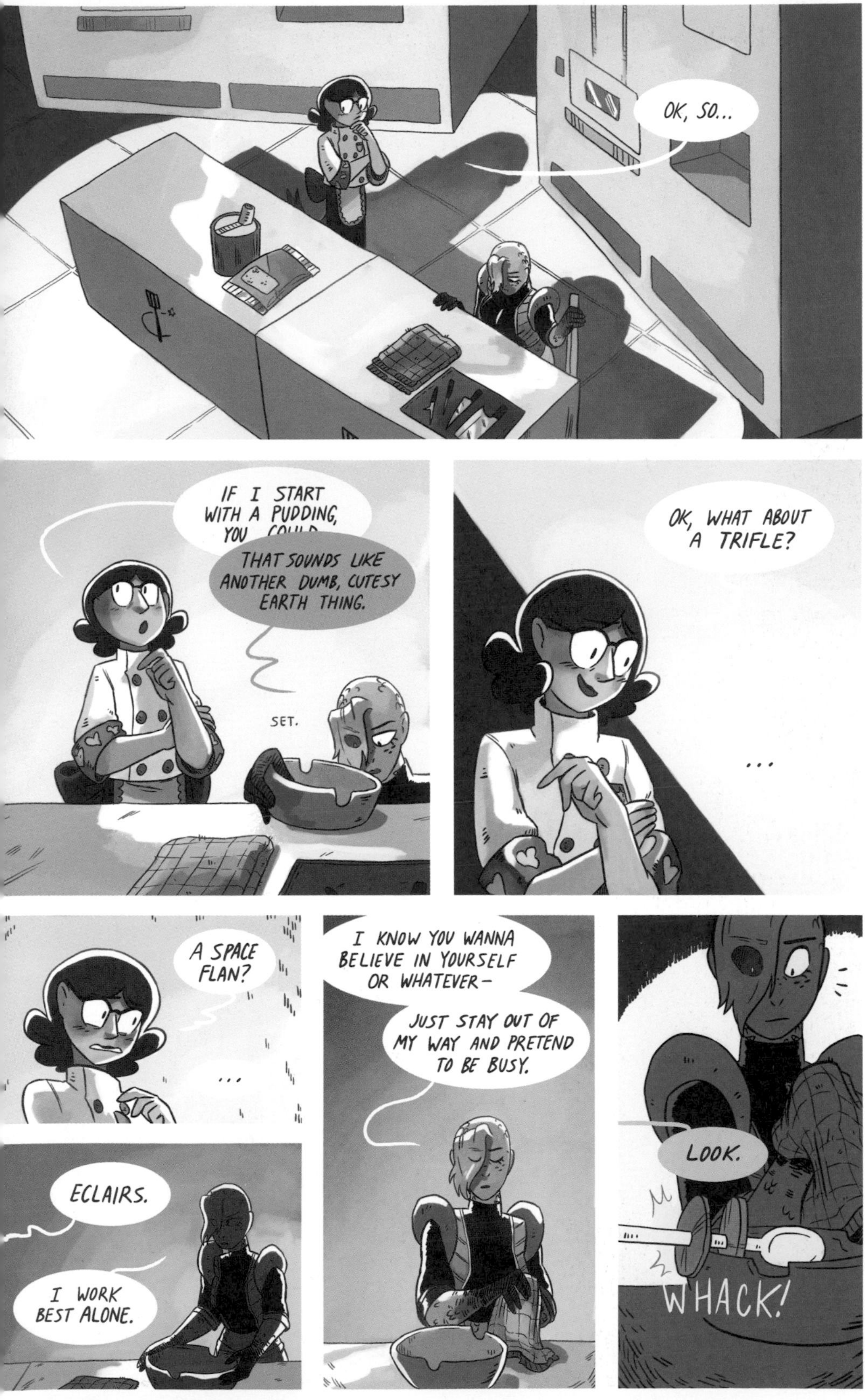
OK, SO...
IF I START WITH A PUDDING, YOU COULD
THAT SOUNDS LIKE ANOTHER DUMB, CUTESY EARTH THING.
SET.
OK, WHAT ABOUT A TRIFLE?
...
A SPACE FLAN?
...
ECLAIRS.
I WORK BEST ALONE.
I KNOW YOU WANNA BELIEVE IN YOURSELF OR WHATEVER–
JUST STAY OUT OF MY WAY AND PRETEND TO BE BUSY.
LOOK.
WHACK!

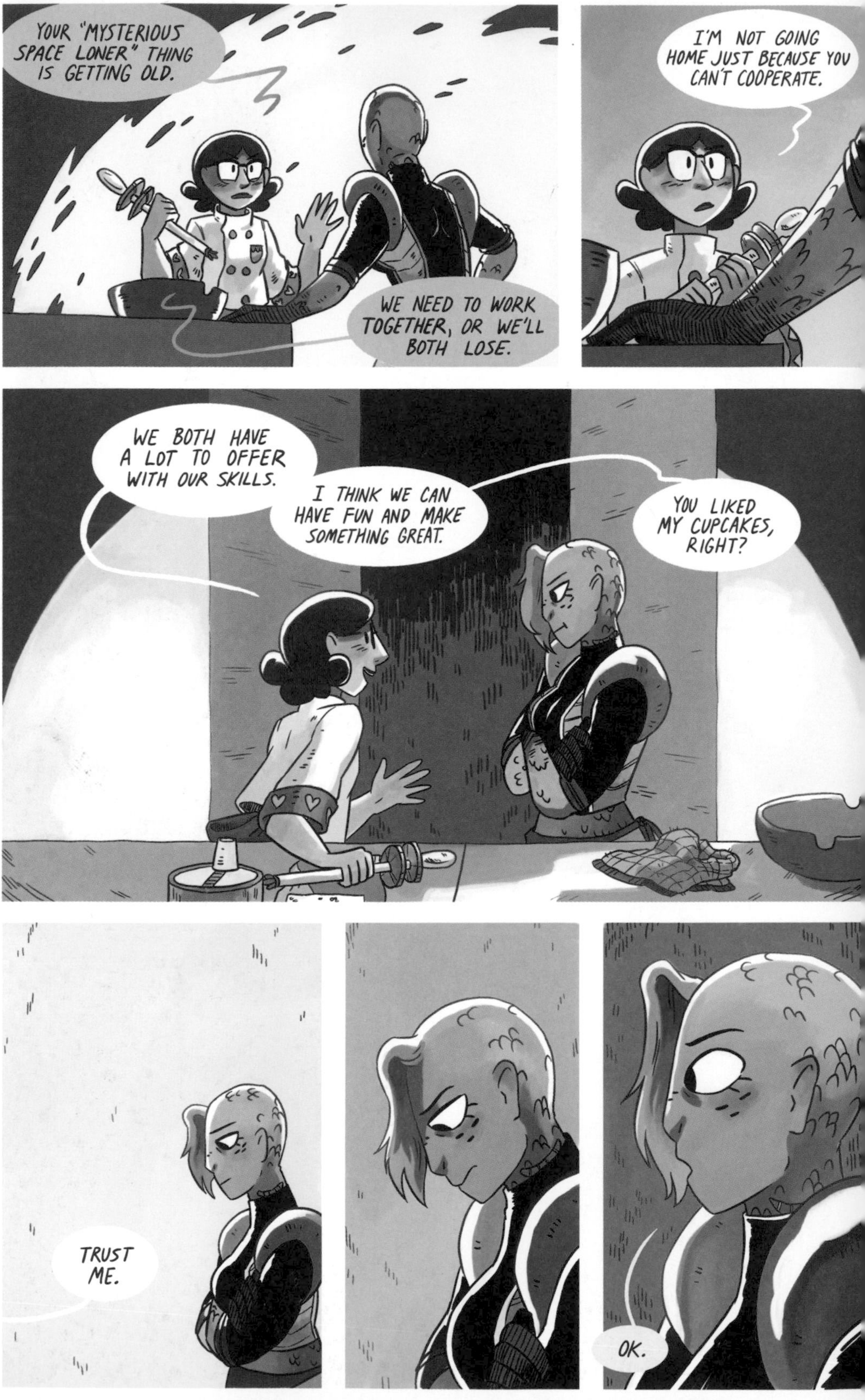
YOUR "MYSTERIOUS SPACE LONER" THING IS GETTING OLD.
WE NEED TO WORK TOGETHER, OR WE'LL BOTH LOSE.
I'M NOT GOING HOME JUST BECAUSE YOU CAN'T COOPERATE.
WE BOTH HAVE A LOT TO OFFER WITH OUR SKILLS.
I THINK WE CAN HAVE FUN AND MAKE SOMETHING GREAT.
YOU LIKED MY CUPCAKES, RIGHT?
TRUST ME.
OK.

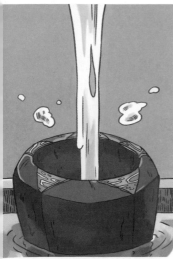

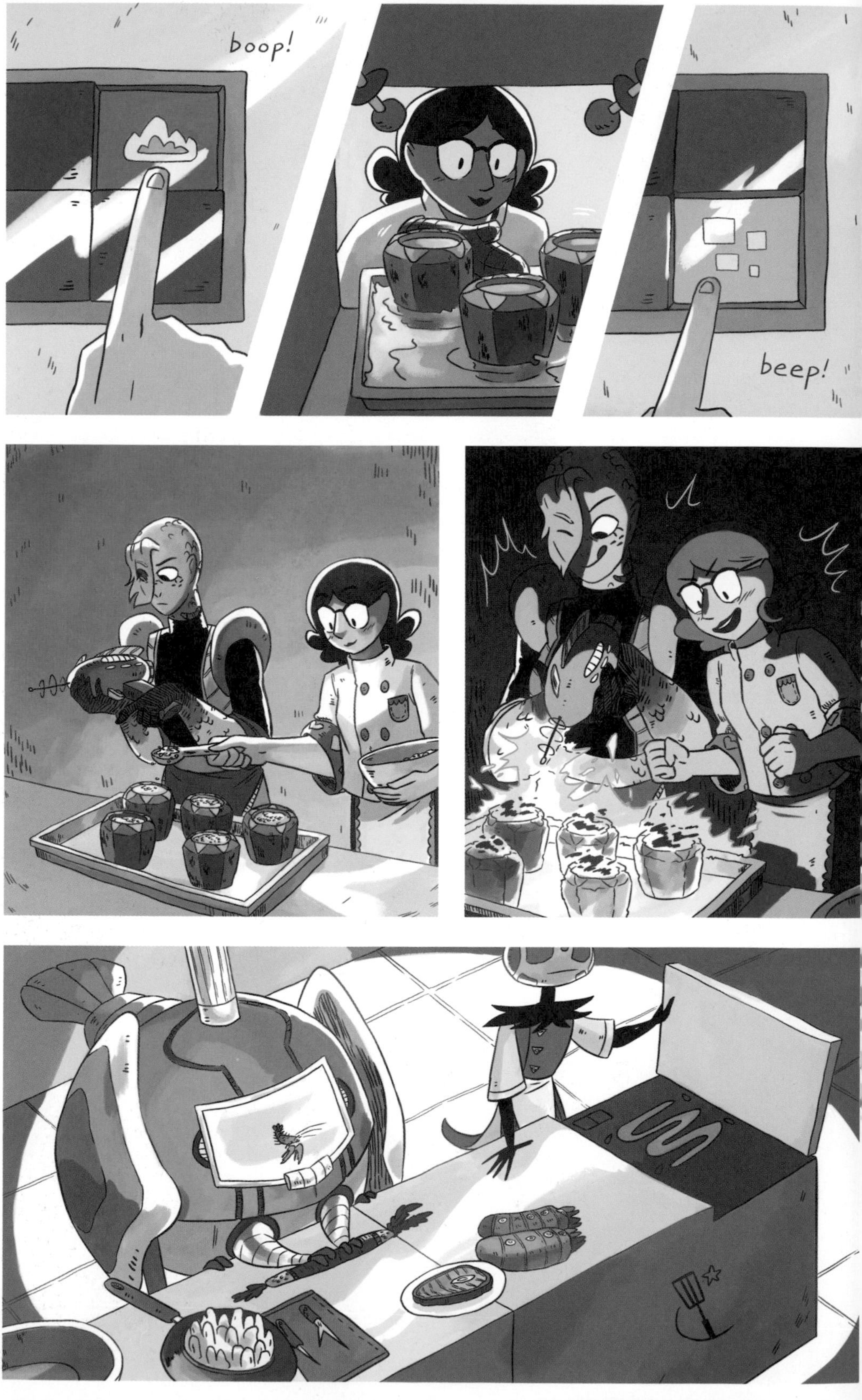
boop!
beep!

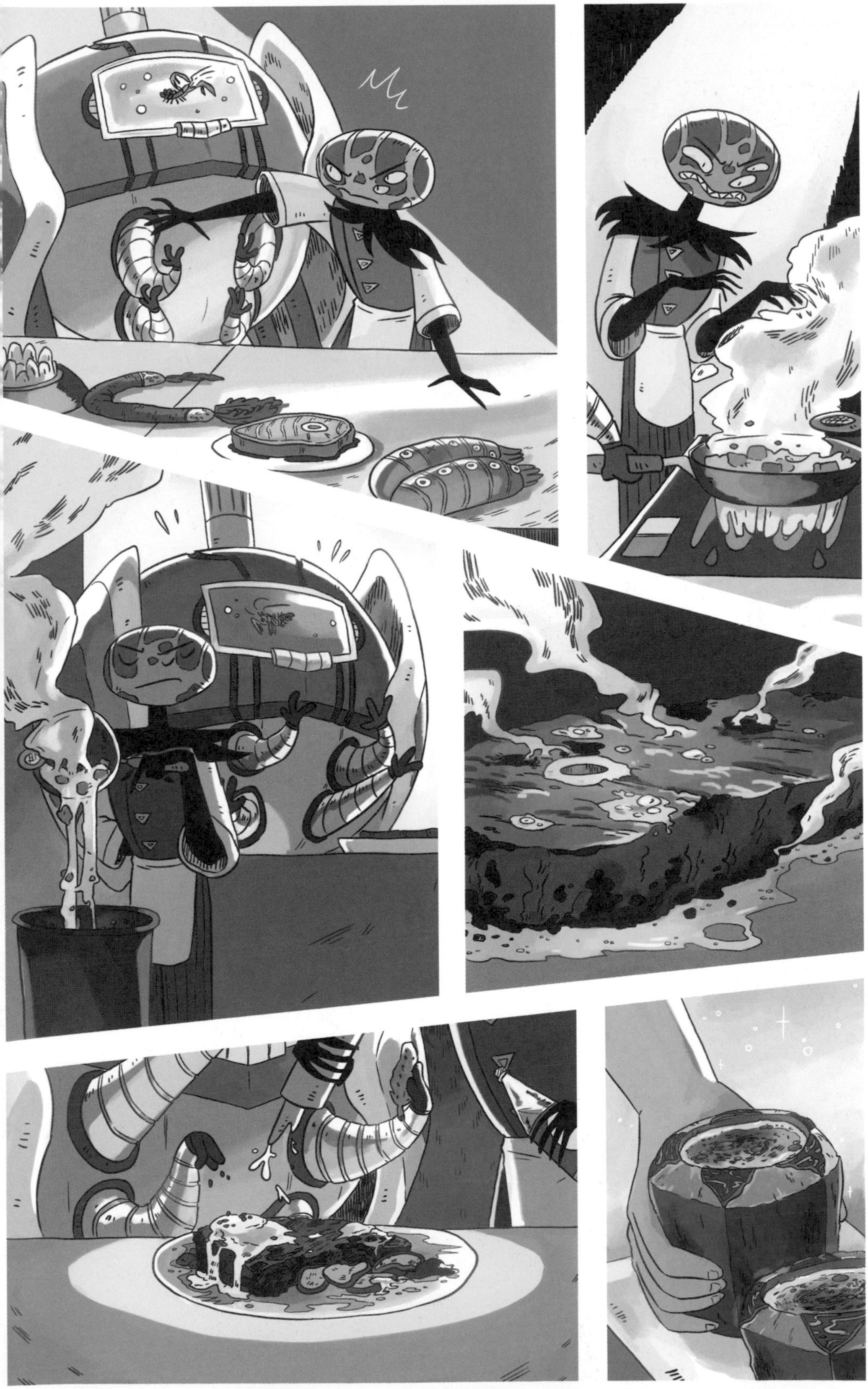

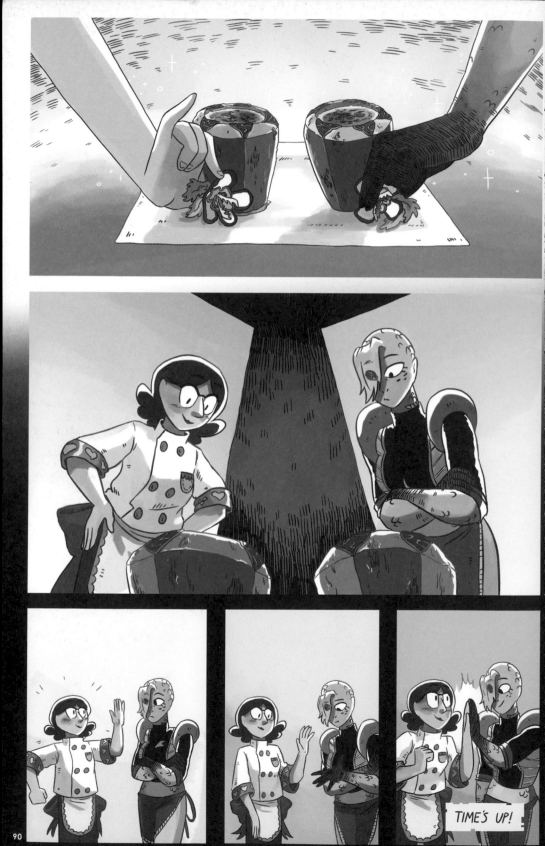

TIME'S UP!

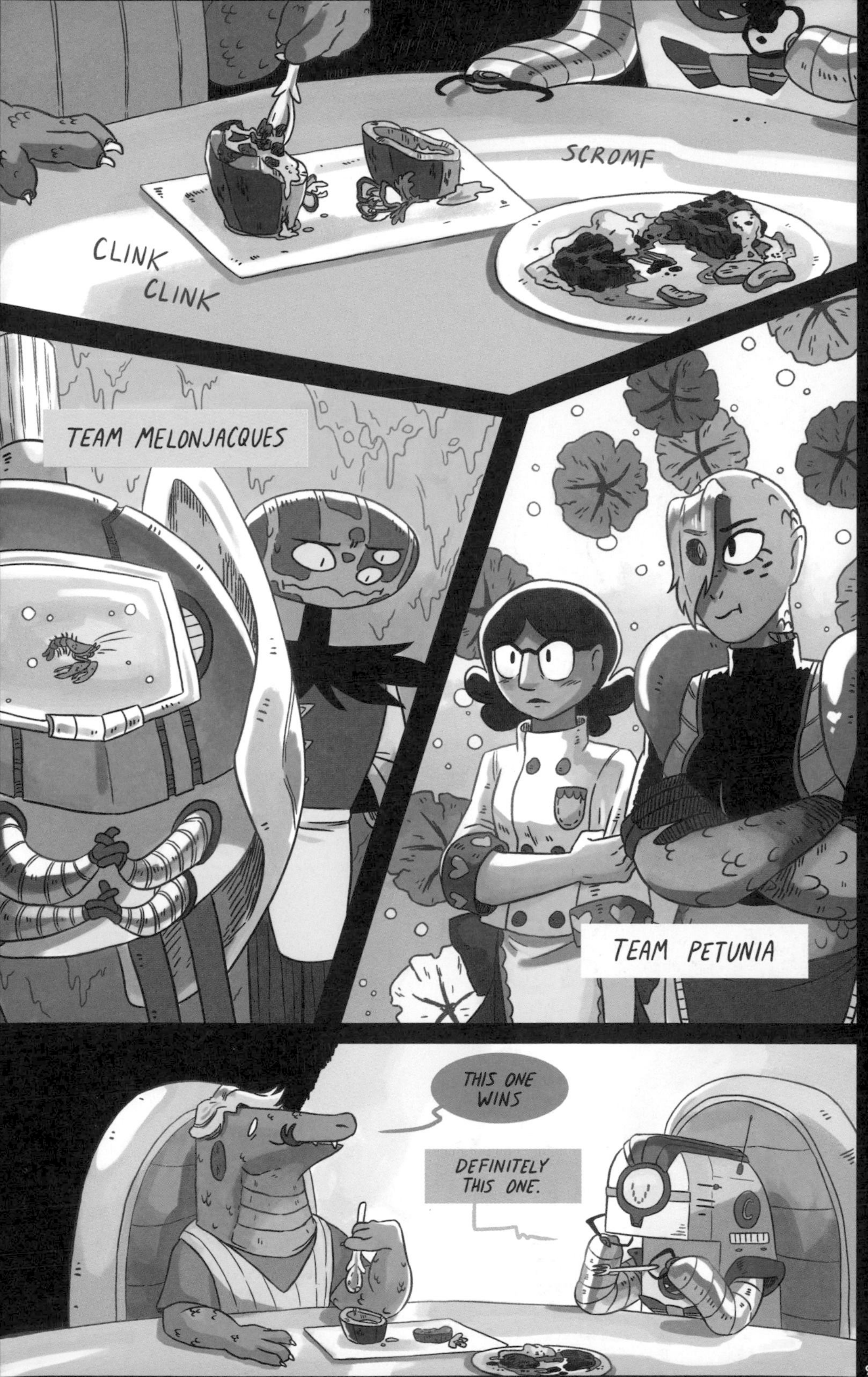
SCROMF
CLINK
CLINK
TEAM MELONJACQUES
TEAM PETUNIA
THIS ONE WINS
DEFINITELY THIS ONE.

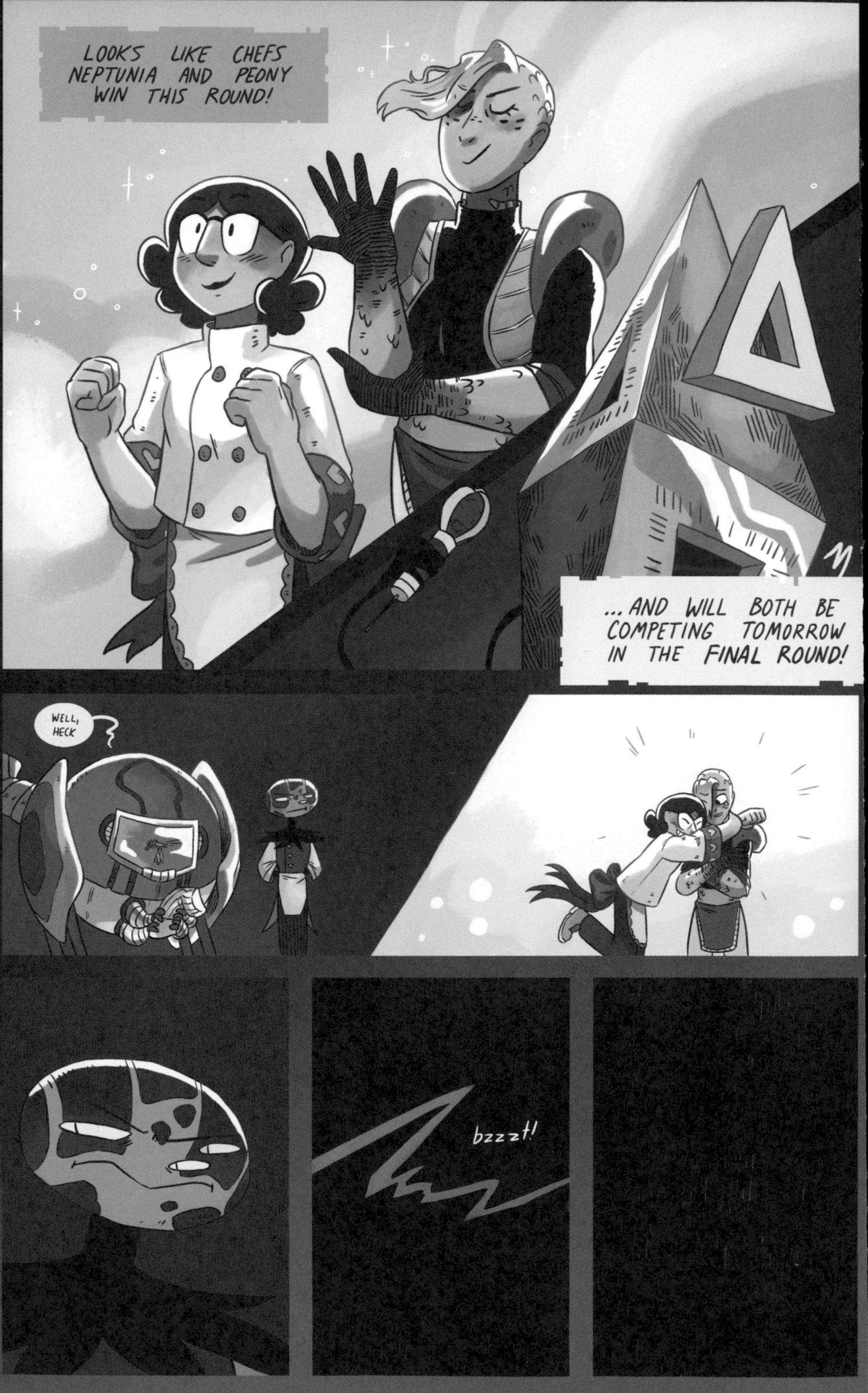
LOOKS LIKE CHEFS NEPTUNIA AND PEONY WIN THIS ROUND!
...AND WILL BOTH BE COMPETING TOMORROW IN THE FINAL ROUND!
WELL, HECK
bzzzt!

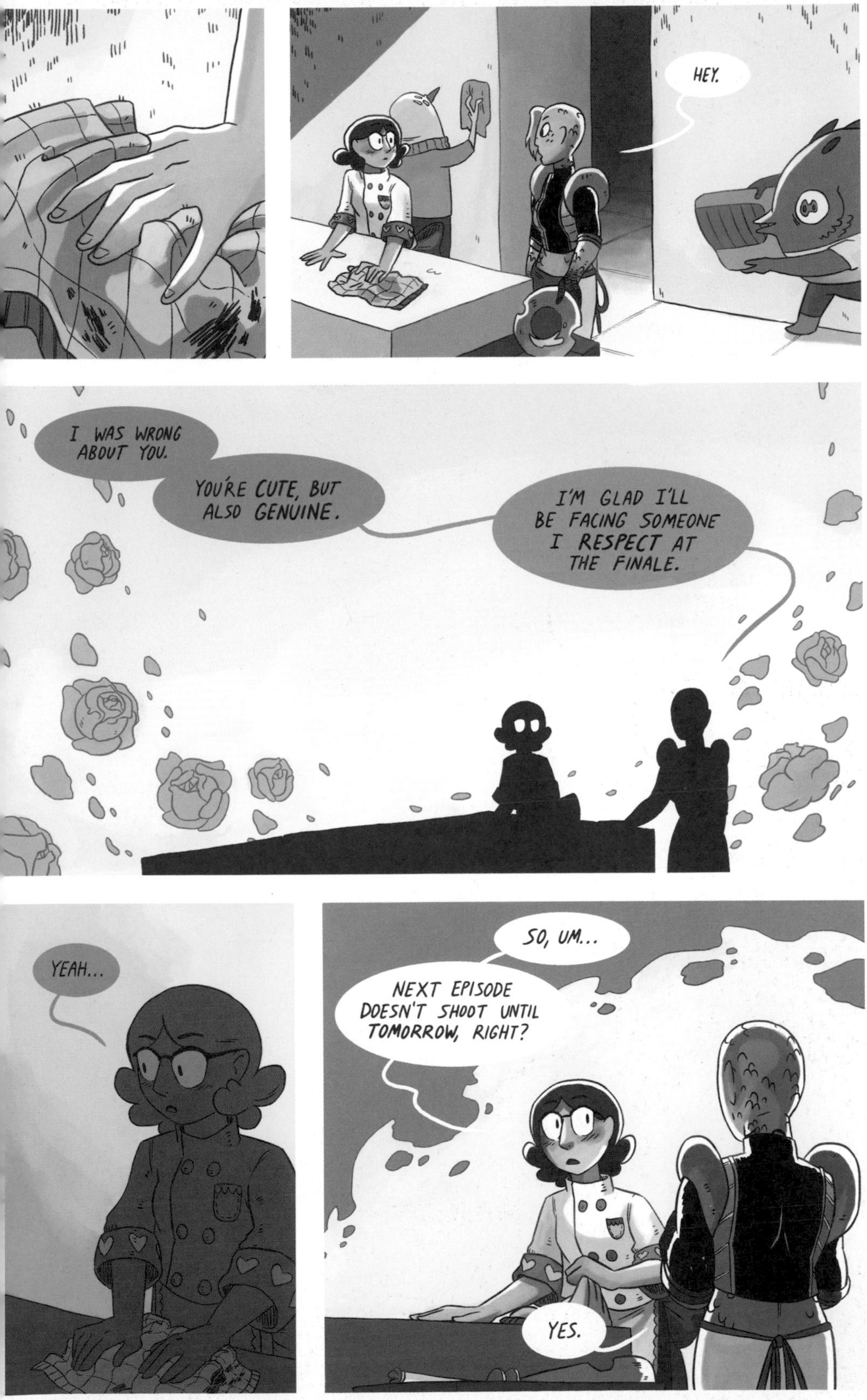
HEY.
I WAS WRONG ABOUT YOU.
YOU'RE CUTE, BUT ALSO GENUINE.
I'M GLAD I'LL BE FACING SOMEONE I RESPECT AT THE FINALE.
YEAH...
SO, UM...
NEXT EPISODE DOESN'T SHOOT UNTIL TOMORROW, RIGHT?
YES.

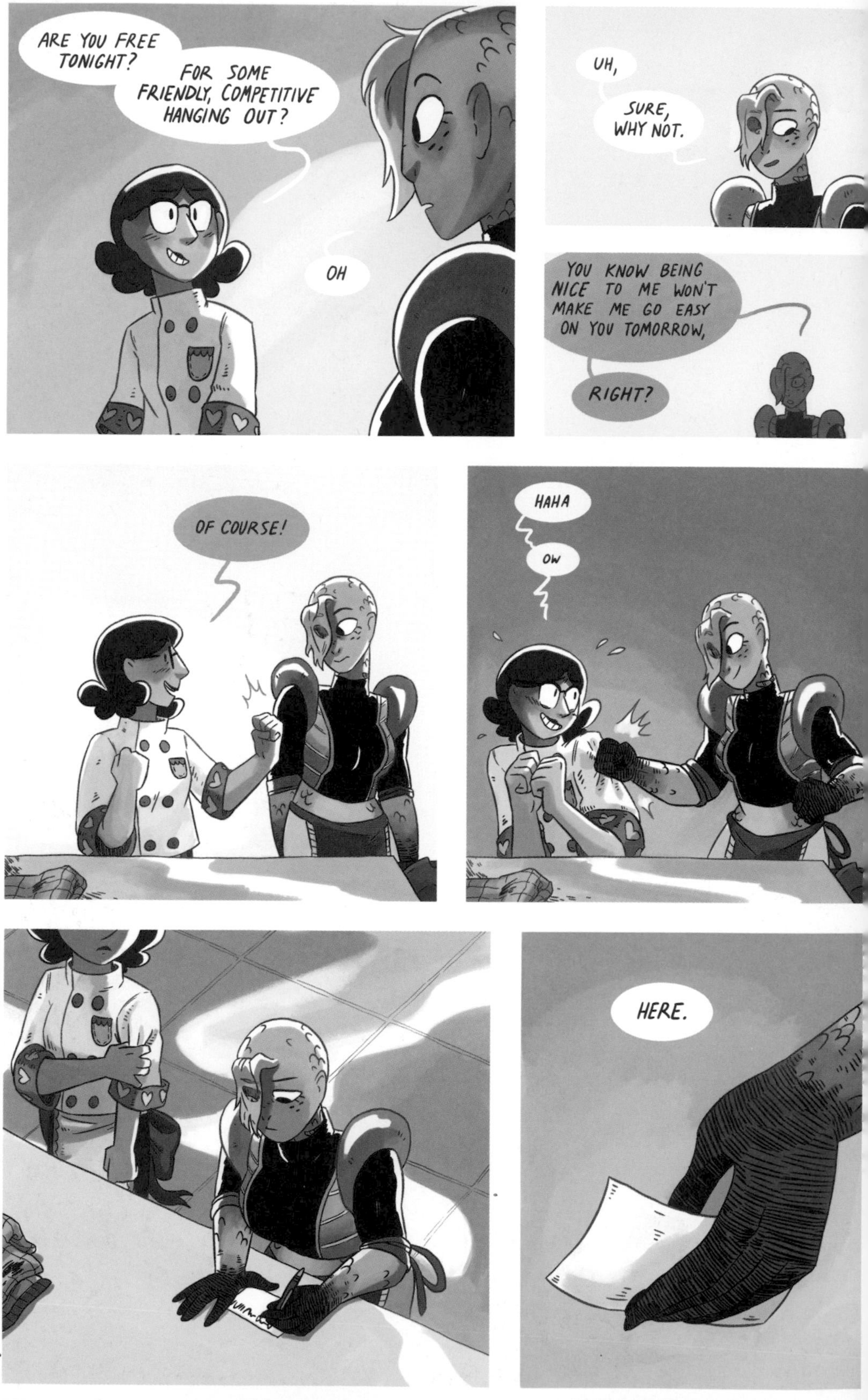

ARE YOU FREE TONIGHT?
FOR SOME FRIENDLY, COMPETITIVE HANGING OUT?
OH
UH,
SURE, WHY NOT.
YOU KNOW BEING NICE TO ME WON'T MAKE ME GO EASY ON YOU TOMORROW,
RIGHT?
OF COURSE!
HAHA
OW
HERE.

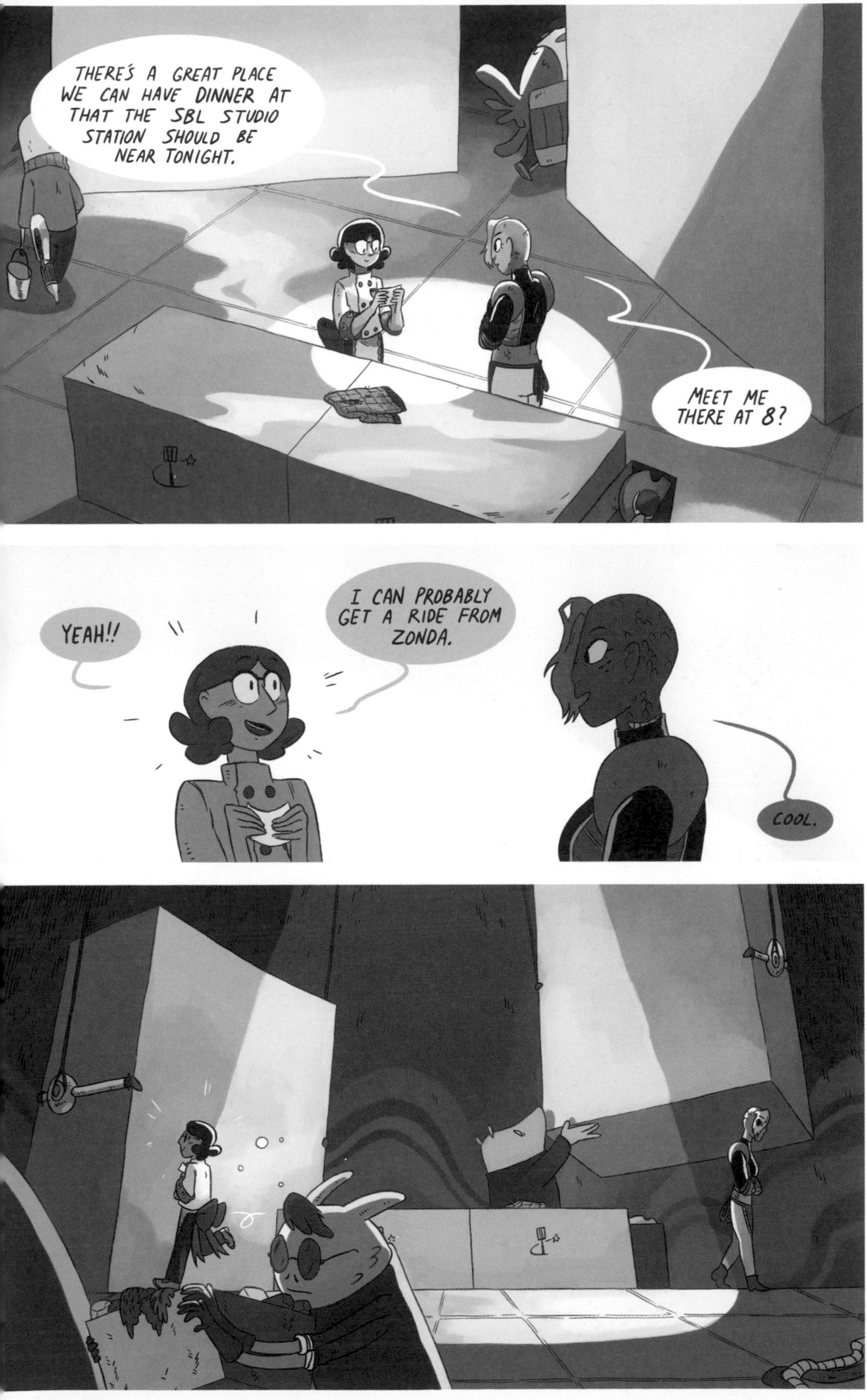
THERE'S A GREAT PLACE WE CAN HAVE DINNER AT THAT THE SBL STUDIO STATION SHOULD BE NEAR TONIGHT.
MEET ME THERE AT 8?
YEAH!!
I CAN PROBABLY GET A RIDE FROM ZONDA.
COOL.

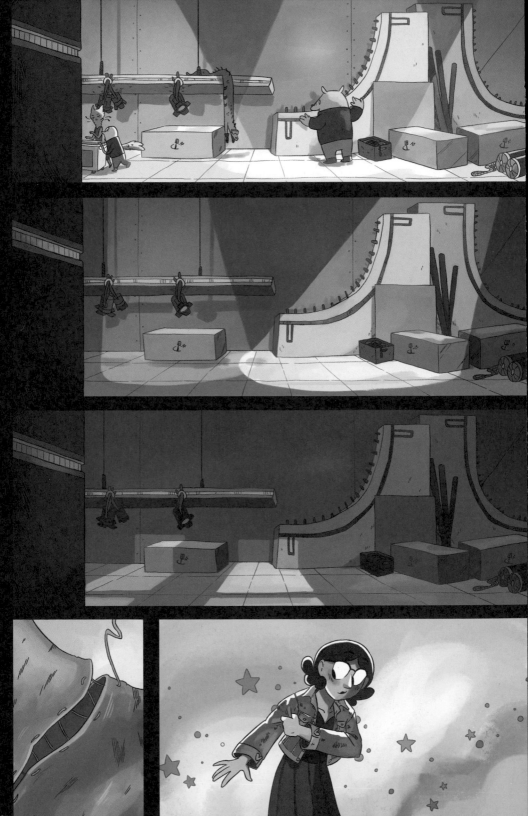

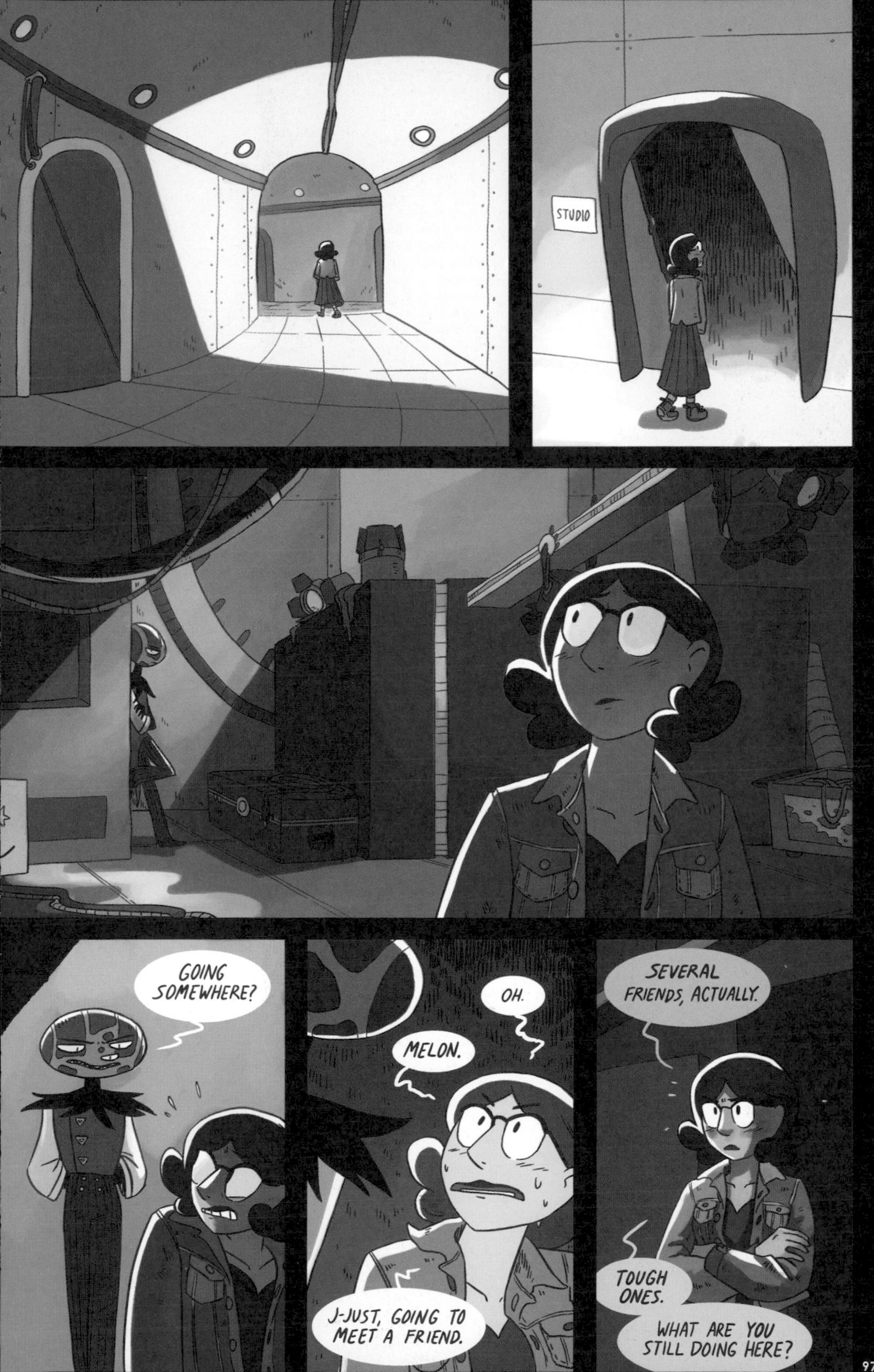
STUDIO
GOING SOMEWHERE?
OH.
MELON.
J-JUST, GOING TO MEET A FRIEND.
SEVERAL FRIENDS, ACTUALLY.
TOUGH ONES.
WHAT ARE YOU STILL DOING HERE?

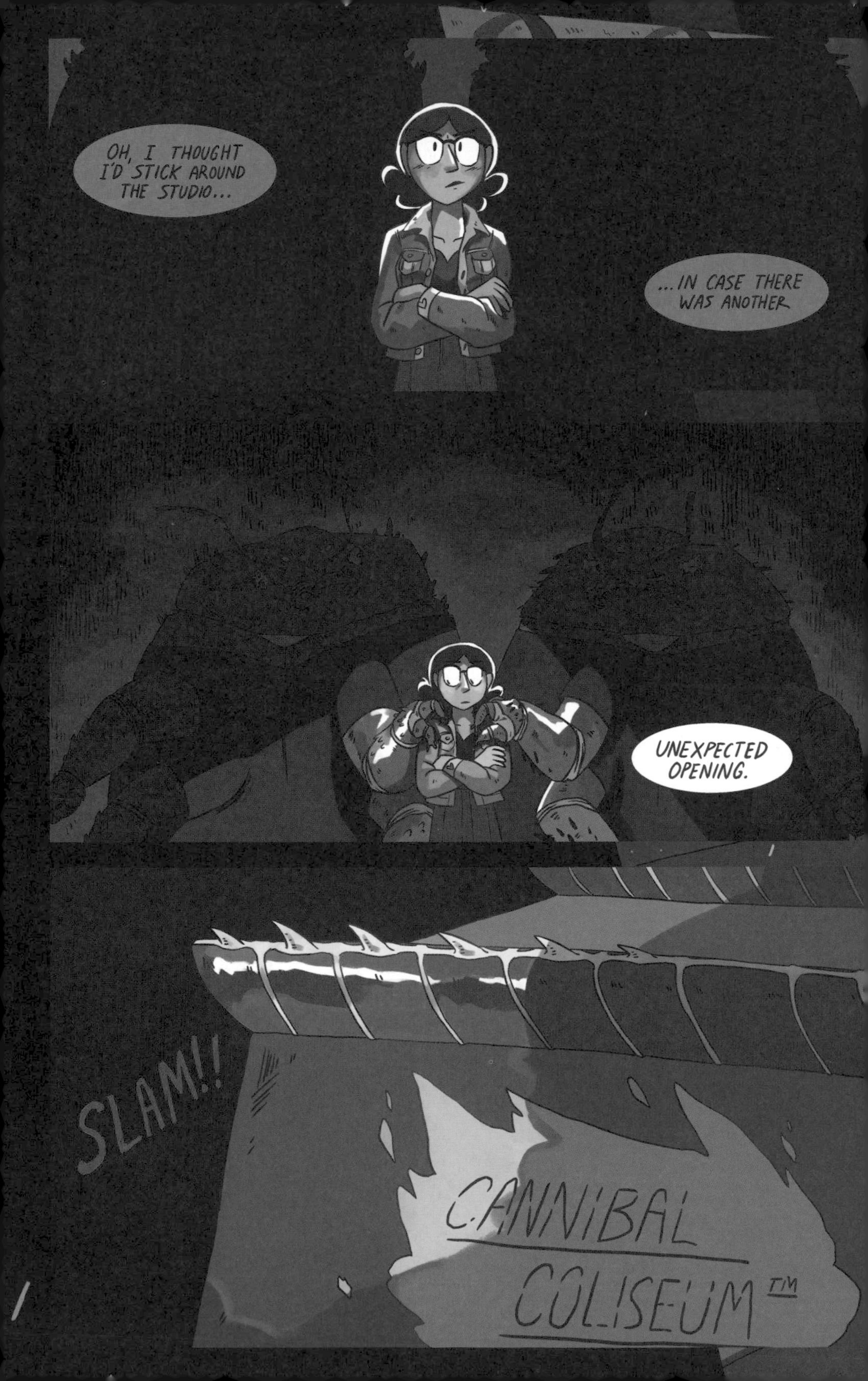
OH, I THOUGHT I'D STICK AROUND THE STUDIO...
...IN CASE THERE WAS ANOTHER
UNEXPECTED OPENING.
SLAM!!
CANNIBAL COLISEUM™

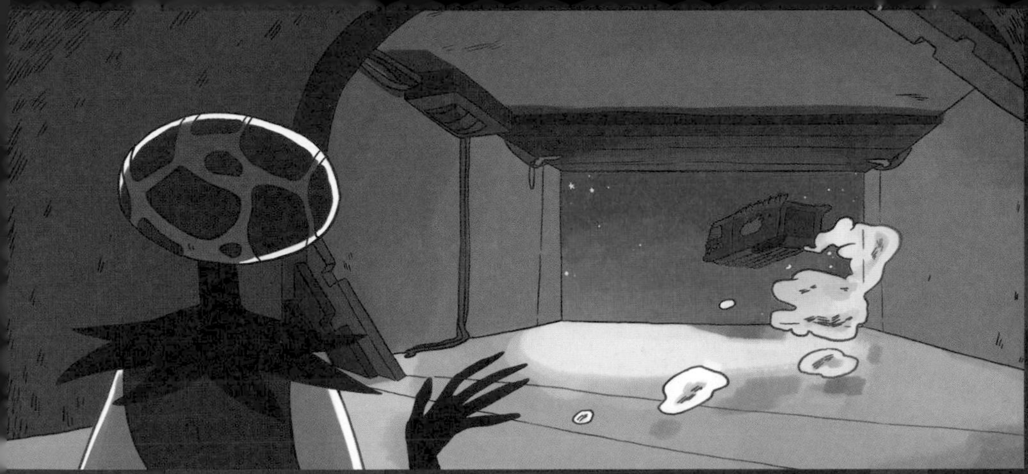

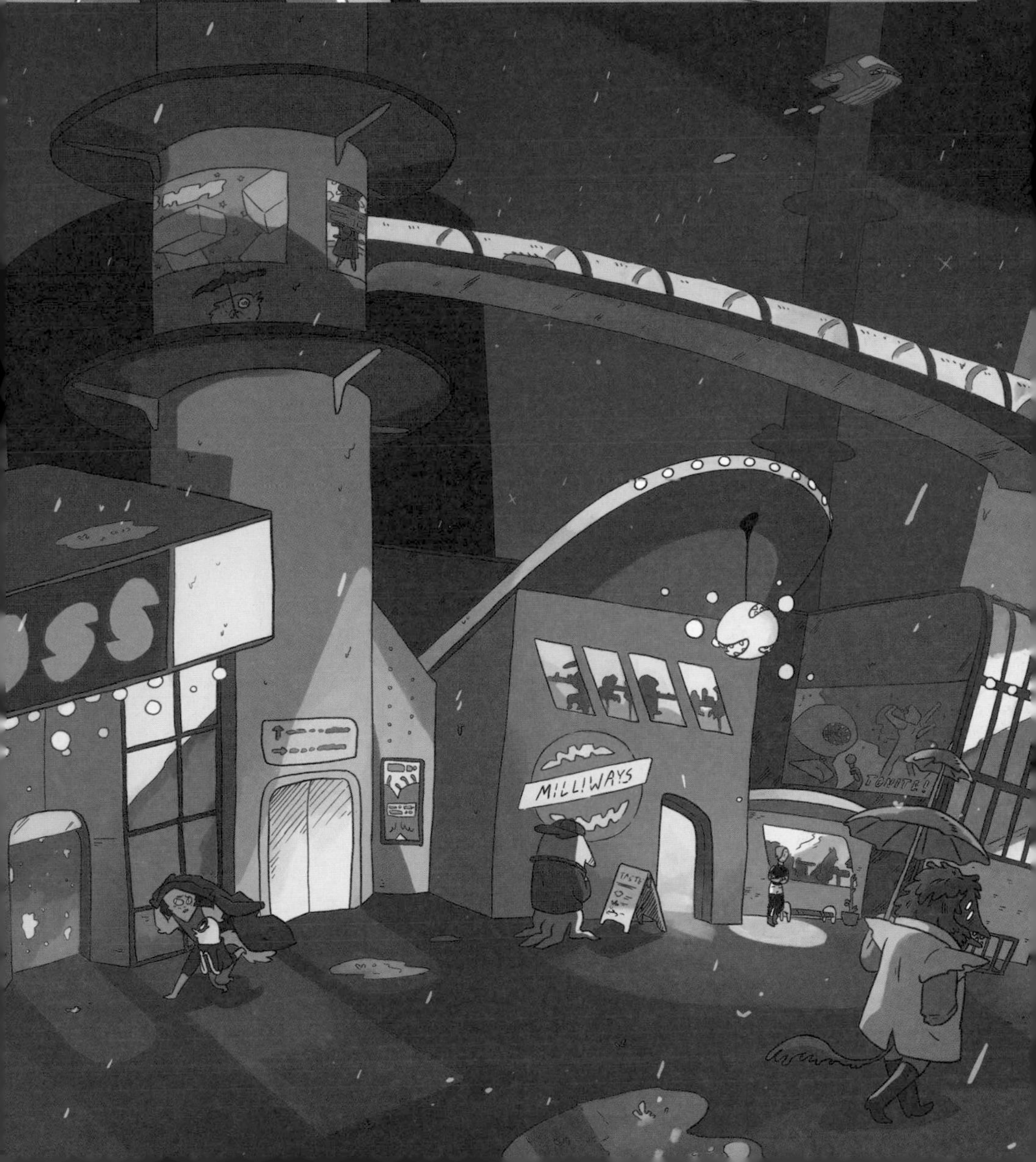
MILLIWAYS
TONITE!

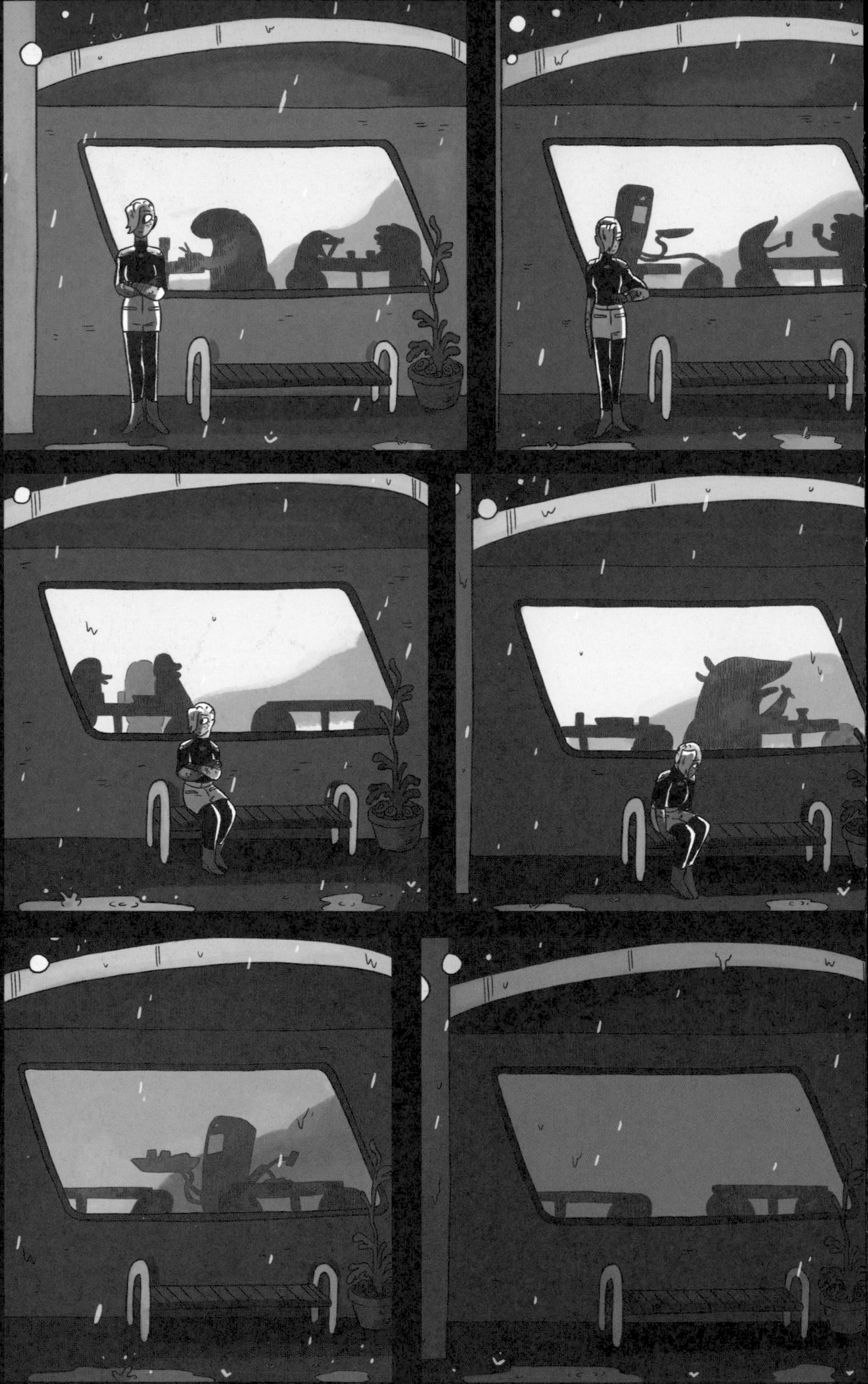

TO BE CONTINUED!

ABOUT THE CAST!

Curious about the alien chefs on Space Battle Lunchtime? You're in luck! Turn the page for some spectacular insight!

CHEF NEPTUNIA

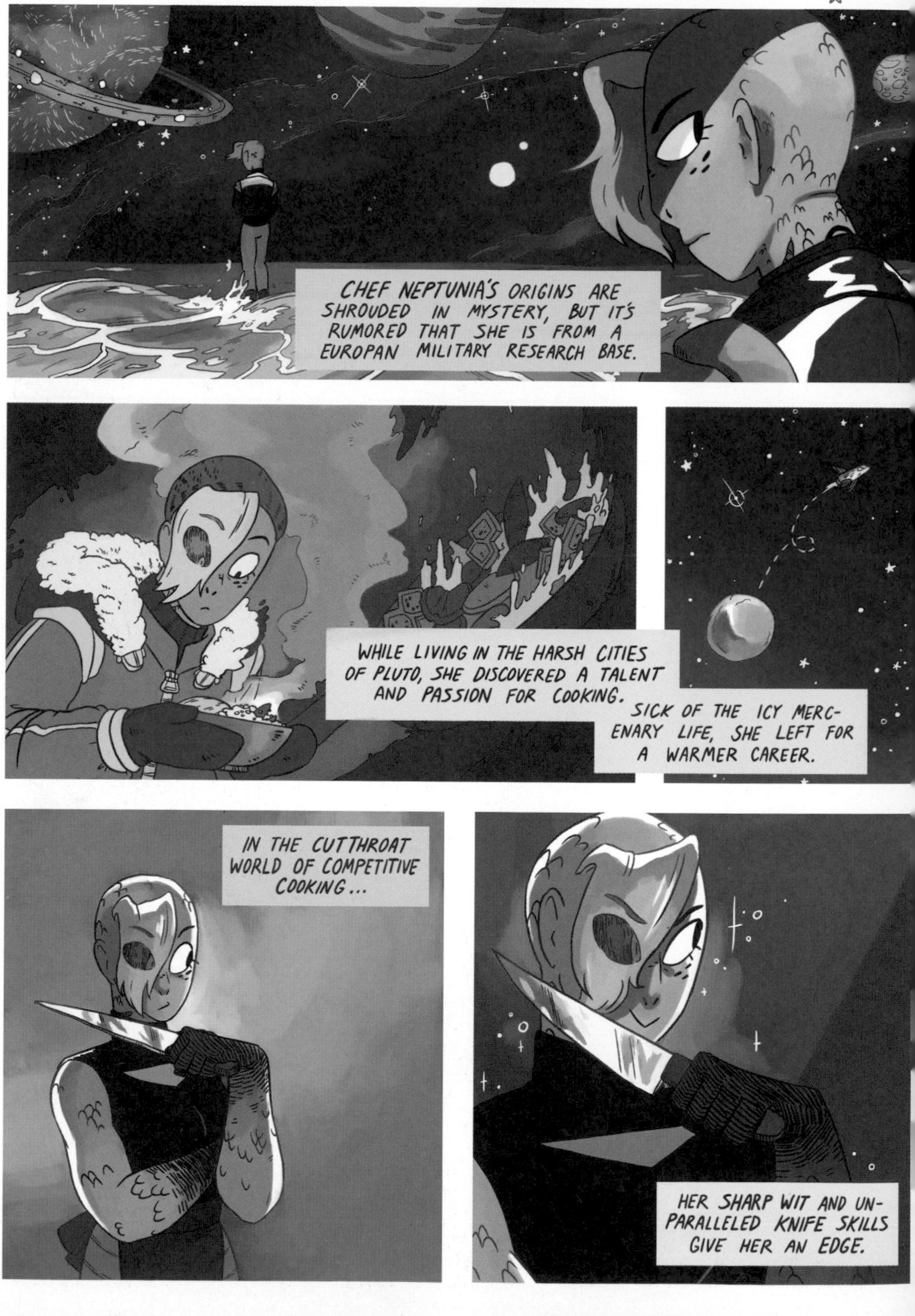

CHEF NEPTUNIA'S ORIGINS ARE SHROUDED IN MYSTERY, BUT IT'S RUMORED THAT SHE IS FROM A EUROPAN MILITARY RESEARCH BASE.
WHILE LIVING IN THE HARSH CITIES OF PLUTO, SHE DISCOVERED A TALENT AND PASSION FOR COOKING.
SICK OF THE ICY MERC-ENARY LIFE, SHE LEFT FOR A WARMER CAREER.
IN THE CUTTHROAT WORLD OF COMPETITIVE COOKING...
HER SHARP WIT AND UN-PARALLELED KNIFE SKILLS GIVE HER AN EDGE.

CHEF MELONHEAD

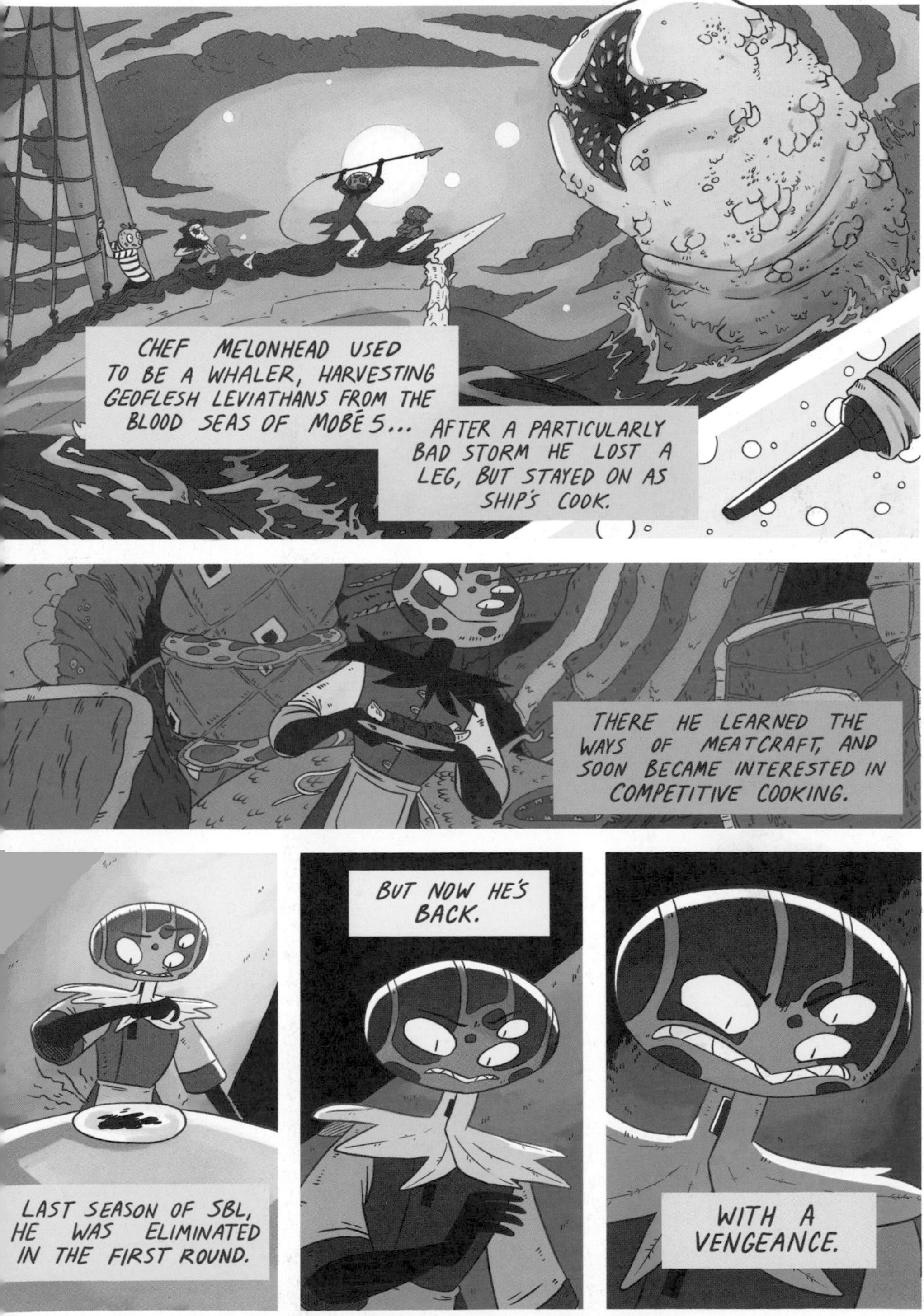
CHEF MELONHEAD USED TO BE A WHALER, HARVESTING GEOFLESH LEVIATHANS FROM THE BLOOD SEAS OF MOBÉ 5...
AFTER A PARTICULARLY BAD STORM HE LOST A LEG, BUT STAYED ON AS SHIP'S COOK.
THERE HE LEARNED THE WAYS OF MEATCRAFT, AND SOON BECAME INTERESTED IN COMPETITIVE COOKING.
LAST SEASON OF SBL, HE WAS ELIMINATED IN THE FIRST ROUND.
BUT NOW HE'S BACK.
WITH A VENGEANCE.

CHEF JACQUES

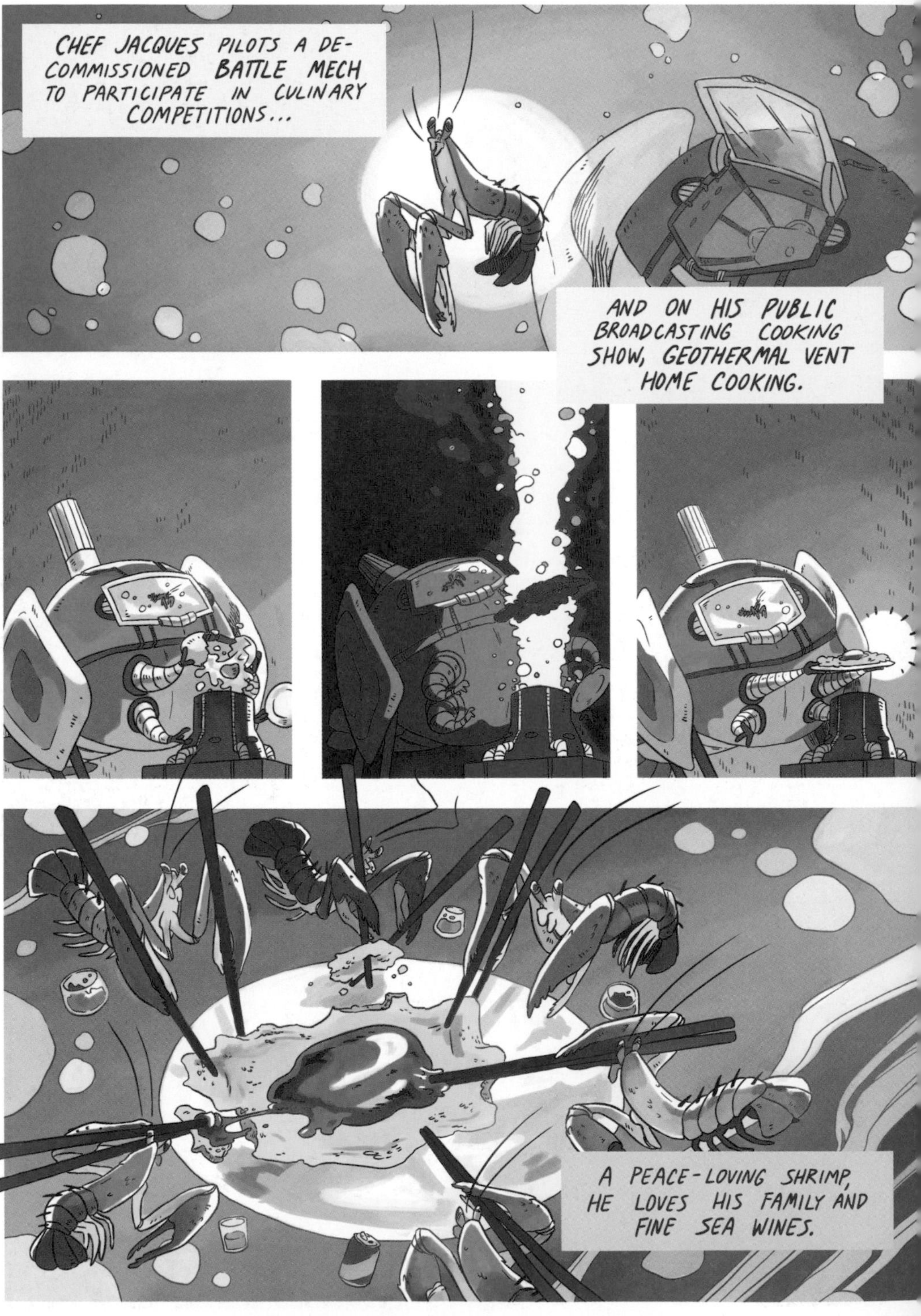

CHEF JACQUES PILOTS A DE-COMMISSIONED **BATTLE MECH** TO PARTICIPATE IN CULINARY COMPETITIONS...

AND ON HIS PUBLIC BROADCASTING COOKING SHOW, GEOTHERMAL VENT HOME COOKING.

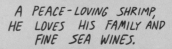

A PEACE-LOVING SHRIMP, HE LOVES HIS FAMILY AND FINE SEA WINES.

CHEF OWLINE

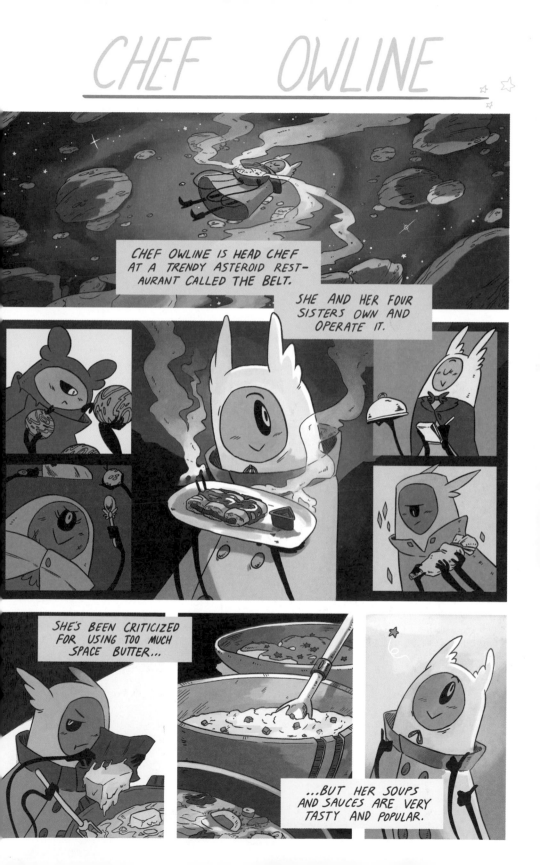

CHEF OWLINE IS HEAD CHEF AT A TRENDY ASTEROID REST- AURANT CALLED THE BELT.

SHE AND HER FOUR SISTERS OWN AND OPERATE IT.

SHE'S BEEN CRITICIZED FOR USING TOO MUCH SPACE BUTTER...

...BUT HER SOUPS AND SAUCES ARE VERY TASTY AND POPULAR.

CHEF MEATABAX

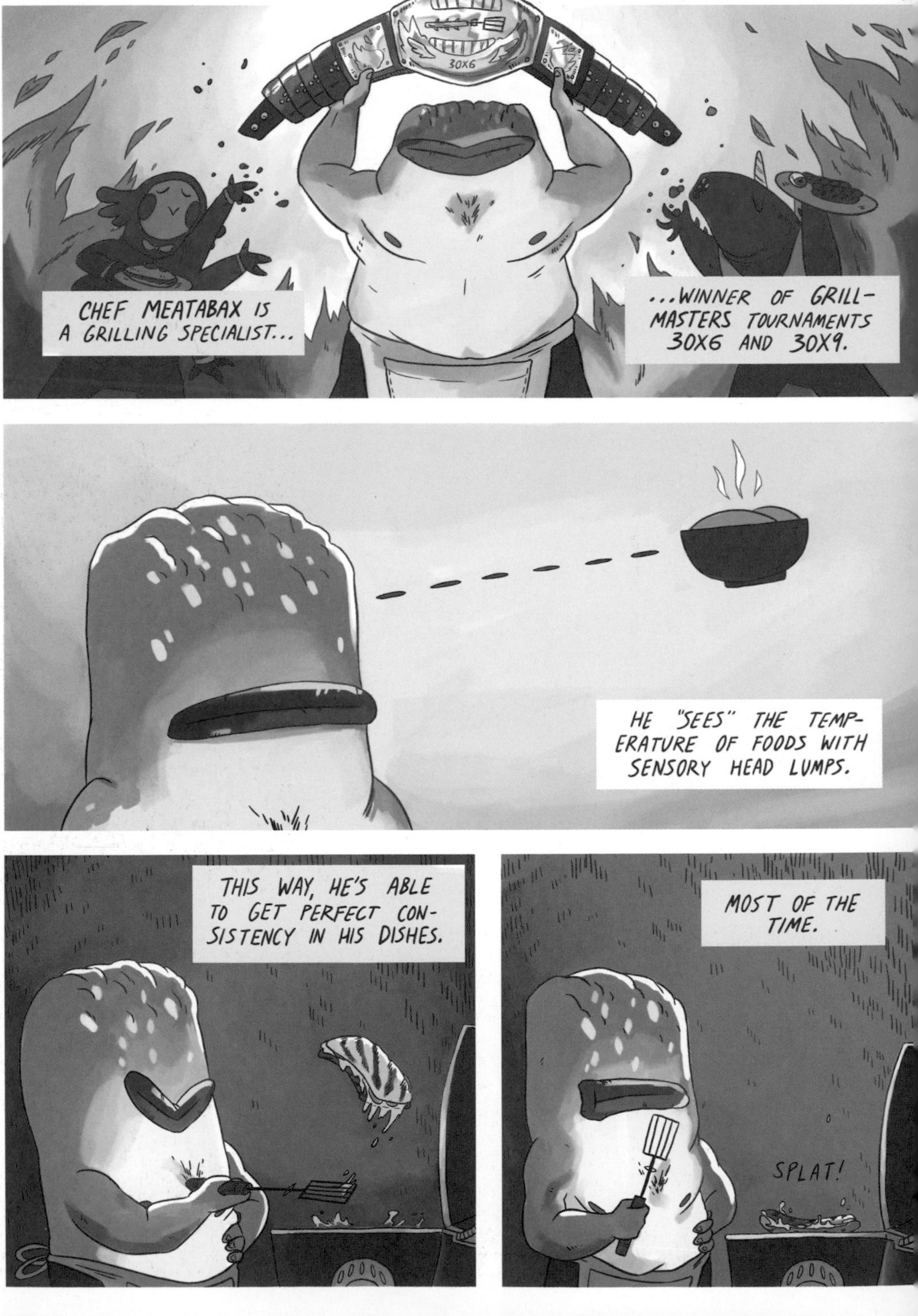

30X6
CHEF MEATABAX IS A GRILLING SPECIALIST...
...WINNER OF GRILL-MASTERS TOURNAMENTS 30X6 AND 30X9.
HE "SEES" THE TEMP-ERATURE OF FOODS WITH SENSORY HEAD LUMPS.
THIS WAY, HE'S ABLE TO GET PERFECT CON-SISTENCY IN HIS DISHES.
MOST OF THE TIME.
SPLAT!

CHEF CHERISA

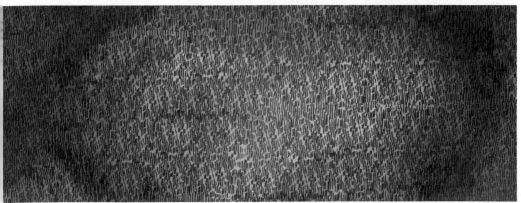

BONUS FEATURES!

Including concept art, bonus sketches, and a look
at the making of Space Battle Lunchtime!

PROCESS

Issue 3

• Peony goes back to a room the studio's set up for her on the station. A quiet moment. (p 1-3)
• Peony wakes up, gets ready and heads down to the studio where there is some 'friendly' ribbing between contestants (p 4-6)
• The second challenge is explained (involves using a gross nutrient health brick), and remaining contestants are warned to cool it on the sabotage (p 7-8)
• Peony thinks, and decides to grate it into a cupcake batter and gets started (p 9-10)
• Jacques makes a cold soup, Melonhead sautees it as a steak side dish, Neptunia uses some fancy knifework to carve it into appealingly shaped slices. Owline tries to make it into some kind of pie... (p 11)
• ...but, her sugar has been replaced with salt, and she didn't notice. (p 12)
• Peony finishes her cupcakes, and gets harassed a little (p 13)
• Neptunia almost drops her dish, but Peony catches it for her and gives it back (p 14-15)
• Judges taste the dishes, Owline gets booted, as her pie seriously injures an alien space slug judge (p 16 -20)
• Everyone is asked to leave the studio for a short break between challenges, Peony shares the rest of her cupcakes (p 21-22)

OUTLINE

↳ PACE OUT PAGES, FIGURE OUT WHAT EVENTS NEED TO HAPPEN

ROUGH SCRIPT

WRITE DIALOGUE AND ACTION, COMICS ARE A VISUAL MEDIUM

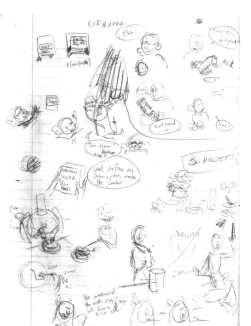

Page 14

Panel 1: Above angle of Peony's workspace, covered in half-finished cupcakes.

Panel 2: Mid shot of Peony concentrating on frosting one of the cupcakes.

Panel 3: Zoom in on the cupcake being frosted.

Panel 4: Peony's hand placing the last star-shaped garnish on top of a tray of cakes. They're very cute and look good.

Zorp (off panel): Time!

REGULAR SCRIPT ↰

LEGIBLE, FINALIZE DIALOGUE

LAYOUTS ⟶

PLAN THE PAGES

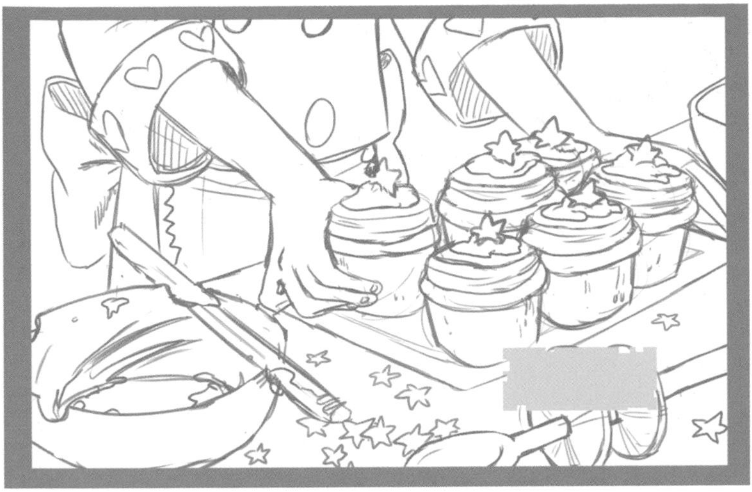

PENCILS

INKS

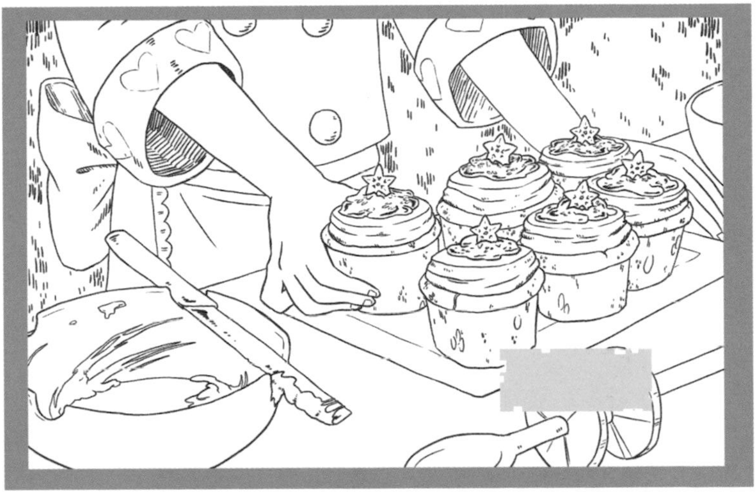

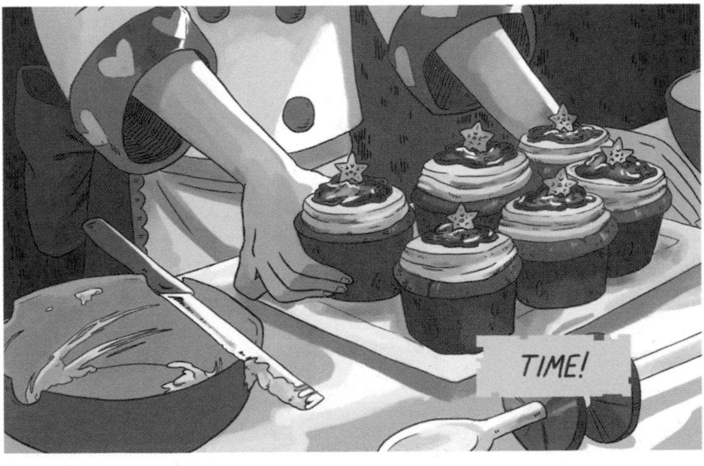
TIME!

COLORS AND LETTERS

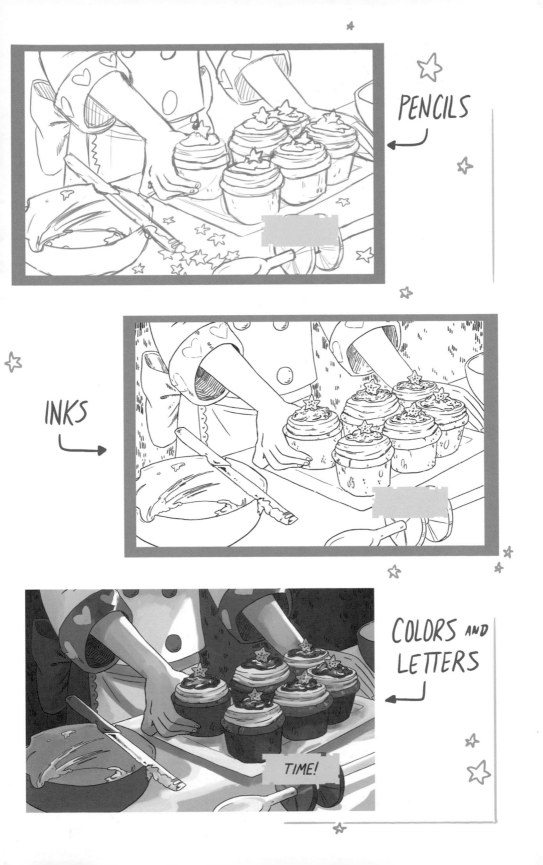

COVER SKETCHES! Many of these never made it to print, but a few did.

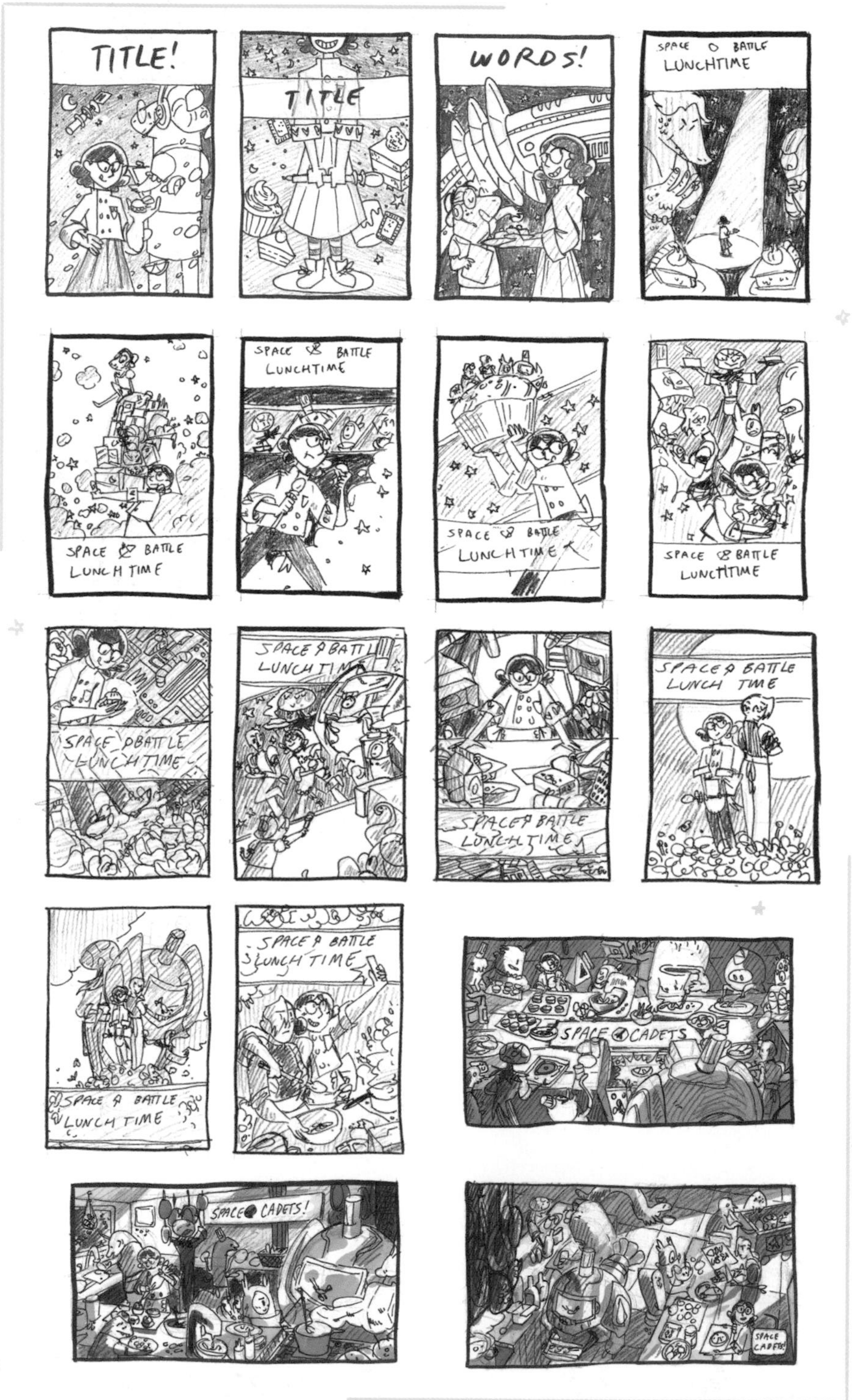
TITLE!
TITLE
WORDS!
SPACE BATTLE LUNCHTIME
SPACE BATTLE LUNCHTIME
SPACE BATTLE LUNCHTIME
SPACE BATTLE LUNCHTIME
SPACE BATTLE LUNCHTIME
SPACE BATTLE LUNCHTIME
SPACE BATTLE LUNCHTIME
SPACE BATTLE LUNCHTIME
SPACE BATTLE LUNCH TIME
SPACE BATTLE LUNCH TIME
SPACE BATTLE LUNCH TIME
SPACE CADETS
SPACE CADETS!
SPACE CADETS!

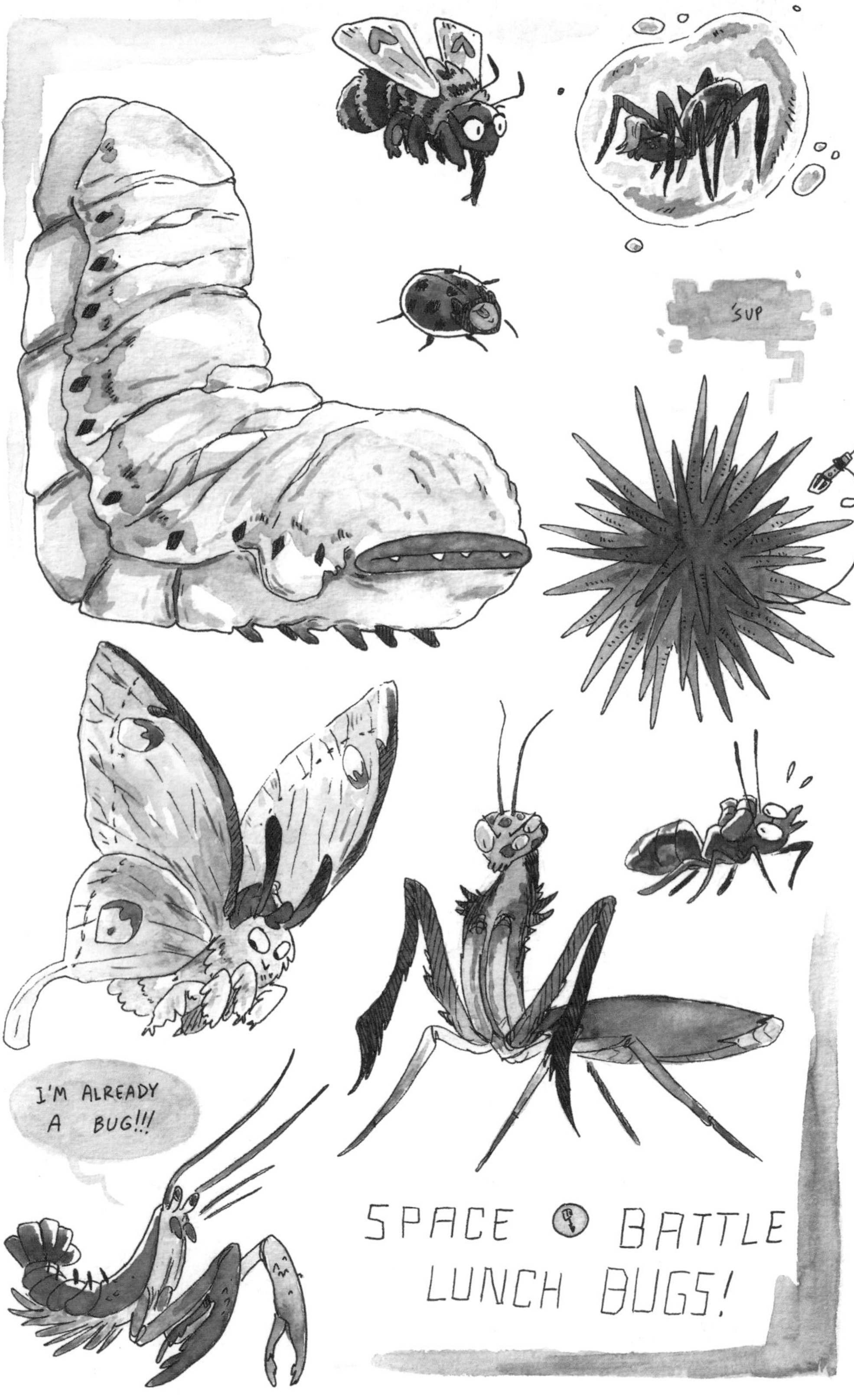
'SUP
I'M ALREADY A BUG!!!
SPACE BATTLE LUNCH BUGS!

SPACE FOOD: requests taken from Twitter.

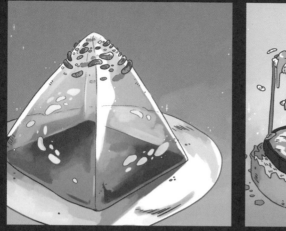

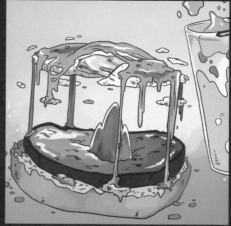

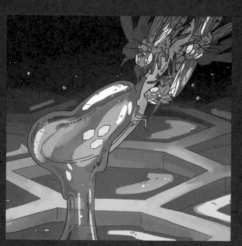

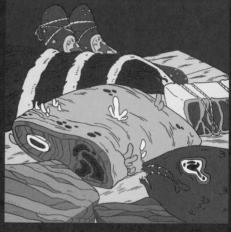

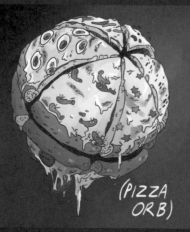

(PIZZA ORB)

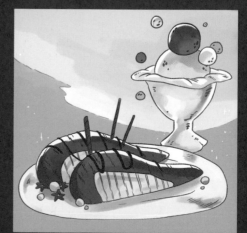

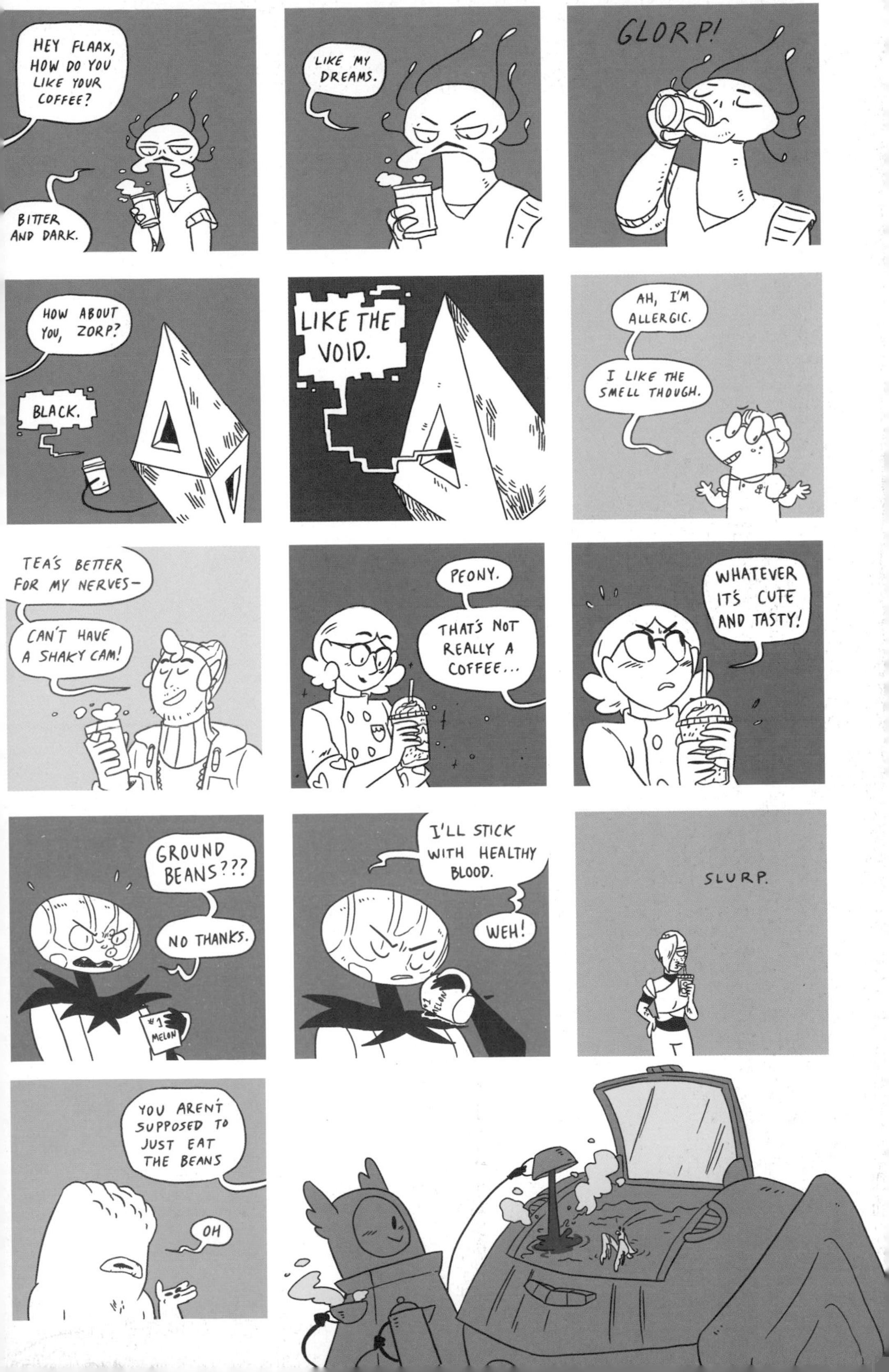

HEY FLAAX, HOW DO YOU LIKE YOUR COFFEE?
BITTER AND DARK.
LIKE MY DREAMS.
GLORP!
HOW ABOUT YOU, ZORP?
BLACK.
LIKE THE VOID.
AH, I'M ALLERGIC.
I LIKE THE SMELL THOUGH.
TEA'S BETTER FOR MY NERVES—
CAN'T HAVE A SHAKY CAM!
PEONY.
THAT'S NOT REALLY A COFFEE...
WHATEVER IT'S CUTE AND TASTY!
GROUND BEANS???
NO THANKS.
#1 MELON
I'LL STICK WITH HEALTHY BLOOD.
WEH!
SLURP.
YOU AREN'T SUPPOSED TO JUST EAT THE BEANS
OH

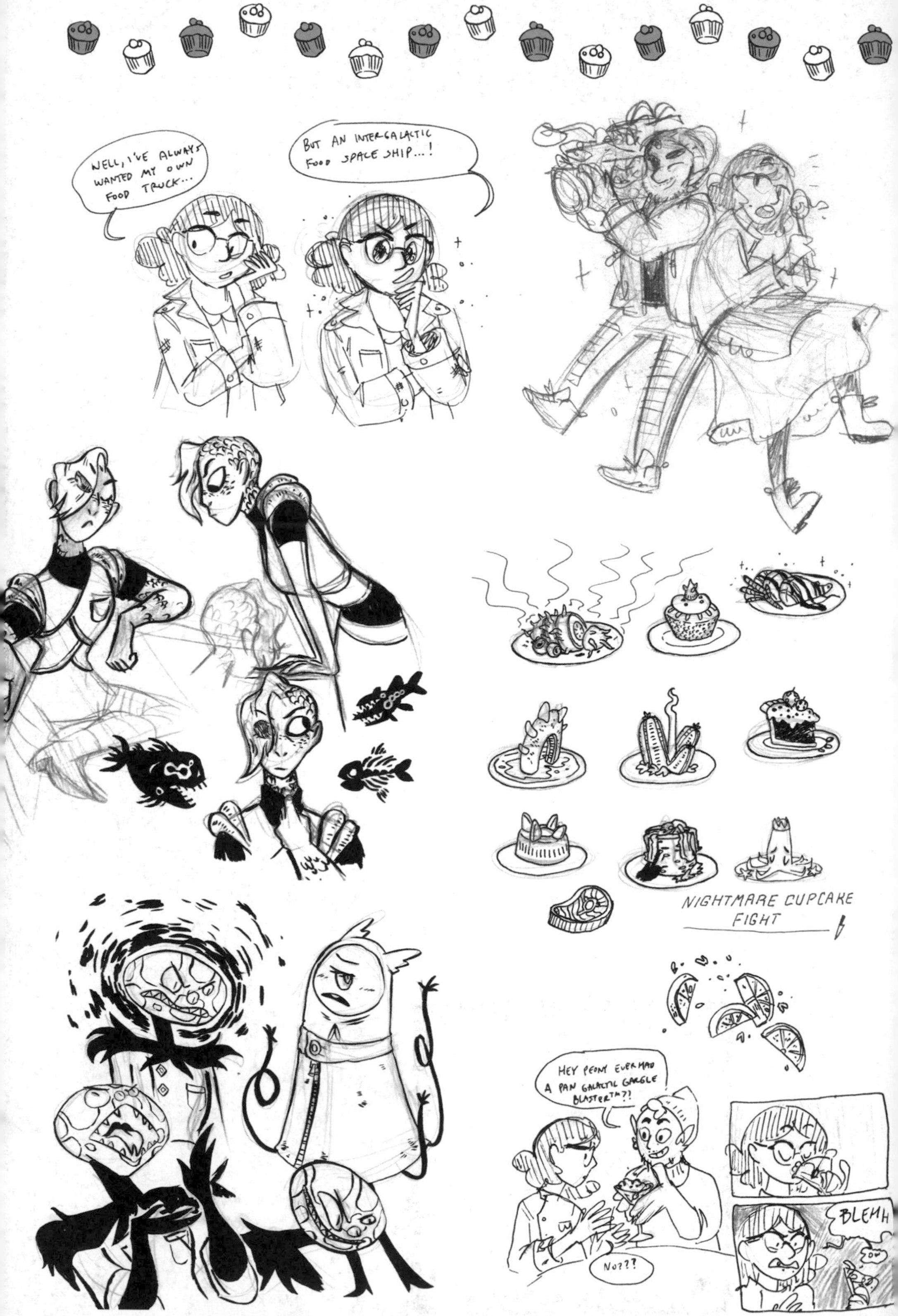
WELL, I'VE ALWAYS WANTED MY OWN FOOD TRUCK...
BUT AN INTERGALACTIC FOOD SPACE SHIP...!
NIGHTMARE CUPCAKE FIGHT
HEY PEONY EVER HAD A PAN GALACTIC GARGLE BLASTER™?!
NO???
BLEHH

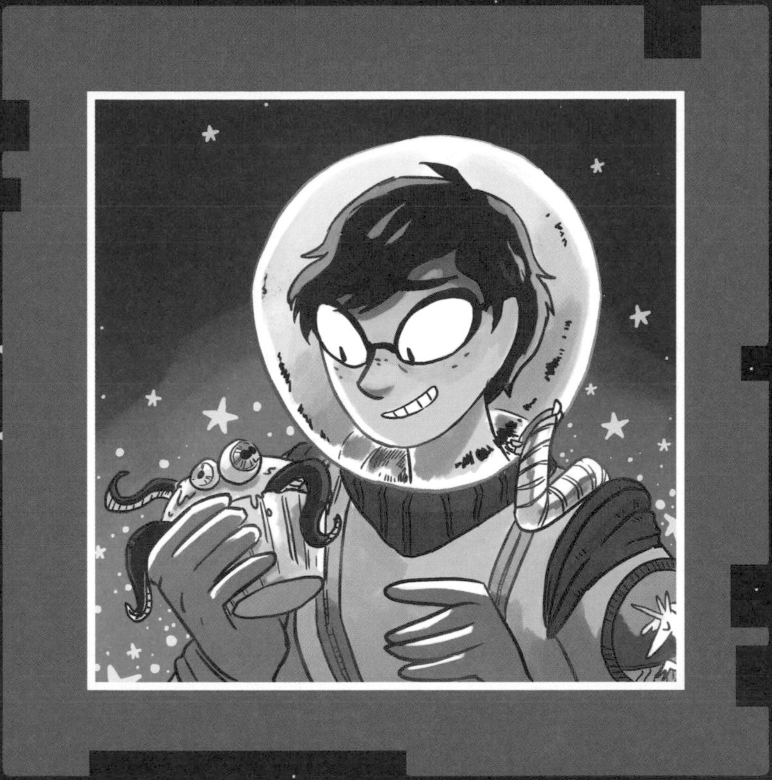

NATALIE RIESS is from a distant, unknown star. Her motives are unknown, but she seems to like drawing weird cats and comic books. She lives in Pennsylvania.

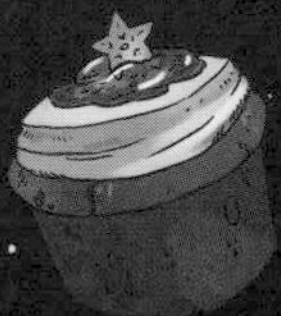

MORE BOOKS FROM ONI PRESS